ASYLUM LAKE

R.A. Evans

Marilyn –
   As Todd's better half
you must have a true
appreciation for horror!
   Welcome to my nightmare!

                    R.A. Evans

Chapbook Press

Chapbook Press
Schuler Books
2660 28th Street SE
Grand Rapids, MI 49512
(616) 942-7330
www.schulerbooks.com

Printed at Schuler Books in Grand Rapids, MI on the Espresso Book Machine®

ISBN 978-1-936243-10-5
ISBN 1-936243-10-5

DEDICATION

**For mom – all those paperbacks
from Gruber's were worth it after all.**

**Mel – thank you for holding us together while
everything was falling apart.**

Author's Note

The stigma associated with mental illness is real. It creates an enormous hurdle for many who truly need help. Regardless of what most people believe, statistics confirm that individuals with a mental illness are much more likely to be the victims of violence than to actually be violent offenders themselves. I encourage you to learn more about mental illness and join the fight against its stigma by visiting the National Alliance on Mental Illness website at www.nami.org.

Asylum Lake has been a team effort. Without the vision of Wendy Mersman of Moon Designs, LLC. the eerie images associated with both the website and cover design would never have been possible. For better or worse, she saw into my dark mind and captured what haunted me. Ashley Box was also an integral part of team Asylum Lake. A sharp yet delicate red pen is always a writer's best friend, and Ashley wielded hers with both strength and compassion.

To the fans, friends, and family members who believed in me long before I believed in myself – I thank you. It is for you and because of you that I continue to ask the dark and terrible questions that have spawned this story and others not yet written.

To my own April and our first awkward kiss – it's funny how that one frozen moment in time can bring inspiration.

And finally, much love to Eddie Vedder and his Pearl Jam band-mates for unknowingly providing me the soundtrack to my life.

Chapter 1

THE BEFORE AND AFTER

April 10, 1972
Bedlam Falls, MI

Six days squirreled away inside the small room behind the clerk's office had angered, divided, and eventually broken the juror's spirits to the point of surrender. The exhausted procession of wrinkled suits and downcast eyes shuffled to the jury box as hushed whispers swept across the anxious gallery.

Three sharp raps of the gavel brought the courtroom to near silence; the Honorable Orrin J. Huntley's steely glower finished the job. He was a sour old man with pruned lips and deep lines that crisscrossed his face. With his thin neck jutting out from the top of his black robe and talon-like fingers grasping the gavel, he surveyed the courtroom like a vulture perched menacingly over dying prey. Leaning forward from his roost, he placed his elbows upon the bench and pierced the jury box with his unblinking stare.

"Mr. Foreman, has the jury reached its verdict?"

Sonny Diedrich, Jury Foreman and Bedlam's only insurance salesman, slowly rose to his feet. "Yes, your Honor, we have."

Huntley shifted his attention from Diedrich to fix his eyes on the stoic boy seated at the defense table. His words scraped like sandpaper from his dry mouth, "Will the defendant please rise."

Dressed in a crisp white shirt that buttoned tightly at the neck and shark-grey trousers, the youth rose alongside his attorney. Awaiting the verdict with the unfailing faith of a supportive father, the Reverend James Collins, stood directly behind his wisp of a son. Delicate features defined the lad's fair-skinned face, while hair the color of autumn leaves spilled down over his forehead. But beneath the maze of curls, brown lifeless eyes stared – as cold as two pennies rusting in a late November rain; the boy's eyes could chill blood.

Shaken, Huntley tore his eyes from the defendant, recasting his focus toward the jury box. "Mr. Foreman, as of count one of the indictment, the murder of Joanna Reed, how does the jury find?"

"Your honor," he hesitated, "We find the defendant g-g-guilty." The words passed through Diedrich's trembling lips with cowardly hesitation.

Both joyful tears and heart-wrenching sobs erupted from the gallery. Huntley lurched to his feet and banged the gavel on his bench. "Order, I will have order," he cried, "or I will clear this court!"

The commotion subsided, to a degree. Soft murmurs hung in the air. Huntley collapsed back into his chair as the hum of cameras and recording devices reverberated throughout the courtroom. An army of reporters from across the state had invaded the small town weeks before - asking questions and digging for answers. But answers had been elusive, and each detail that had emerged throughout the trial had only posed more questions. The reporters, for now, had the answer that mattered most to them and were salivating at the prospect of sharing it.

In a matter of moments, young Lionel Collins, the same boy who had shoveled driveways and mowed lawns, and with whom Sunday sermons and meals with most everyone had been shared, had been found guilty on all five murder charges; he had been convicted of brutal crimes committed not only against his neighbors and community, but against humanity itself.

He was led by deputies from the courtroom; the chains that were clamped tightly about his wrists and ankles jingled with each unbalanced step. He peered over his shoulder into the gallery – a sly smile curved his thin lips.

In the wake of people rushing from the courtroom, a nondescript man rose from a hard wooden seat in the back of the gallery. His presence during the trial had gone unnoticed, as it had been at the funerals months before. Not that anyone should notice. More than a decade had elapsed since he had last walked the streets of Bedlam Falls.

The man was pale with a tuft of dark hair atop his head and rail-thin; his natty black suit hung from his bones eerily similar to the way clothes hang on a scarecrow. His sunken and red-rimmed eyes, appearing to have stared into the bottom of one too many a whiskey bottle, darted around the empty room as he made his way forward to the oak table where Lionel returned each day to sit with his attorney.

Resting on the desk's polished surface lay a bracelet. The man's whiskey-soaked eyes widened as a look of recognition, then horror, crept over his face. With a palsied hand, he scraped it from the table.

Much as a painful sliver slowly works its way from one's flesh, this sinister token had somehow surfaced from the murky depths of Asylum Lake. Alone in his knowledge of how it had come to rest on the rocky lake-bed, the man looked down at the words stamped on its battered surface and winced as he traced a trembling finger across the cold plastic. He stood there, trance-like. Suddenly, his gnarled fingers closed around the bracelet, quickly hiding it away inside his breast pocket.

As the stranger walked from the empty courthouse into the damp air, a chilling wave wracked his entire body. He paused on the steps, steadying himself against the handrail. The spring breeze, which usually held the promise of brighter days to come, today carried an ominous scent.

With more than a passing suspicion that Lionel's verdict, and the evidence introduced throughout the trial, had been an omen of a long-forgotten darkness looming on the horizon, Douglas Wyatt shambled from the courthouse. Breathing slow and deep, he placed a protective hand over his heart and headed south into the afternoon chill -- The Lord's Prayer falling from his lips.

August 18, 2010
Bedlam Falls, MI

There was Bedlam Falls before the trial of Lionel Collins and Bedlam Falls after the trial of Lionel Collins. Del's Grocery had been replaced with Kroger and thirteen miles outside of town a McDonald's now greeted the tourists exiting off US-31. On the surface, little had changed in the quaint, northern Michigan town.

However, buried deep in the marrow of Bedlam Falls, malignant wounds from the town's dark past were beginning to fester.

Four years after Lionel's conviction, FORD Motors Company had decided the sleepy town would be as good a place as any to build a stamping plant. As new jobs and unfamiliar faces flocked to Bedlam Falls, the close-knit community transformed. Gone were the days of unlocked doors and neighborly chats over hedges. Within just a few short years, the town's backwoods charm and personality were replaced with the same malaise that people had once come to Bedlam Falls to escape.

Brady nearly missed the exit. His mind had gone numb four hours into the six-hour drive from Chicago. As he pulled out of the McDonald's, a brimming cup of too-hot coffee cradled between his thighs, anxious knots began their tug-of-war inside his stomach.

Six months ago, he had been the young ace at the Chicago Tribune. His investigation and coverage of the shocking murder of Janie Pearce, a twenty-eight year-old pregnant mother of three who had been beaten to death outside a downtown Chicago eatery, had been picked up by the Associated Press and made headlines across the country. The perpetrator, a homeless schizophrenic who had claimed that voices had urged him to commit the crime, had been a familiar figure within the revolving door of Cook County's over-burdened mental health system.

The case had resulted in swift and sudden changes in how the chronically mentally ill received treatment in the State of Illinois. *Janie's Law*, as the legislation would later be named, mandated monthly psychological testing be performed and evaluated by a team of state-certified medical specialists before and after a patient's release - as well as bi-weekly reviews of a patient's medical history and medication usage.

The goal of the new enforcements was an attempt to safeguard the general public, as well as the patient, from the physical and psychological strains associated with their reintroduction to society.

Although some measures met with opposition -- the so-called *draconian measures* coined by human advocacy and civil-rights groups -- most were lauded by neighborhood organizations and law-enforcement agencies alike. Illinois crime statistics linking Cook County mental health discharges with violent crimes had risen steadily since the 1980s. But only after Janie Pearce's untimely death, and Brady's thorough and meticulous exposes, was the fact illuminated.

Brady's critically acclaimed work, which had been a catalyst in the institution of Janie's Law, resulted in his name and the *Pulitzer Prize* being talked about in the same conversation. The award had never materialized, but Brady's reputation had still transcended itself. The buzz around the newsroom had him being groomed for the city desk -- all this before age thirty. Although most of the Tribune's elder statesmen found his boyish good looks and casual style more than a bit off-putting, his new-found yet well-deserved celebrity had provided a much-needed boost to the paper's slumping circulation. His female co-workers, however, were all in agreement; Brady Tanner was very easy on the eyes.

His reporting had also garnered attention from the publishing front and before long a book deal had been discussed with a signing bonus large enough to finally move out of their shabby one-bedroom apartment above the bakery on Lexington. New dreams could be realized moving to the suburbs; a home office for Brady and a home large enough for a budding family for Karen.

As negotiations with a small publisher intensified, the couple collectively crossed their fingers and toured a gorgeous 2,100 square-foot Colonial, located in the quiet, northern Chicago suburb of Morton Grove. While walking down the hall toward the second-level master bedroom, Karen had already mentally decorated the first room on the left; the perfectly-sized nursery room would be done-up in greens and yellows since they had already decided to keep the baby's sex a surprise. Even though she desperately wanted to paint the room cotton-candy pink, Karen knew that boys ran in her family. She prayed the baby feet that one day in the not-too-distant future would be scuttling across the floors would belong to an "Allison" or an "Audrey" and not to a "Brady Junior." Not that she would be disappointed if she had a son. She just wondered, how does a *girl* raise a *boy*?

Brady raised the coffee to his lips and took a slow sip. "Damn!" At the sound of his voice, Brady's passenger sat up. "I guess I won't be using my taste buds for awhile, eh, Gruff?" He reached over and began to stroke the yellow lab that rode beside him. Gruff smiled the way only a dog owner could recognize and curled back into a ball.

Gruff had been Karen's security system. Three break-ins and a handful of muggings in their Southside Armour Square neighborhood had spooked her. More than anything, she had wanted the sense of security that would come from having a house with a fenced yard and vigilant neighbors. But Brady's salary could barely cover rent, let alone the expenses of owning a home, and Karen's parents had already been paying her way through law school - a fact that relentlessly had been the topic of conversation whenever the in-laws visited. The thought of borrowing down-payment money for a house from the Greene's sickened Brady.

His temporary solution for abating Karen's fears, while also avoiding further indebtedness to her parents, had been to sneak thirty dollars from the cookie jar where Karen had kept the grocery money. He scampered off to the animal shelter and returned two hours later with a puppy under one arm, and a bag of dog food and adoption papers under the other. The new addition to the Tanner family would be dubbed McGruff for his supposed crime fighting abilities -- never again would security be an issue.

Less than a year later, Brady guided his Volkswagen through the winding roads that led to Bedlam Falls. Gruff warmed the passenger seat, his oversized paws tucked under his chin. Yawning, Gruff raised his head and looked at Brady with the "pet me" look. Brady lovingly obliged and ran his fingers down Gruff's neck, scratching and petting the soft fur. As he drove, Brady's thoughts continued to drift.

The book deal had been inked just a month after it had been first proposed. The process culminated with a final meeting in New York City that had gone well too well, in fact. A celebratory drink with his new editor, coupled with cross-town traffic, had caused him to miss his 5:30 p.m. flight back to Chicago. Brady had planned to treat an unsuspecting Karen to a night at Abuelo's, a Mexican restaurant on the city's trendy Westside. Although Brady wasn't sure how Karen's second-trimester tummy-bundle would react to spicy enchiladas, Brady thought Karen definitely deserved a four-star meal -- pickles and pineapple cheesecake just weren't cutting it! Besides, what better place to tell Karen how much he had missed her than at a romantic candle-lit table surrounded by serenading mariachis? But, as misfortune would have it, Brady's *surprise* would have to wait 'til the weekend. His 6:45 p.m. alternate flight had been delayed as well; it wasn't until 10:30 p.m. that the plane finally touched down in the Windy City.

"Brady! Brady!" a familiar voice called. He scanned the throng of travelers merging to his left and spotted Will, Karen's brother. With a smile tugging at the corners of his mouth, Brady burrowed through the congested terminal toward his brother-in-law, expecting to see an echo of excitement on the man's face. Instead, Will's eyes were red and puffy, and he looked as if he hadn't slept in days. Brady's smile vanished.

"Damn you, Brady. Where the hell have you been?" Will asked, grabbing Brady's shoulder with one trembling hand and steering him away from the crowd. Before Brady could respond, Will continued, choking back tears. "There's been...an accident."

"What do you mean an accident?" asked Brady, his mind stuttering over the pain in Will's voice. "What's happened to Karen?"

Will's grip tightened on Brady's shoulder. "She's gone, Brady. Karen is dead."

The sound of a blaring horn roused Brady from his reverie. A sharp turn of the steering wheel brought his car out of the lane of oncoming traffic. He peered into the rear-view mirror, his heart still pounding. A pale face and eyes brimming with tears stared back at him. "Get a hold of yourself," he demanded under his breath.

Brady wiped the salty wetness from his hazel eyes. With his vision restored and heartbeat once again nearing normal, he caught sight of a road sign — Bedlam Falls: A Great Place to Land.

"Hokey," he scoffed aloud. Brady's voice roused Gruff from his slumber. At the sight of his yawning companion, Brady pushed a button to lower the passenger window. Assuming his canine co-pilot position, Gruff poked his head toward the sky, lapping the fresh breeze.

Brady turned his attention from his passenger to the buildings and landmarks that were coming into view. The sight of *The Hayloft* brought a hint of a smile to his lips. Standing just outside the city limits, the dilapidated tavern hadn't been governed by the blue laws that had once banned the sale of alcohol. Brady's smile widened at the memory of swigging his first beer behind that dusty-red barn.

The parking lot was empty, save for an odd-looking man on a bicycle. Unkempt and unstable, he rode fruitlessly in wobbly circles that cast long shadows across the barren blacktop. Scrawled across the tattered sandwich-board sign that hung loosely around his neck was a single word – REPENT. With a snow-white beard hanging in a tangled mess between his knees, the haggard rider looked like a strung-out Santa -- Bedlam Falls had definitely changed.

Chapter 2

HOMECOMING

The house was cradled by rolling hills in a thick copse of trees overlooking the lake. To those who had recently settled in or visited the area, the small body of water was known as Half-Moon Lake for its crescent shape, but the locals knew it as Asylum Lake – an odd homage to the enormous psychiatric hospital and grounds that loomed on its northern shoreline. Abandoned and empty, Lake View Asylum stood as a silent reminder of the town's dark history.

One of only a handful of homes with lake-frontage, the *Up North House* as Brady's family fondly referred to it, had been built by his great-grandfather in the 1940s. Its log construction gave the appearance of a rustic hunting lodge.

Brady paused in the driveway and stared through the dusty windshield down the overgrown pathway to the house. Although the afternoon sun left much of it in shadows, it was evident the *Up North House* had seen better days. Trees blocked the lake from his view, but not the sound of the gulls in the distance; their cries echoed through the silence.

He stepped from the Jetta and kicked the tangled grass and fallen branches that had collected through the changing seasons of neglect. The house, once meticulously kept, looked not merely vacant, but forgotten.

Has it really been 14 years? Brady rounded the car to let Gruff out to stretch his legs. The dog bounded through the open door, pressed his nose to the ground and started swinging his tail back and forth. He found "the spot" and relieved himself.

Brady pondered his next move. He had never walked through that door without at least one of his parents in tow. The years since his last visit felt like a lifetime ago. *Really, only half a lifetime*, he thought. His mother had lost her battle with breast cancer here in 2005, while watching the sun rise one last time over the lake, dad's hand gently holding hers. Brady was miles away in Chicago chasing his dreams…and Karen.

His father had broken the news to him over the phone. "She's gone," was all he could muster. Brady thought he could hear the splash of a tear through the receiver. "Come home."

So Brady had returned to Grand Rapids for his mother's funeral. Although his parents had retired to Bedlam Falls following his mother's diagnosis, they kept their roots in Grand Rapids. His brief and infrequent visits had always been to their home in the city. He had become a connoisseur at brushing aside both their subtle and not-so-subtle invitations to spend time with them at the lake.

Walking alongside his father to his mother's graveside memorial, Brady had been struck by how, over the years, time had chipped away at the man's chiseled features. The elder Tanner's sky-blue eyes were downcast and clouded with grief. His slumped posture and wilted gait had punctuated the utter emptiness and loss that now entombed him. Feebly attempting to bridge the distance that had grown between them, Brady awkwardly placed a hand on his father's shoulder.

After the service concluded, the Tanner men had returned to an empty house. Rolling into the driveway, the sight of the For Sale sign in the front yard had fractured Brady's reservoir of strength. His head slumped onto the steering wheel, tears finally spilling from his eyes. His father sat in the passenger seat, the distinctive scent of his aftershave providing a quiet comfort. A short while later, Brady felt the touch of his father's hand gently settle on the back of his neck; a meaningful yet brief gesture that infused both of them with a renewed sense of hope. Without a word, Brady traced his father's footsteps up the paved walkway and into the house, a last chance to cling to the memories inside.

Although a smorgasbord of casseroles, deserts and other comfort foods crowded the refrigerator -- courtesy of neighbors and friends -- the elder Tanner and his son ate bologna sandwiches from TV trays while sitting in front of the television.

The Tigers were at home playing the third game of a four-game series with the Indians and losing horribly. Brady stretched out on the couch and watched Detroit come from four runs down in the ninth to beat the Indians in extra innings.

From where his father was sleeping in the worn-out leather recliner, a rumble of snoring drowned out the sound of the play-by-play. The rocking chair his mother had always warmed, which flanked the fireplace and was within easy reach of her yarn basket, now sat idle. Brady caught himself several times stealing glances in its direction -- sure that he could hear the clinking of her knitting needles.

The next day, Brady escaped from Grand Rapids, relatively intact emotionally, yet unsure of when, or if, he would return. He had glanced back only once as he made the long walk down the gate to board his flight. His father smiled weakly, nodded, and then turned and disappeared into the crowd. There was no tear-filled goodbye or final embrace; merely a silent acknowledgment of the loss they both felt. Brady never expected that nearly three years to the day, he would be walking down that same gate into Grand Rapids' Gerald R. Ford International Airport for yet another tearful goodbye -- this time for his father. Fitting though, that both parents, had drawn their last breaths at the *Up North House*; the sound of the loons singing them to their final sleep.

And now, here he was, at the one place he had sworn he would never return. The key in his hand felt like an anchor. It contained the weight of years of regret. He jiggled it nervously inside his closed fist. "Okay, boy," he called to Gruff. Then, muttering under his breath, "Only thing we have to fear...and all that nonsense."

They made their way slowly down the path to the front porch. Gruff, oblivious to the anxiety growing inside his seemingly stalwart companion, followed behind distracted by the sights and sounds of nature -- a city dog taking in his first dose of country life.

Wildflowers and grass grew between the planked floorboards, up over the wooden handrail and posts. Leaves and other debris collected in the corners and sinewy webs hung from the weathered timbers overhead. The boards beneath his feet groaned as Brady stood motionless at the door.

With a nervous hand, he scraped the key into the rusted lock and felt the click as the knob turned. The door opened into the den. Brady paused, breathing in the stale, musty air. It was mixed with a pine scent, evidence of a recent cleaning. Frank and Maddie Griggs, the closest thing his family had to neighbors on the lake, lived four miles away. Brady's father and Frank had been friends since childhood, and Maddie and mom had been as close as sisters.

Since his father's death, the Griggs' had kept in touch with Brady through an occasional card or phone call to let him know they were, as Frank put it, *keeping an eye on things*. Brady had always pledged to visit the next weekend or the next month, but time flew by and the seasons changed.

The surprise in Frank's voice was unmistakable when Brady phoned him to say, "If you see the lights on this weekend, don't come in swinging your golf club – it'll just be me." They shared a laugh, followed by an uncomfortable silence, before Frank promised to have things in order for when Brady arrived. Having made good on his pledge to return, Brady felt as if somehow, his mission had been accomplished. As if now, he could turn tail and drive back to Chicago as fast as his Jetta could go.

Then he noticed something. The blinds were drawn, providing just enough light to see a note taped to the wall by the switch. Brady reached for the note as he flipped on the light.

Brady,

Maddie ran a dust cloth around the place and I made sure the plumbing was kosher. Everything else seems to be in order. There's a pie and some groceries in the fridge – just enough to welcome you back. We'll be up north this weekend enjoying the view from the island - we'll call when we get back.

Frank

Brady smiled -- Michiganders always go north to get away from it all – even those already living in the northern-most parts of the state.

The Griggs, year-rounders on nearby Bass Lake, were no exception. Mackinac Island, located midway between the state's Upper and Lower Peninsulas, had been their favorite vacation place for years.

Padding into the house, Gruff brushed past Brady, stirring him from his thoughts. Brady's gaze rose from the note. Opening that door had been like breaking the seal on a time capsule. Brady's life had moved on, yet inside these all-too-familiar walls, it was 1995 all over again.

Brady scanned the den. Trophies and photos lined the shelves and walls -- each capturing a moment in time, freezing it for display. His eyes retraced the years of his life, from diapers and toothless smiles to kindergarten graduation, Little League, family vacations and...braces. *God, how I hated those braces*, he mused. Brady had spent the better part of two years not smiling because of those damn braces, convinced that he looked like James Bond's steel-toothed, arch-nemesis Jaws. To this day he turned the channel in disgust any time a Bond movie came on TV.

A loud clatter, issued simultaneously with a sharp bark and low growl summoned Brady from his musings and sent him sprinting down the hall and through the kitchen to the source of the commotion.

The shadows gave way to light as the afternoon sun poured itself in through the massive windows overlooking the lake. Gruff, hackles raised and tail lowered, stood in the center of the room staring at the coffee table. Scrabble pieces were spread across its surface while others lay scattered on the floor.

"It's okay, boy," Brady said leaning down to soothe the dog with a scratch behind its ears. "That tail of yours just swept 'em right off the table." Chuckling, he continued "We'd solve the world's energy problems if we could harness the power of that wag." Brady stretched out his hand and picked the pieces up from the floor and tossed them on the table.

Scrabble had been a Tanner family tradition. Instead of church on Sunday mornings, it had been dad's chocolate-chip pancakes followed by a heated game of Scrabble. The game had remained a coffee table fixture both here, at the Up North House, as well as at their home in Grand Rapids. While Brady and his father had spent countless hours debating the rules surrounding the usage of slang and proper names, mom used her background as a nurse for an endless supply of medical terminology that proved insurmountable to the Tanner men. Brady could count on one hand the number of times either of them had beaten her at a game of Scrabble.

The memory lifted Brady's spirits as his focus drifted to the board, a bit surprised that Dad hadn't packed it away. *Why would he keep it out after Mom was gone?* Then, from among the tile pieces scattered across the tabletop, five squares stared up at Brady. Starting from the center square and traveling downward was a single, perfectly-placed word:

The blood drained from Brady's face, as a strange yet familiar sensation crept over him. Gruff's rumbling growl returned.

In an instant his mind leapt from one possibility to the next. *The tiles in the middle of the board would be the least likely to get disturbed when bumped. Simple physics, right? Or maybe dad had started a game and never finished it -- but with whom? No, Maddie probably set the pieces there when she was dusting – it would be like her clever way of welcoming me back.*

"Please allow me to introduce myself. I'm a man of wealth and taste," The Rolling Stones lyric erupted from out of nowhere, causing him to jump with a girlish squeal. The tension broken, Brady fished his i-Phone from his pocket. *Sympathy for the Devil* was the ring-tone he had assigned to his in-laws. He was far more impressed with the selection than Karen had been and promised to change it out for something less dramatic, but...

"Ooh, Ooh -- hope you guess my name," the song continued. Only because you saved us from this B horror movie Gruff and I were trapped in do I answer this, he thought as he reluctantly pressed the button to accept the call. "Hello," he answered, his voice containing more contempt than he intended to reveal.

"Brady, Thomas Greene, Karen's father. I didn't catch you at a bad time, did I?" His tenor clearly implied that he could care less if Brady was performing brain surgery. There was a message to be delivered and deliver it this moment he would.

"No, Tom," Brady replied emphasizing the name. He imagined steam pouring from his father-in-law's ears. He was *Thomas*, he had told Brady the first time they had met. They had been shaking hands across a crowded Thanksgiving table packed with Karen's relatives.

"Thomas Greene," was the introduction. Both the words and the handshake were cold and brief. "Welcome to our table."

"Thanks for inviting me, Tom," Brady replied, a lopsided grin sealing his fate. Karen had cautioned him about her father. But like watching a movie despite its negative reviews, Brady had refused to believe all that Karen had warned about her father. Determined to sit through scene after awkward scene, Brady would undoubtedly learn the long and hard way.

"Thomas, Mr. Tanner," was the curt reply. Then straightening his posture nearly to the point of snapping his spine, the man continued , "as my father and his father before him were named. Not Tom. A Tom is a cat of some sort I believe," he had smirked darkly.

Soft snickers from around the table trailed the remark. The home crowd, if you will, was a receptive one. Brady's face reddened as Karen's father had looked down his long nose at him.

"Or a turkey," Brady said, his tongue outpacing his brain. He averted his eyes and looked at the enormous bird gracing the center of the table, packed with stuffing. The silence that followed was deafening and seemed to last forever. From the far end of the table however, laughter broke, conquering the tension.

"Cheers, Brady. Come, sit here by me. Fill your plate and your glass. It's Thanksgiving for heaven's sake."

Brady turned to see a lanky, suit-clad thirty-something-year-old standing and motioning with one hand toward an empty chair to his left. In the other, he held a glass of wine. Brady recognized Will immediately from the countless photo albums Karen kept. She spoke of him often, and kindly.

"Let Karen catch up down there with mom and dad," he added. "I'm Will." He added, extending his hand, "Karen's brother. Welcome to our happy home." With the last syllables he shot a brief, yet frosty glare at his father.

Brady's grip on the phone tightened as he tried to bring his anger under control before continuing. "What can I do for you, sir?"

"It's regarding the Trust, Brady," the contempt thick in his voice. "We must get this resolved. Did you receive the paperwork from my attorneys? They assured me that everything was hand delivered."

Hand delivered my ass, Brady thought. If by hand delivered he was referring to the three suits with matching briefcases and attitudes that came to The Tribune last month to bully him into signing a set of documents that made War and Peace look like a children's book, then yes, it had been hand delivered.

"Yes, yes, of course I received them," he said, "right to my desk at work – all very convenient." *And right at deadline*, Brady wanted to add, but didn't. *Why give him the satisfaction?*

"Good. Good," Greene continued and then added a long pause for dramatic effect. "Then may I ask what the problem is? I assure you it is all very straight forward, and generous I might add."

The Trust that Mr. Greene had been part of Karen's inheritance from her grandparents. The stipulations divided the payments into three installments, the first to be made available to Karen on her twenty-fifth birthday. The second installment would be paid out when she reached thirty years of age, and the last, thirty-five.

Brady and Karen had been married shortly before Karen's 24th birthday. Just over a year later they had celebrated her 25th birthday in their tiny apartment while watching Jeopardy and eating frozen pizza. Brady had even sprung for a bottle of wine. Her inheritance was never mentioned. Less than a week later Karen was dead and Brady was named as sole beneficiary in her will.

"No problem at all, Tom," now Brady was emphasizing the name, poking at the angry grizzly bear with a very short stick. "I'm sure you can understand that a decision like this should be given time to...marinate." He smiled, feeling quite proud of his word choice. It was a self-important word -- one that Thomas Greene would have chosen. "My attorney is currently looking into the matter and I plan to discuss it with him in the very near future. Now is there anything else I can do for you?"

A long silence ensued, and when he spoke, his words carried the weight of a man who was not used to being trifled with. "Tanner, let's not mince words here. My daughter's...curiosity with you aside, we both know the right thing to do here is to settle this Trust. Fifty thousand dollars is more than fair compensation for a single year of marriage, wouldn't you agree?"

The nerve of this man discussing Brady's marriage as if it had been little more than a business transaction infuriated him. Hell, Brady didn't want the money. He'd love nothing more than to give it to Gilda's Club, the cancer support organization his mother had joined after her breast cancer diagnosis. What a difference $5.3 million could make there. But the money was locked in probate, and would be for years -- or so the attorneys had assured him. Years for Thomas Greene and his cronies to peer under every rock, to find anything and everything they could use against him and the people he cared about.

People like Greene disgusted Brady. The prick had money to waste on armies of attorneys and could afford to wage imaginary wars and fight petty battles. Brady's attorney advised him to settle and move on. Not surprisingly, Brady was just stubborn enough not to heed the advice.

"Sorry, Tom, I'm getting another call," Brady lied. In his best Thomas Greene impression he added, "It's my accountant. We're discussing some very exciting investment opportunities. Strike while the iron is hot, right? What do you say we put a pin in this and reconnect in about a week? I'll have my people get in touch with your people." Brady hit END, silencing his former father-in-law in mind-rant.

Brady wanted to scream, but instead lost his breath in laughter. In the span of five minutes he had gone from nearly wetting himself over an uncompleted game of Scrabble to basically telling the man who served on the Board's of Directors of some of the most prestigious Fortune 500 companies and cultural foundations to go fuck himself! Already he felt more alive than he had in ages.

Despite the interruption of the heated phone call, Gruff was still staring intently at the coffee table. "Come on, boy," Brady said, reaching over and sorting through the Scrabble tiles, "nothing to be afraid of." Pleased with himself, Brady laid out six tiles on the board.

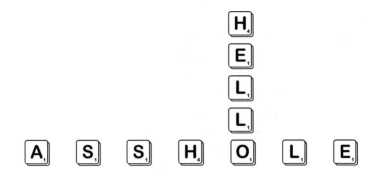

"Double word score that, TOM!" he announced triumphantly to the empty room. "Now Gruff, let's go get some of Maddie's pie."

Chapter 3

LOOKING BACK TO LOOK AHEAD

By 4:30 p.m. Brady could barely keep his eyes open. After the long drive from Chicago to Bedlam Falls and the rollercoaster of emotions of the afternoon -- not to mention the devouring of half of Maddie's famous apple pie -- he wanted nothing more than to rest his eyes. Gruff shared the same thought and had already claimed a patch of floor in the den near the stone fireplace.

Brady retrieved his bags from the car and migrated upstairs to what used to be his old bedroom. Maddie must have anticipated his choice of sleeping arrangements and had his bed ready with fresh linens and blankets. Kicking off his Chuck Taylor's, he plopped down on the twin bed and stretched out, arms resting behind his head and feet nearly dangling off the edge.

Cindy Crawford, wearing nothing but a tiny black bikini and a smile, stared down at him from the poster that was stapled to the ceiling. *Ms. Crawford*, he thought, *fancy meeting you here*. He stared into her deep brown paper eyes and instantly felt like a teenager again.

The walls were covered with the eclectic interests of his misspent youth. A Pearl Jam poster hung prominently over the small desk by the window. Many fans and musicians, both past and contemporary, considered them to be the Led Zeppelin of his generation. Brady's iPhone was filled with every track they had ever recorded -- even the unreleased versions that he secretly pirated off the Internet. He and his roommate had spent an entire summer after their sophomore year in college following the band on tour.

An autographed Barry Sanders Lions jersey hung unaccompanied in the open closet. Mere words couldn't describe the best running back the NFL had ever seen. Of course, the Lions had still sucked, but at least with Barry they sucked with style. Now that the star running back was retired, they weren't even worth watching.

Brady's gaze settled on his once-impressive, now horribly outdated boom-box resting on the dresser. He rose and approached the dust-covered radio wondering which CD had been entombed in the machine for over a decade. Pressing the PLAY button made him feel like he was playing an odd version of Russian Roulette. *Please, no Vanilla Ice*, he joking plead, as the soothing voice of Darius Rucker from Hootie and the Blowfish began to drift from the tinny-sounding speakers. Closing his eyes with relief, he collapsed back onto the bed to dream the dreams of a teenage boy celebrating summer vacation.

It was nearly midnight when Brady woke. Gruff had tracked him down, settling into the space at the foot of the bed. It was a habit he had picked up after Karen's death -- letting Gruff sleep in the bed with him. He wasn't sure who felt more comforted -- him or the dog.

Brady swung his feet off the bed, careful not to disturb his loyal companion, and stepped into his shoes. Guiding himself by moonlight and memory, he made his way down the hall to the bathroom. He hoped a quick splash of cold water on his face would wash the sleep from his eyes.

Why do I let that prick get to me? Brady wondered. But as much as he would like to blame his former father-in-law for the growing anxiety he was feeling, Brady was insightful enough to recognize that their heated exchange about Karen's trust was only part of what had his mind doing somersaults. He knew it had much more to do with being back here with all of these... memories.

Sadly, Brady was only partially right about the cold water; the fog of partial wakefulness still clouded his vision as he emerged from the bathroom and paused in the hallway. To the left waited his parent's bedroom. Back to the right would take him past the guest room to his own, and then beyond to the stairs. *Some things are best tackled in the light of day*, he concluded as he turned back to his right.

"Come on, boy," he called from the doorway. "Let's take a walk." Gruff responded with all of the energy a one-year-old lab could muster and bounded from the bed. Apparently the dog's slumber had been more peaceful than Brady's own.

Together, the pair made their way down the stairs and through the kitchen. The half-eaten pie remained on the counter. There was no plate in sight -- just an apple-encrusted fork resting in the pie pan.

Brady couldn't remember the last time he had used something other than paper plates. Most of the time he ate his meals standing at the kitchen sink -- a leftover piece of cold pizza or take -- out Chinese from the night before. Surprisingly, Gruff preferred the Szechwan Beef to pizza. "You'll be the first dog to master the art of chopsticks," Brady often joked as the dog sat at his feet licking the remnants of rice and vegetables from the carryout containers.

French doors opened off the kitchen to a small deck overlooking the lake. He had helped his father hang the doors during spring break of his freshman year of high school. The old maple tree along the side of the house had been split by lightning during one of the worst storms to hit the area since the *Big One* of 1958 -- famous for knocking out power for three months across three counties.

The strike had sent the business-end of the tree crashing through the roof, demolishing half the house. Between the mess in the kitchen, the wind-blown rain, and the resulting water damage throughout, the place was a complete and utter disaster. Surprisingly, his father took it all in stride. He had seemed almost excited by the family's misfortune. His parents had talked for years about wanting to remodel the kitchen, fix the aging roof, and maybe even adding some extra space for an office.

Brady wasn't sure how much his parents had sunk into the renovations, but there was no way insurance had covered everything. His father had used that lightning strike as an excuse to rebuild that old log cabin into his mother's dream house. In the span of a few short months The *Up North House* was transformed from the place they spent their summers and long weekends, to the home where his parents would someday spend their retirement. Not that any of that mattered now.

Brady walked through the French doors with Gruff in tow. Wind blew in from across the lake causing the tree limbs overhead to bend and sway. A set of chimes fashioned from old forks and spoons hung from the deck's lattice over-hang. *Sixth-grade Bible camp*, Brady thought, as the rusty silverware clanked in the breeze above him -- *worst week of my life*.

While Brady was growing up, a Seventh Day Adventist family had moved in next door to their house in Grand Rapids. The much-too-friendly neighbors made it their mission to "save" the Tanner family. His parents were able to politely decline their repeated invitations to attend Bible studies or Saturday services, but somehow they convinced Brady's mother that a week at Bible camp would be "a good thing." Seven days without television, radio or any-thing that resembled real food, equated to the worst form of torture a young boy could endure. Not to mention all of the singing and praying. The only lasting impressions Brady had taken from the experience were those damn chimes and a severe distaste for organized religion.

Stairs descended from the deck to an area of brick pavers with a fire-pit ringed with stones. His father had carefully arranged a collection of tree stumps around the pit for seating. A few short strides from the fire-pit lay the beach where an old wooden dock extended out over the lake.

Brady paused at the fire pit. The remnants of fires past still rested inside; the charred logs and debris-covered memories were burned recognition. The wind off the lake warned of a coming storm, and the gathering clouds played hide-and-seek with the moon allowing just enough filtered light to reflect off the lake's choppy surface. In the distance, the Asylum stood silhouetted against a backdrop of trees and hills. Brady was surprised to see that the building, which had shuttered its doors and windows half a century before, hadn't been leveled and replaced with a condo development or golf course.

Sweeping his gaze across the lake's shadowed waves, Brady was struck by surprise -- *the float is gone*.

When Brady was eleven, he and his father had strapped sections of the old dock to a couple of barrels and swam them out to the middle of the lake. They used chains tied around cement blocks to keep them in place. Most mornings they would race from the beach, swim to the float, then stretch out to bake in the sun. They'd talk about sports, life...and girls. He was twelve when Dad tried to give him "the talk" out on that float; he wasn't sure who had been more horrified. Now, like his dad, the float was merely one of a collection of memories that Brady rarely, if ever, revisited.

I guess I don't blame them. It would have been a tough reminder to have around. He sighed -- this was the part he had been dreading for the past fourteen years; standing here and looking out as the lake brought the memories of his last days at the *Up North House* all rushing back.

It was 1995 and shaping up to be the best summer of his young life. *A summer of firsts*, he thought, and *almost of lasts*. His first beer and kiss happened within a week of each other. Her name was April Mayer -- a combination which Brady had found so cute, yet April had hated with a passion. To this day the smell of cherries reminded him of her chapstick. The stale, albeit exciting, taste of that warm beer came in a distant second to that kiss.

They had met at Charlie's, the small ice cream place in town. Summer never officially began for his family until they enjoyed their first cone from Charlie's. Maybe it was the way she kept tucking her light brown hair behind her ear as it fell across her face when she leaned over to scoop ice cream or how her blue eyes sparkled under the visor she wore, but April took both his order - medium chocolate chip in a sugar cone - and his breath away. It was a wonderfully uncomfortable feeling, much like getting the wind knocked out of you from a punch to the stomach – only a million times better.

Every day for the next week he pedaled more than five miles each way for a banana split. His rationale: a banana split takes much longer to prepare than a simple cone, giving him more time to steal glances at her from behind his sunglasses. Twice he had waited in line only to have Maude, the heavyset woman who owned the place, swap-out April's station behind the counter to take his order. Aside from the obvious disappointment, Maude was also known for being very stingy with the toppings.

It took a week, and nearly all of the birthday money from his grandmother, to muster the courage to say something other than "Banana split, please." And even then, it wasn't as if he had cleverly delivered a witty ice-breaker; although he had spent enough time in front of his mirror practicing. The best he could do was, "I like bananas." He cringed as he thought back to what he had pathetically said so many years ago.

Brady nearly fainted when she replied with her own nervous giggle. "That's good, because you sure do eat a lot of them." *She noticed*, he shouted inside his head, and smiled. From that moment on they were nearly inseparable.

Gruff walked down to the water's edge, careful to keep Brady within sight. Ever since Karen's death the dog had suffered from some kind of canine anxiety disorder. Sometimes, he would pace from room to room in that small apartment, as if he would somehow find her if he just kept searching. And whenever Gruff was left alone for more than a few hours he became destructive – chewing and clawing at the flooring and curtains.

NBC's Dateline did a segment on pet anxiety disorders once and Brady remembered sitting on the couch with Karen and laughing at the people who took their pets to psychiatrists who treated them with antidepressants. But on the advice of a friend, Brady had set up his camera and caught it all on video. Watching it made him crumble inside. Although, in some odd way seeing Gruff grieve for Karen gave him permission to grieve, too. And part of his grieving process was letting her go – in ways both big and small.

Maybe that's why I'm here, pondered -- still unsure of why he had decided to come back to the Up North House -- *to put some distance between me and my memories of Karen.*

That's the funny thing about memories, however -- they can attach themselves to places…and things. No matter how much time or distance you give them, they wait for you to return. And since his return to the *Up North House* Brady could feel the memories pulling at him. Fourteen years is a long time to wait, and some memories are less patient than others. The impatient memories, he had learned, eventually start searching for you.

Now, staring out at the windswept lake, Brady knew they had found him and it was finally time to remember.

June 29, 1996
Bedlam Falls, Michigan

Brady knew before his father even opened his mouth what was coming. Maybe it was the devilish look in the man's eye or the way he was clutching the bag of marshmallows, but for whatever reason, Brady felt his face reddening in anticipation of the embarrassment that was fast approaching. "Did Brady ever tell you about the time he tried to roast marshmallows with the hair dryer?" his dad asked, passing the marshmallows around the fire.

"Now, John," his mother interrupted before the infamous hair-dryer story could be told. *A son can always count on his mother to come to the rescue.* "Don't you think the time he got into my make-up bag is a much better story? I know I do." And she gave Brady a sly wink.

Across the fire pit, April covered her mouth and giggled. Next to her Tammy Matthews leaned over and whispered something into April's ear. Brady could only imagine what they were discussing. Those two were trouble. At fourteen, Brady had already learned that girls were confusing enough on their own, but when you get two or more together, all bets were off.

On a stump to Brady's left, Jeff eagerly awaited the conclusion of the marshmallow story, as if there was an important moral to be learned. Jeff's own father had died in a car accident while Jeff was still in grade school, and in his absence it was clear to anyone who took the time to notice that Brady's friend practically worshipped John Tanner. The fact that Brady's father had spent fifteen years as the Chief of Detectives for the Grand Rapids Police Department probably factored into it. Jeff had grown up watching *COPS* on television and made no secret of his desire to wear the shield one day.

"You know, sir," said Jeff while pushing a marshmallow down onto a roasting stick, "I made a grilled cheese once with my mom's iron. I bet you could roast a marshmallow better with that than a hair dryer."

Brady's dad responded with a look of confusion and slowly nodded his head as he smiled. "Jeff, you just might be right." Something about Jeff Ryder, although always polite and by all accounts an all-around good kid, rubbed John Tanner the wrong way. But, much like family, a father doesn't get to choose his child's friends; his long years in law enforcement gave him the wisdom to realize that an annoying friend was significantly better than some of the alternatives.

John rose to his feet and reached over to rest his hand on Jeff's shoulder. "Linda, I think the kids are in very capable marshmallow roasting hands here." Squeezing the boy's shoulder, he continued, "What do you say we go watch some television?"

Jeff beamed at the compliment, missing the slightly sarcastic overtone. Not that he was a dim bulb; on the contrary, Jeff was extremely bright and the kind of athlete that comes around once every decade or so. More importantly, he was Brady's best friend in the world – even if it was only for three months every summer with the occasional long weekend mixed in.

"All right, dear," mom agreed. She leaned over and gave Brady a kiss on his cheek. "But we're not watching the game tonight. The Tigers will just have to lose without you. What do you say we pop some corn and rent a movie?" she suggested, sashaying over to her husband's outstretched arms.

Brady's father wrapped her in his arms and waltzed her in a slow circle that culminated in an awkwardly cheesy dip. "Groovy, baby."

The girls giggled again from across the fire. *Why do they have to be so embarrassing?* Brady cringed as he watched his parents make their way towards the house holding hands. "Goodnight," he called after them in a tone that clearly meant *Good Riddance*, too.

"G'night, kids," a waving reply over his father's shoulder, "TV says there's a storm coming in - don't stay out here too long."

"You're parents are so cute," Tammy teased as she moved over to the stump next to Jeff and grabbed a marshmallow from a stick he had been roasting. She picked it apart with her brightly painted fingernails and popped the gooiness into her mouth. Today her nails were lime green to match her shorts.

Brady always wondered what she did first – pick out her clothes or her nail color – they always seemed to match. "Nothing like my parents," she continued, "they hardly speak to each other."

The last thing a teenage boy wants to hear is how cute his parents are. To Brady, his parents were just mom and dad. He had been around enough of his friends' parents to understand his weren't much different than most, only in the small and embarrassing ways.

"Trust me," Brady responded as he raised a can of Coke to his lips. "My parents aren't so cute when I forget to clean my room or take the garbage out." He took a long drink and then added, "That reminds me, what's with the trash bag, Jeff? I saw you shove it behind the bushes when your mom dropped you off. You don't have severed heads or something in there, do you?"

"Gross," April groaned and raised herself off the stump and stretched. She was tall, taller than Brady anyway. Not by much, but just enough to have bragging rights. She had insisted once that they stand back to back just to prove it. Brady watched her turn and look out over the lake. "It's so quiet,'" she noted, turning to look at Brady through the dancing flames of the fire. "These crickets and frogs would drive me nuts," she declared over the usual sounds of a northern Michigan shoreline. "I thought the reason people choose to live out in the middle of nowhere was for the peace and quiet. Besides, don't you miss having neighbors?"

April lived in a trailer park with her parents and younger sister. Brady could understand how not having neighbors would seem so foreign to her. In a trailer park you couldn't sneeze in your kitchen without having your neighbor's next door say bless you from theirs.

"I guess you get used to it after awhile," Brady shrugged. "Besides, I get enough noise and people in Grand Rapids," he added, referring to his family's house in the city. "It's nice to have quiet for a change."

"You've got neighbors here," Jeff said as he retrieved the trash bag from its hiding place in the bushes. And then gesturing to the lake, "That old nut house across the lake isn't as empty as people think. You know it's haunted, right?"

"What are you talking about? You mean that old hospital?" Brady remembered asking his father about it once as they sat on the float enjoying the morning sun.

"It's just an empty building, Brady," his father had replied casting a nervous glance at the hospital. "Just promise me you'll stay away from it," he continued – his gaze returning to Brady. "I'm not saying that the place is dangerous." His father paused, "But old buildings are like teeth, Brady. They rot from the inside out when they're not cared for."

His father had hesitated before reaching over and playfully wrapping his arm around Brady's shoulder. "Which reminds me – did you brush this morning?" Without warning, his dad wrestled Brady off the edge of the float into the water. "Race you back," he shouted and began swimming for shore. "Loser has to mow the lawn."

Brady pulled his attention from the darkened hospital to Tammy as she added, "Yeah, the hospital. You do know what happened there, right? Why it closed and everything?" She finished the marshmallow and wiped her sticky fingers on her shorts as she, too, stood. Brady shrugged in ignorance. "He really doesn't know," she said, turning to Jeff as he returned with the trash bag.

April came around the fire and stood next to Brady, sliding her hand into his. "Stop it, Tammy. It's really not funny." She squeezed Brady's hand as she turned to face him. "We always thought you knew. I mean, it's no secret."

Brady didn't know how to respond. He'd never given that place across the lake so much as a second thought, and now a million questions formed in his mind but none came to his lips. His eyes moved from April's face and drifted again to the hilltop structure silhouetted against the moon. Her hand slid from his, moving up his arm to rest on his shoulder. He felt Jeff and Tammy draw closer, too. For a brief time they all stood quietly, gazing out into the moonlit darkness. Brady's frightened expression drew smiles from his friends.

It was Jeff's voice that broke the silence. "So what if you live next to a hospital full of soul-devouring ghosts who're just waiting to eat the flesh from your bones?" he laughed and then added, "You, at least, have cable TV!" and burst out laughing. The girls joined in.

"You really are way too easy, Brady," Tammy said as she stepped forward and playfully punched him in the arm. Brady watched her turn to April and soon the two were whispering and giggling again.

"Not cool," he muttered to Jeff as he turned from the girls and grabbed the bag from his friend's hand. He dropped down on a stump near the fire to examine its contents and instantly his spirits brightened. "Hey girls," he called out as he dumped the bag's contents on the ground. "I hope you brought your suits."

Chapter 4

BENEATH THE WAVES

As is the case with most daring adventures planned at the spur of the moment, the act of doing the deed rarely measures up to the anticipation. Swimming out to the float to light off fireworks seemed like a great idea while standing on the shore near the warmth of the fire, but actually doing it had some serious drawbacks. For one, climbing out of the warm water into the cool air was more than a little uncomfortable. The wind had also picked up, bringing with it low hanging clouds that suffocated the moon's pale light. The clincher, however, was that nobody had thought to bring a lighter or matches.

"So let me see if I have this right," Tammy asked as she stood shivering on the edge of the float with April, teeth chattering and water dripping from her hair. "You dragged us all the way out here to light off fireworks and you didn't even bother to bring a lighter?"

Brady was smart enough to know a rhetorical question when he heard one. Sadly, however, Jeff stumbled right in. "How was I supposed to know that aquaman here," jerking a thumb in Brady's direction, "would swim us all out here? I figured we'd light 'em from the shore." He took a step forward and reached for her, offering his most innocent smile. "Besides, it's really not that bad once you get used to it."

Tammy responded with a look of disgust and more chattering teeth, but she took his hand and let him bring her into his arms. She buried her head in his chest as he stroked her arms and shoulders in an attempt to generate some heat.

Smooth, Brady thought. His plan to impress the ladies with a romantic fireworks display out on the lake was blown, excuse the pun. But sure enough, Jeff had turned misfortune to his advantage. He stood there watching them, one hand folded across his chest for warmth and the other still clutching the trash bag full of fireworks. He was so lost in thought that he didn't notice April's approach.

"Well played. Most guys would have been happy cuddling by the fire, but not you. You maroon us out here in the middle of the lake." Smiling now, she moved closer, "All part of your master plan, I suppose?"

Brady could see the water running down her goose bumped arms and legs. He had seen her in a bikini before, but always safely in the light of day. Out here, at night, she looked…different. His first inclination was to take a step back, but his heels were already at the edge. "I – uh – um - I," came his stammering reply as he fidgeted with the bag and his words.

She leaned in and pressed her shivering lips to his, sending warmth through him like a bolt of lightning. The last thing he remembered before closing his eyes to her kiss was the touch of her hands to his face and the passing thought that even without a lighter, these fireworks were amazing.

A short time later, the fireworks from their make-out session behind them, Brady and April sat together. She rested her head on his shoulder. Behind them Jeff and Tammy were also cuddled - the sound of their conversation drowned out by the splashing of the water against the barrels supporting the float. The prediction of stormy weather appeared to be coming true as the raft rolled on the wind-blown and choppy surface of the lake.

"I wish the wind would just blow us back," April snuggled closer into Brady's chest. "I really don't want to get back in that water. I just want to fall asleep right here in your arms."

Brady didn't blame her. The air had cooled at least ten degrees since they had been out here and there was no telling how much colder the water would feel. He had already resigned himself to the fact that the night was going to end with a very cold swim back to the shore. Fortunately, however, there was a warm fire waiting for them. He could see it flickering in the distance.

Without warning a jagged finger of lightning splintered across the sky. It was quickly followed by a clap of thunder that shattered the silence and swept over the lake like the blast from a shotgun. Jeff jumped to his feet. "Holy shit - that was close!" He seemed almost excited by the prospect of re-enacting Ben Franklin's famous kite and key experiment. "Look at the hair on my arm, dude – its standing straight up!" He held out his arm begging for someone to notice. "That-was-fucking-awesome," he screamed into the night and raised his arms into the air, as if urging the storm overhead for an encore.

Tammy grabbed him by one outstretched arm and spun him around. "Correct me if I'm wrong, but isn't being in the middle of a lake like the last place you want to be during a thunderstorm?"

As the reality of her comment sunk in, Jeff lowered his arms and sheepishly looked from Tammy's face and over to Brady and April as they rose to their feet. "Maybe we should just – um – head back," he added and jerked his thumb back in the direction of Brady's house.

"There's really nothing to worry about," Brady said, and then slouching slightly as he stood next to April he added. "As long as the Amazon Woman here," nudging her with his hip, "is out here with us we're safe. Lightning always strikes the tallest tree, right?" He knew April would one day regret that half-inch advantage she held over him. For the briefest of moments he stood with that lopsided grin on his face – the one that his mother claimed always meant mischief.

Her response was quick and not altogether surprising. The Amazon Woman easily shoved him off the edge of the float and into the water. His lop-sided grin quickly fell from his face as he plunged beneath the waves. He sunk like a stone.

Brady found himself in the lake's frigid grasp, his very life being squeezed from his lungs as he sank further into the darkness. It seemed an eternity that he fell. He knew from the amount of chain it had taken his father to secure the float that the lake bottomed out at nearly forty feet; Brady had the sensation that he was fast approaching its limit. And then, just as quickly as he had descended, Brady was belched out and upward as if the lake had thought better of swallowing him whole. He sputtered and splashed as he broke the water's surface.

"Brady! Brady!" He heard Jeff's frantic call from the darkness somewhere to his left. The storm had finally broken and sheets of raining were ricocheting off the lake's choppy surface. The water ran from his hair and into his eyes nearly blinding him to the cries of his friend. As he felt the air rush back into his lungs he responded to Jeff's calls with a stuttering whisper that was no match to the sound of the wind blowing across the lake, "H-h-ee-re. O-ov-e-rr...he-e-re."

Without warning, the lake reconsidered and, with its icy tentacles, pulled Brady back down beneath its surface. What little air was left in his lungs emerged as a silent bubbling scream as he struggled against the force that was pulling him deeper into the inky blackness. His last thought before giving into whatever awaited him at the bottom of Asylum Lake was of April...the taste of her cherry Chapstick...and fireworks.

The clouds, which had hung gray and threatening most of the night, fully opened above him, sending sheets of rain across the once placid surface of the lake. The drops washed over Brady and traced salty lines as they ran down his face. He wiped the back of his hand across his eyes and shook his head in disbelief as he realized the rain was mixed with his tears.

Brady turned to find Gruff standing in the shallow waters near the shore. The dog's tail was tucked and its eyes were locked onto some distant point out on the horizon. Brady could read the anxiety in Gruff's body language. A slow and silent spark of lightning arched through the clouds overhead, and for the briefest of moments the asylum across the lake stood illuminated against the menacing backdrop of the surrounding hills and trees. The sight made Brady's skin crawl.

The feeling was familiar and it brought his thoughts back to that night on the float, and more specifically to what he had experienced beneath the waves. Quickly, his thoughts jumped forward to the next thing he had remembered after surrendering to the cold darkness of the water – waking up two days later at a hospital in Traverse City, courtesy of a twenty-five minute aero-med flight. The helicopter ride and everything else in between and right after was lost or at least buried in a way that he hadn't quite found a way to uncover...yet. It gnawed at him from just below the surface of his memory.

Maybe this journey would be little more than a failed attempt to reconcile himself with the painful memories from his past but, as he stood at the end of the dock and gazed out through the wind and rain of a summer storm into the muted grays of the midnight hour, Brady felt both oddly cleansed and at the same time as if he were on the verge of something great...and terrible. It brought neither a feeling of fear nor comfort, but turning to make his way back to the *Up North House*, he knew at least the few remaining hours of this night would be filled with dreams of a far happier and less complicated time.

As Brady began the trek back from the sandy beach, he was unaware that his was not the only spirit searching for answers and in need of cleansing. Mere yards away, strewn along the rocky and forgotten bottom of Asylum Lake, the unremembered were growing restless.

Chapter 5

CRIMES AGAINST HUMANITY

November 2, 1971
Bedlam Falls, MI

Blood spilled by violence leaves a stain far different from blood which is shed in any other way. As Lionel stood on the tips of his toes at the kitchen sink, he was surprised by how much more difficult blood was to wash away than the dirt he was accustomed to. The dish rag had done little to clean the gore from beneath his fingernails. It had taken a fork from the drawer to scrape most of it out. As for the streaks and spatters that coated his forearms, neck and face - they seemed to be a lost cause. Lionel had considered showering, but that would have meant removing what was left of Mrs. Reed from the bathtub. In the end he did what he could with a wet towel and decided not to worry about the rest.

Not that the mess was limited to the kitchen; bloody tracks led from one end of the small Cape Cod to the other and smeared fingerprints were on everything from the kitchen knives to the golf club he discovered in the hall closet. Even the hedge clippers he had picked up in the garage were bloodied ... and broken. The blades had actually bent and snapped clear off from the wooden handles. The dull and rusty shears had worked just fine on the kids, but Mrs.

Reed was a big woman with thick bones – and thick bones, he learned, required a hacksaw. Lionel had to make the long walk from the bathroom to the garage three times for new blades.

The white plastic bracelet hung loosely on his wrist throughout the entire ordeal. It, too, had been stained beyond any hope of coming clean. Most of the words, however, were still legible beneath the smears of blood.

```
Ellis Arkema        #00981
SOUTH WING, LAKE VIEW ASYLUM

DOB: UNKNOWN    Age: NA  Sex: M
SSN: UNKNOWN    Dos: NA  Dr. W. Clovis
```

Lionel liked the feel of the cool plastic against his skin. He had found the bracelet while fishing with his father. It was the only thing he had hooked all day. He felt compelled to hide it away in his pocket before his father could notice. Ever since then he had gradually set aside most of his other interests – everything from comic books to baseball cards – and instead found himself spending his time alone in his room imagining stories about who Ellis Arkema was and how he may have lost that bracelet in the lake.

At times it almost felt as if he were listening to someone else tell these stories – a faceless and shadowy voice inside his head that was both scary and reassuring. Sometimes the stories made him cry and other times he laughed out loud. It all seemed to make his parents more than a bit uncomfortable. He had thought, and the voice agreed, that maybe he should keep the bracelet a secret.

He turned from the sink and decided to make one more trip through the house before leaving. He followed the trail of blood and gore from the hardwood floor in the kitchen to the orange shag carpeting that led through the living room and down the hallway. A dead body is difficult thing for anyone to move, and at only twelve, it had taken quite an effort for Lionel to drag it all the way to the bathroom.

The door to the nursery the twins shared was wide open. He could see their small forms huddled close together on the floor as he paused in the hallway. The pools of blood that spread from under their lifeless bodies formed giant wings in the carpet. It was an oddly beautiful sight – the pale light coming in through the window falling gently across their outstretched wings. Their bodies, he reasoned, were mere cocoons from which he had helped them escape. He envied the flight of their spirits.

Slicing their tiny throats had proven to be much more difficult than he had anticipated, but the hedge-clippers had taken away their hands and feet quite easily. As he continued down the hall, Lionel tried unsuccessfully to remember where he had put them.

The bathroom looked like someone had flung red paint violently across the walls and floor. Spattered blood ran down and across the mirror hanging over the vanity and onto the toilet nearby. The broken hedge-clippers had been thrown into the corner near the trash. Dull hacksaw blades and an assortment of knives and other tools lay scattered coldly on the tile. The back of the toilet reminded him of the meat case at Dell's Grocery – filets and various other cuts of the late Mrs. Reed were neatly stacked into three identical, gooey rows. Blood trailed from the oozing stacks down the side of the tank and onto the floor, forming clotted pools.

Lionel drank in the coppery smell of the blood and gore, a devious smile flashing across his innocent lips.

Stepping carefully toward the tub, he attempted to avoid the slick pools of blood. He had slipped and fallen once already, banging his elbow painfully against the toilet. It had sent a jolt throughout his entire arm that throbbed with every step he took.

Looking up, Lionel noted sadly that the shower curtain had been torn aside and hung clumsily by the three remaining rings that still encircled the pristine rod – the one part of the bathroom that remained untouched by the gore around it.

He stared into the red soup of bones and chunks as they floated on the surface of the nearly over-filled tub. Others pieces rested at the bottom and clung to the sides of the tub; he fought the urge to reach in and stir them around with his hand. Instead, he raised his eyes to look at the shower wall. A single lonely word, written in blood, glistened on the white tile:

REPENT

The sound of heavy footsteps approaching from down the hall roused him from admiring his handiwork. Lionel's knees wobbled and his thoughts became fuzzy as a wave of dizziness washed over him. He closed his eyes and rubbed at his temples in an attempt to ease the feeling. When he opened them and caught sight of the grotesque display that surrounded him, a mixture of bile and recently eaten cookies rose in his throat. It burned as he swallowed it down.

"What the...Oh, Lord no!" A pained cry came from the next room.

His heart began to pound so heavily he thought for sure it would beat right through his chest. The room was spinning now as fear swept through him. He felt the earth shift beneath his feet and thought for sure he would faint. Just as he was ready to give in and let go the voice inside his head began to scream. "Kill him! Kill him now!"

His arm shot forward involuntarily and grabbed the broken hedge-clipper shear from where it lay on the floor. As he caught sight of the bracelet on his wrist his racing heart slowed. He took in a single deep breath and blew it out releasing it in a slow and soft hiss. A quiet calm settled upon him.

The sound of more footsteps, this time retreating quickly towards the living room, urged him forward. He stepped into the hallway and silently made his way towards the twin's room. Anger rushed through him as he looked at their once perfectly posed bodies now lying disturbed on the floor. Their butterfly wings had been trampled by large booted feet.

He followed the fresh tracks from the room. He could hear movement ahead and emerged to see Mr. Reed standing at a small desk in the living room with one hand pressing the phone to his ear as the other frantically tried to turn the rotary dial. His blue work overalls were stretched across his large frame and his dark brown boots creaked as he shifted his weight nervously from foot to foot. Below the soles of his sneakers, red patterned designs etched themselves deeply into the carpet.

The dull shear bit into the palm of Lionel's tiny hand as his grip tightened around it.

"P-p-pl-ease...something has happened," he cried into the phone. They're dead...my babies...they're dead." And then the revelation that he hadn't seen his wife lying with the kids dawned on him. He dropped the phone and quickly turned, ready to run back into the bloodied mess he had just retreated from. Lionel struck quickly and brought the rusty shear up and across the much taller man's throat with one quick and surprisingly powerful stroke. The dull blade tore into his neck as he cried out for his wife. Her name rose in a gurgling spray of blood that spread across the room and onto the bookshelves and wall. It ran down the screen and across the top of the large console television that sat nearby. Reed fell to the floor at Lionel's feet where he lay twitching…and finally, dying.

Lionel dropped the blade and casually stepped over the body. He reached down and pulled the knob on the television and then turned the dial until the theme song from Gilligan's Island began to waft from the set. He walked to the sofa and plopped down on the edge of a freshly blood-spattered cushion. Beneath a thick coating of blood that now included both the dried and fresh varieties, an impish grin played across his delicate features. His eyes remained frozen on the gore-covered television screen as he absently worked at wiping the bracelet clean on his pants. Within minutes the sound of sirens outside drowned out Gilligan and the Skipper arguing about coconuts. Lionel heard neither, however. He was lost to the voice inside his head.

Deputy John Tanner was the first to arrive at the Reed residence. He knew Ken Reed only in passing, mostly from Sundays at church. They shared polite handshakes and brief, innocuous conversations about everything from the weather to the current sad state of the Lions. Ken was a big man and quiet - definitely not one to be rattled easily. Tanner was at the station when Ken's call came in and the voice he heard over the line carried with it neither the size nor strength he had always attributed to him. It's tone had left the deputy rattled and more than a bit curious about what could panic the mountain of a man so horribly.

From the outside, at least, he found the Reed home to be nothing less than ordinary. Piles of leaves dotted the large yard and a single rake leaned precariously against the mailbox. The garage door was open and no vehicles were in the driveway. He parked on the street and cut the sirens – leaving the lights on.

He reached for the radio and pressed it to his lips. "Maddie, you read me? It's John. Where the hell is Frank?" Maddie worked dispatch for the Bedlam County Sheriff's Department, and Frank – simple words couldn't describe Deputy Frank Griggs. He was…an experience. And John had been experiencing Frank's antics since they were in grade school together. He had long suspected that Frank and Maddie were more than merely co-workers, which was frowned upon by the Sheriff, but he hadn't the courage to inquire. If they were happy then he was happy for them.

"Loud and clear, John." Maddie's voice crackled through the speaker. "Frank's been," a pause, "delayed."

It was more in the way she said it than what she actually said that sounded so odd. Frank had once been "delayed" to a drunk and disorderly call in the parking lot at The Hayloft. It was opening day of firearm season and the story went that he had spotted a fourteen point buck running along the side of Country Road 22 just outside of town. Frank took it down from the driver's seat with his service revolver, the steering wheel cradled between his knees. He pulled into The Hayloft an hour later with the monster tied with yellow caution tape across the hood of his cruiser. The once angry crowd erupted into cheers and high fives. They dispersed peacefully a short time later with most retreating back into the smoky confines of The Hayloft to toast the sharp shooting Deputy Frank Griggs.

John tossed the radio onto the seat next to him and flung open the driver's door of the cruiser. A polite rain was falling – a fine but cold mist accompanied by a sharp breeze that brought with it the warning of a heavier storm in the very near future. He rounded the back of the car and briefly gazed up at the western sky where dark clouds gathered on the horizon. His hand moved instinctually to unbuckle the sidearm holster on his hip as he leaned into the wind and started down the driveway.

He was halfway down the driveway when he caught site sight of the footprints. They were small and red and seemed to double back and forth across themselves both entering and exiting the partially open door that led from the garage into the house. Deputy Tanner paused and drew his weapon. He briefly debated returning to the car for his radio, but at the site of the blood in the garage, Ken Reed's words, "They're dead...my babies are dead," came pounding back into his head, leaving him shaking with fear as the reality of the situation swept over him. His sweaty grip tightened around the gun as he crept forward fearful of who had left those footprints, but convinced he would soon find out.

Deputy Griggs pressed his face against the window and peered inside. The cold rain ran down his neck and back. "Shit," he cursed as he stepped back and pulled the hood of his yellow slicker over his head. It was the fourth time he had bent down to look into the window, as if he somehow expected the keys would be magically removed from the ignition and safely in his hand instead. Finally, after resigning himself to the fact no magic key fairy was coming to his rescue, he crossed his arms across his barrel chest and leaned against the locked door of the cruiser, listening to the sound of John Fogerty's raspy voice singing Credence Clearwater Revival's *Have You Ever Seen The Rain* echo from the comfort of the dry interior of the car. *Yeah, I've seen the fucking rain*, he thought, letting the heat from the idling car warm his stiffening back.

Fortunately, he thought to himself, it had been only a half a mile walk to the nearest house. The old couple seemed quite understanding when he explained that he needed to use their phone. Police emergency, he had assured them. If only he had thought of a police emergency that involved asking to use their bathroom before he had decided to stop and take a leak on the side of the road; hindsight. If only -- he wouldn't be standing out in the rain right now. He could only imagine what Johnny would say when he arrived.

He heard the siren long before the car came into view over the rise. The flashing reds and blues cut through the pouring rain as the cruiser sped towards him. Puzzled, Frank walked to the front of his car as he watched the lights draw closer. His heart fell as he saw the Sheriff Buck Tanner's face tighten into a scowl behind the windshield wipers as the car rolled to a stop. "Fuck a duck," he muttered as he shook the rain from his slicker and braced for the verbal barrage that was sure to come.

"Get your ass in here, Griggs," the Sheriff yelled as he rolled the driver's side window down. The deputy hesitated momentarily, "Now, Frank – there's trouble!"

The confused deputy sprinted to the passenger door and threw himself into the car. If he didn't know better he would say the Sheriff was scared -- and that was something that just didn't happen. His scowl had been replaced by a very pale and blank expression.

"Sheriff, let me explain," Griggs began, lowering his hood and removing his cap. He ran a shaking hand through his slick hair and continued. "I've been in that car all day, sir and I knew I wouldn't be able to make it all the way back to the station…"

He was interrupted by the crackle of the radio. "Sheriff, can you read me? Power's out here in town and we're running off the generator." It was Maddie's voice, and Griggs thought she sounded as nervous as the Sheriff looked.

The sheriff's hand shot forward and grabbed the radio from its cradle on the dash. "Here, Maddie." A pause and then glancing at his drenched passenger, "We're right here."

Maddie exhaled into the radio with obvious relief and then continued. "John's on-scene, sir – he called in looking for Fra – I mean Deputy Griggs."

"Well, get him on the horn and tell him we're on our way," the Sheriff ordered, glancing again at Griggs, who seemed to have shrunk at least six inches as he sank down into the seat trying to disappear into the upholstery. "I've been trying to reach him, but with this storm I think there's some kind of interference."

Silence, and then, "Sheriff," another pause and then with a quivering voice, Maddie said, "I've been trying for the past ten minutes and he's not responding."

Frank straightened in his seat. "What's going on, sir? Where's John?"

Sheriff Buck Tanner reached down and hung the radio back in its cradle as his foot pressed down even further on the accelerator. His eyes blazed from beneath the trademark Stetson hat atop his head but said nothing. They sped away – leaving Griggs' still-running car along the side of the road. Griggs looked into his side view mirror and watched the cruiser disappear from sight.

He sat in silence waiting for an explanation and watched the speedometer out of the corner of his eye begin to bounce as it shot passed ninety and blew towards one-hundred miles per hour. Trees and fields zipped by outside the rain streaked windows as they sped along the slick country roads back towards town.

They drove without speaking as if hypnotized by the scraping of the wipers across the windshield - keeping perfect time with the blaring siren overhead. Grip tightening on the steering wheel, Buck Tanner's instincts turned from his responsibility as Sheriff to protect and serve the public, to those of a father trying to save his son.

John Tanner entered the garage and approached the open door. He carefully stepped over the bloody footprints, taking note of their relatively small size. He saw no obvious signs of a struggle, only what appeared to be an ordinary garage. An old riding mower was parked in the corner next to a giant snowmobile. The place was clean and orderly, except for the busy trail of bloody prints mapping paths to and from the house. They appeared to lead to the workbench.

Tools sprawled across its surface. The blood became visible as the deputy drew closer. He plucked a claw hammer from the bench and held it up in the light. Torn bits of flesh riddled with long dark hair clung to its claws and both the head and handle were slick with blood. As the realization of what he was looking at sunk in, the hammer slid from his hand landing and bouncing from the workbench with a thud. Revulsion overwhelmed him as he stumbled backward.

Trying to escape the sickening horror as he stumbled away, the young deputy failed to notice the small shadow creep up behind him. As John Tanner turned, however, he could feel the stab of something very sharp and cold bury itself into his chest. The pain dropped him to his knees, bringing him face-to-face with his attacker. The warm spread of blood flowed down his arm and over his hand. He attempted to raise his gun to ward off a second blow but instead felt it slide through his weakening grip.

As his world gave way to blackness, the deputy looked into the eyes of his small, blood soaked assailant. It was like looking into the bottom of an endless well of darkness. He felt small hands on his body -- pulling and tugging -- and then closed his eyes. The wail of an approaching siren gave Deputy Tanner hope – even as piercing flashes of pain about his face and chest tried to steal it away.

Chapter 6

HOUSE OF THE DEAD

Deputy Frank Griggs didn't know what the hell was going on, but he knew from the way Sheriff Tanner was white knuckling the steering wheel that it must be serious. More than once the cruiser had swept into an oncoming lane of traffic as it sped around slower vehicles. They were breaking every rule of the road, and Griggs could feel his stomach lurch at the thought of what they might be hurrying toward.

The Sheriff eased his foot off the accelerator as they entered the city limits. Their speed dropped from well over one hundred down to just over seventy. Bedlam's lone stoplight hung dark and heavy over Main Street as the cruiser passed beneath it. Without power, storefronts and lawns were enveloped in a murky grayness. The flashing reds and blues of the lights atop the car cast eerily hypnotic shadows against the quiet backdrop of the sleepy little town. Somewhere in the storm clouds overhead the sun was nearing the horizon. Below however, Bedlam Falls was entombed in premature nighttime.

Buck Tanner's voice cut through the silence, "I came into the station right after Johnny left." He paused, choosing his words carefully. "Maddie took a call from Ken Reed – something about his babies being dead." He spoke as if he were testifying at court – brief answers that revealed simple facts and little else. "Something happened and she lost him…Ken, that is. The line was open but all she heard was… a thump."

The cruiser skidded from the pavement onto the rough and rocky gravel of Sigler Road as Buck cranked the wheel hard to his left. They could see the flashing lights of Johnny's car in the distance through the sheets of rain. Once again, the Sheriff pressed his foot down hard on the accelerator and then added in a rough whisper that sounded like sandpaper as the words scraped between his lips, "She spent fifteen minutes listening to Gilligan's Island…till the storm knocked the power out," a final pause as he set his jaw and turned to Griggs. "And that's about the last time anyone's heard from Johnny."

Griggs swallowed slowly as the full impact of what was unfolding settled over him. He reached for the .38 at his side and brought it out from its holster. With the flick of his wrist the short-barreled pistol snapped open to reveal a full cylinder. It spun as he snapped it closed. In his three years as a Deputy, Griggs had never drawn his gun on a call. Now that he held it in his shaking hand with the very real possibility that he may have to use it, it felt heavy with the weight of responsibility.

Every time you draw your gun you hold a life in your hands, Sheriff Tanner had told him the day he pinned the badge to his chest. *Sometimes to save a life, you have to take one, he added. And then giving his hand one firm shake, And as much as you try to convince yourself that it all balances out in the end – it doesn't. It's best just to let God worry about the math.*

The cruiser skidded to a stop at the end of the driveway announcing their arrival to anyone within earshot. Buck had the door partially open even before the car stopped rolling. "Cover the back," he barked to Griggs as he drew the cannon he kept holstered on his hip. It was a .44 Magnum, the same gun Clint Eastwood would make famous in his Dirty Harry movies. He sprinted towards the house without looking back.

Griggs leapt from the vehicle with his .38 in hand. He leaned into the blowing rain and made his way through the yard as the Sheriff disappeared into the darkened garage. Wind and rain aside, the place felt too quiet. He crept to the side of the house and peered in a window. Shadows on top of shadows greeted him.

He continued along, slowly making his way to the backyard. The faint sound of banging and creaking could be heard. Griggs felt his stomach tighten and paused before rounding the corner, both hands clutching the gun. Through the rain he could see a tire swing dancing in the wind. The limb overhead creaked each time the tire struck the large maple. He exhaled slowly as he surveyed the back of the house. A gas grill stood alone on a small cement patio with what appeared to be outdoor furniture neatly stacked beside the grill.

The yard extended beyond the large maple tree into a densely wooded area. *State land,* Griggs thought as he stared into the trees. It went on for miles – all the way to the lake and old hospital.

His attention returned to the house as a shadow passed quickly behind the window. He approached and stood on his toes to look inside - nothing. He reached for the flashlight on his belt and brought it up to the window. As he contemplated whether to switch it on and alert whoever was inside to his presence, a streak of lightning illuminated the entire yard. It was followed almost immediately by a crack of thunder that pierced the silence. The brightness lasted only a millisecond, but it was long enough for him to see the body of Kenneth Reed laying motionless on the floor inside. Reed's eyes were open and his lifeless gaze burned through the window.

Startled, Griggs jumped away from the window and pressed his back against the house. His yellow slicker provided little refuge as the cold rain soaked him to his core. He shivered as he took a deep breath and exhaled slowly.

Fuck it! He thought, switching on his flashlight. Its beam sliced through the darkness, yet provided little comfort. He ducked under the window and took four long strides to the back door. The locked handle jiggled in his hand.

Griggs stepped back and raised his heavy foot to the door and kicked it in. He entered, full of confidence and ready to kick ass. Shattered glass and splintered wood littered the floor. Ahead, an open door revealed stairs that led down to the basement. As he swung the beam to his right the light fell over the kitchen counter; pooled blood covered everything. The darkened basement could wait, he decided, proceeding into the gruesome kitchen.

The cabinets, countertops and backsplash were encased with gore. Blood-soaked towels were strewn everywhere as if someone had tried, albeit unsuccessfully, to clean up. In the center of this gore sat a plate of chocolate chip cookies. As he stared at the cookies, Grigg's attention was drawn to a lump of towels in the sink. He fought the urge to scream as he looked in horror at a pile of tiny feet and hands stacked in the sink – *there were too many; three feet, four? How many hands?* Griggs' mind couldn't register what he was seeing.

The sheriff's words echoed inside his head, *Maddie took a call from Ken Reed – something about his babies being dead. And then, something happened and she lost him.*

Griggs turned quickly from the sink, wretching, as a distant and muffled groan broke the silence. "Johnny," he whispered as he followed the bloody tracks and drag marks into the living room. And then, "Sheriff, is that you?"

The light fell on Ken Reed's bludgeoned body. His face, neck and chest were slick with blood. The phone rested on the floor beside his outstretched hand. It, too, was bloodied. The deputy scanned the room and saw the streaks and spatters that covered the walls and furniture -- even the television. Looking down at the lifeless body, he instinctively reached down to check for a pulse, although clearly, there was no need. As his fingertips touched the fresh blood and the cooling flesh, he jerked his hand back.

Griggs followed the trail of gore deeper into the house as it led down the hall. Thunder rolled overhead as the wind picked up intensity, sending sheets of rain beating down on the roof and against the windows. Occasional flashes of lightning accompanied the thunder. And, as much as Griggs cringed at the sight of the carnage those lightening flashes revealed, it was what may be waiting unseen in the shadows that sent a cold stab of fear into his heart.

Buck Tanner had seen a lot in his twenty-plus years in law enforcement. As a young deputy in 1959, he had been the first on scene to a wintry twenty-three-car pileup. The stark contrast of the warm blood melting into the cold snow had been almost more than he could take. Luckily, instincts and training took over and it wasn't until hours later after he had returned to the relative privacy of the station that the shakes and tears erupted.

The worst, however, had been a farming accident. Although not uncommon in rural communities, this one had been especially grizzly. It was the summer of 1964, his first as Sheriff, and he had been called out to Dick Reynolds' place. The old man had set off with his grandson in the combine harvester at sunrise. They packed jelly sandwiches, pears from the tree in the backyard and a jug of water. They weren't expected back until late in the afternoon.

Shortly after 7:00 that evening Mrs. Reynolds had grown worried and put in a call to the station. By the time the sheriff had rolled up in his cruiser, a group of five or so neighbors and friends were loading into trucks to drive the fields looking for the pair. Buck climbed into the passenger seat of Dale Watson's truck and for an hour they drove down the dirt gullies and tracks of the farm's four hundred acres. Dusk was falling when they stumbled upon the boy. He was walking aimlessly through the fields, his face red and wet with tears.

It took some time but as the boy led them back to where the combine was parked they coaxed the story out of him. His grandpa had run into a rock or something and got out to see if he could move it away. The combine was old and stubborn and, much like the old man himself didn't take kindly to starting and stopping.

Dick left it idling and went to work digging the rock out of the dry earth. His grandson, just a few weeks shy of his eighth birthday, quickly became bored and restless in the cab of the great reaper. All of those levers and buttons started looking a bit too interesting and before he knew it the combine was roaring to life and once again spitting plumes of black smoke into the air.

In no time, the rotating thresher blades began to shuck the skin from Dick's bones like so much ripened corn from their husks. His screams echoed across and in between the rows of corn, causing great flocks of crows to take flight with shouts of their own. The boy hit the kill switch and jumped from the cab only to find bits and pieces of his grandfather clinging to stalks of corn four rows deep in every direction. The reddened teeth of the reaper smiled menacingly at him as he ran screaming into the stalks.

Now, seven years later, Buck stood staring down into a bathtub filled with…God knows what, and for the first time since that muggy summer night in the cornfield felt his stomach clench, and despite the cold rain clinging to him, beads of sweat spill over his brow. He removed his Stetson and wiped his already damp forearm across his slick forehead.

The beam from his flashlight rose from the butchered remnants in the tub to rest on the single blood-scrawled word on the tiled wall above. The air whistled out of him in a whisper, "I'll be God damned…"

His mind raced to connect the dots. At the sight of that word scrawled in blood an odd sensation of déjà vu washed over him. *I've seen this before*, he thought.

As he stood in the dimly lit bathroom on the verge of clarity his world went black, courtesy of a nine-iron to the back of his head.

Lionel's world was quickly unraveling. Bodies and their assorted parts were now strewn across the entire house. He vacillated between tears and laughter as the voice inside his head screamed instructions. The man from the garage was still alive – although barely so. The steak knife had broken off in his chest. But the garage was full of tools and the screwdriver was sharp and fit nicely in Lionel's small hand as it tore into the man's flesh. The lad's swinging arm had eventually tired from the effort.

The man moaned as Lionel dragged him by his ankles through the kitchen and to the basement steps. It took some effort but he found the strength to kick him down. His limp body rolled to the bottom where it landed with a moist and sickening thud.

Once the first deputy arrived, the voice assured him more would be on the way. Lionel hid in the linen closet and watched through the louvered door as the second officer slowly made his way through the house. The voice screamed in fury as the man passed in front of the closet on his way into the bathroom. *Her blood is on your hands! You let them take her! The price for blood is blood!*

A short while later Lionel sat quietly on the floor in the twins' room, careful not to further disturb their desiccated butterfly wings. The golf club rested beside him, its steel shaft twisted and slick with blood. The voice in his head had grown quiet, leaving him alone with his thoughts and quite exhausted.

When Griggs found him asleep and drenched in blood he assumed the boy was merely one more victim. The deputy wrapped the boy's limp body in blankets and cradled him in his arms until the State Police arrived. Griggs was the only one to walk out of the house that night. Young Lionel and Sheriff Tanner were brought by ambulance to the small hospital in Cadillac, forty-five minutes north of Bedlam Falls.

While they went north, John Tanner was rushed south by ambulance to the nearest trauma center two hours away in Grand Rapids. To keep him alive, paramedics wrestled the rain-slick roads as well as the deputy's assorted stab and puncture wounds.

As for the Reeds – the following morning they crossed the threshold of their home one final time in a parade of black plastic bags.

Power was restored to the area shortly before dawn. Neither the streetlights nor the unexpectedly warm November sunshine could break through the darkness of the storm's aftermath as the fear of a nameless and faceless killer among them settled over the citizens of Bedlam Falls.

Chapter 7

THE AFTERMATH

In the days that followed, it became increasingly difficult to separate rumor from truth. Theories pinned the bloody handiwork on everyone from a lone drifter strung out on drugs to a satanic cult that had graduated from animal sacrifice and cattle mutilations. Each rumor seemed more outrageous than the last, yet still contained enough plausibility that they spread through the small town like wildfire. And as much as opinions varied, there was one area of general agreement; Deputy John Tanner was one lucky son of a bitch – even if he had yet to regain consciousness.

Sheriff Buck Tanner was released from the hospital, against doctor's orders, with a fairly serious concussion and more than sixty stitches keeping his torn scalp pieced together. Thankfully, the Stetson had made it through the ordeal only slightly crumpled, but no worse for wear.

Buck was unofficially coordinating the investigation from his son's bedside in Grand Rapids. With two-thirds of local law enforcement out of commission, the State Police had increased patrols in the area. This was both a blessing and a curse. While this provided much needed support for acting-Sheriff Frank Griggs as he tried to restore some sense of safety, small towns are notoriously private and the presence of more *outsiders* only ratcheted up the anxiety level.

The Collins boy, as he was later identified, appeared to be the unfortunate victim of being in the wrong place at the wrong time. He seemed to be gripped by shock in the aftermath of what he had witnessed and could provide nothing in the way of details. Griggs had tried unsuccessfully to interview the boy both at the hospital that night and then the following day after he was released to go home. Aside from the fairly deep gash on his right palm he was physically uninjured. The extent of his mental trauma, however, had yet to be established. Lionel remained silent.

They were lined up in a solitary row at the front of the Grace Resurrection Church; larger caskets on each end sitting in silent protection of the two miniaturized ones in the center. To the relief of most -- and the disappointment of a curious few -- their flower-laden lids were closed and sealed.

A large photo taken the previous Christmas stood to the side on a wooden easel. The glossy image of Ken and Joanna Reed holding their small children dressed in bright greens and reds for the holiday season provided an odd juxtaposition to the dismembered remains that most imagined resting inside the satin-lined boxes.

Reverend James Collins rose from his seat behind the pulpit and stood in quiet introspection as a hush fell over the congregation. Presiding over a funeral was always difficult – especially when children were involved. But the fact that his child should by all accounts be resting in a box beside them weighed even more heavily on him.

Only by the grace of God, he thought and glanced into the overfilled pews where Lionel sat quietly. *Too young for so much tragedy*, his heart grieved.

Lionel had not only endured the recent tragedy, but the suicide of his mother the previous summer. Her passing had taken more from Lionel than merely her presence; it had taken the best part of his young soul -- leaving a void that nothing seemed able to fill. He was now just the shell of the happy child he had once been.

Although months had passed, the painful memory of that morning was still very fresh in the reverend's mind. He had left shortly after sunrise to share a bit of scripture with Homer Goode. The long-time church deacon had taken a nasty spill while picking up his pipe tobacco at Dell's, leaving him with a broken hip and unable to do most anything for himself.

Normally, the entire family would make the trip across town packed into their tiny green AMC Gremlin. Melody would bring a casserole and do a bit of cleaning while Lionel poured over Homer's old cigar boxes stuffed with photos and souvenirs from his time overseas fighting the krauts and wops in the First World War. It was Lionel's father who had to explain that the "krauts and wops", as Homer so fondly referred to them, were actually the Germans and Italians with whom the allied forces had battled and eventually defeated.

That final Saturday, however, Melody had a touch of whatever bug was going around and wanted nothing more than to stay in bed. Lionel agreed to stay home with her, against his mother's wishes, and the elder Collins set off in the Gremlin alone. He had considered staying home himself, as things around the house had been more than a little strained for the past few weeks. Lionel's newfound sullen attitude had Melody worried, and her own recent mood swings had caused a fair amount of friction between the normally happy couple.

He pulled away from the curb wishing he could turn the clock back just a few weeks to a time before things had started to unravel at home. *Fishing with Lionel*, he smiled, thinking of the last time he could remember things being... normal. He sighed as he looked into the rearview mirror and watched his house slowly fade from view.

The reverend's visit with Homer was cut short by the unexpected appearance of Buck Tanner at the door. The Sheriff lived across the lake from Homer and since the old man's fall the lawman stopped by now and then to check on things. Collins wasn't anxious to get home, but seeing the view of the lake through Homer's kitchen window reminded him of that fishing trip with Lionel. *Maybe all the boy needs is some father-son time*, he thought and then excused himself with a handshake and promise to return the following Saturday. His spirits remained hopeful until he turned onto the street that led home.

With each passing block his stomach tightened into anxious knots. As the white Colonial came into view all thoughts of a happy ending out on the lake vanished. There was no fairytale ending to this, he knew. Something dark had crept into their lives and its hold over his family was only tightening.

Collins parked in front of the house and killed the ignition. The minutes ticked by as he sat in the car debating what he would be walking into. Chances were good that Melody would be in a foul mood. Moodiness often followed her headaches. It was a routine that was quickly wearing on him...and Lionel; it must be wearing on him, too, as the boy's moods had been unpredictable, as well. Clutching his antique Holman Bible, the reverend stepped from the car into the sunshine and let its warmth wash over him. Dating back to 1865, the family heirloom weighed just over five pounds and was covered with rich gold-embossed leather.

The walk from the car to the front door gave him just enough time to collect his thoughts and mutter a brief prayer under his breath. The windows were open throughout the house and he could see the curtains in the front room dance in the late morning breeze. Given the current state of family affairs, he didn't expect to hear conversation, but was anticipating the monotonous tones of the radio or television. Instead, he was greeted by a near-deafening silence as he opened the screen door. It snapped shut behind him with a sharp bang that echoed throughout the house.

"Melody," he called as he walked through the living room and into the kitchen. The remnants of his breakfast still cluttered the counter; half-filled cup of coffee and toast crumbs. He continued on through the house and approached the back stairs leading to the second floor.

The muffled sound of whispers greeted him as he began his climb. *At least they're talking*, he thought and smiled. His mood instantly brightened as the steps creaked beneath him with the weight of each step. The stairway opened into the hall. He turned left to Lionel's room, peering into the empty space through the open door. Retracing his steps, he returned down the hall and past the stairs. The master bedroom was closed. The whispers were louder here, although still unintelligible.

"Honey," James called, grasping the handle and pushing the door open. For a moment his mind could not process what lay before him. The bible fell from his hands and landed at his feet with a thud as his mind raced to grasp the image that greeted him.

The large antique light fixture was ripped from the ceiling, its twisted metal and exposed wires dangling precariously over the bed he shared with his wife. Looped around the base of the fixture was a belt; the opposite end of which was cinched tightly around Melody's neck. Her body swayed slowly back and forth, the tips of her toes bloodied as they traced lines through the shards of broken glass that covered the rumpled bed sheets. Lifeless eyes bulged from their sockets as a silent scream split her lips. Her swollen tongue lay blue and unmoving from the corner of her mouth.

Lionel sat on the floor under the window slowly rocking back and forth. His incoherent muttering was lost as James' cries for help shattered the silence; echoing through the open windows and into the blue-skied morning beyond.

Less than six short months later, Reverend James Collins stood before his parishioners and tried, once again, to give reason to something beyond reason. His gaze shifted from Lionel and moved to the caskets before him; a lone tear spilling down his cheek. It landed on the dog-eared pages of his great-grandfather's worn Bible spread on the pulpit before him -- falling across *Ecclesiastes III* with a silent splash. When he spoke it was in a voice barely above a whisper, yet it carried throughout the small church with a soothing strength and purpose. *"To every thing there is a season, and a time to every purpose under the heaven: A time to be born, and a time to die; a time to plant, and a time to pluck up that which is planted; A time to kill, and a time to heal..."*

Lionel could feel the eyes boring into the back of his head as he fiddled absentmindedly with the plastic band that encircled his wrist. The voice in his head did its best to reassure him that everything was alright, but Lionel knew from his interviews with Deputy Griggs that the man just wasn't convinced by what he was hearing – or not hearing for that matter.

He did his best to stay focused on his father, but instead found himself stealing glances behind him in hopes of catching sight of the deputy. Rather than the deputy however, he caught the gaze of an odd man seated near the back of the church. A poorly fitting shirt hung loosely around the man's thin neck and the black suit he wore had definitely seen better days. He wasn't a member of the church, nor could Lionel recall seeing him before, but the man smiled and nodded at him with familiarity. It made the boy's skin crawl.

Fortunately, Lionel's father was nearing the end of the eulogy. The homily was a familiar one and it brought a smile to the young man's face as he closed his eyes and envisioned red wings spreading out under the lifeless bodies of Joshua and Jacob Reed. He listened to the words his father spoke and imagined soaring among the clouds on blood-red butterfly wings.

And the reverend spoke,

In the tall grasses of a wide valley a lone caterpillar crawled slowly about the base of a large tree. Like countless caterpillars before, this caterpillar's entire life had been spent traveling from the small pond on the eastern end of the valley to this very tree on the slopes of the western hills. The caterpillar often wondered what happened to its brethren who had climbed up the mighty Oak only to never return.

The caterpillars had agreed among themselves that the next one who was called to the dizzying heights of the tree would come back and report to the others what lies beyond.

Not long after, the lone caterpillar found itself drawn up the tree by nature and began to make its way slowly skyward. After some time the caterpillar found itself out on a large leafy limb overlooking the valley. Here, in the comfort of the tree, the sun shined brightly. It had been so dark on the ground in the shadow of the Oak and the view from within the tall grasses of the valley floor were far less beautiful. As the caterpillar looked down on where its friends still toiled on the ground it smiled and then slowly drifted off to sleep – exhausted from its long journey.

After a short while something began to happen. The caterpillar began to change. Two brightly colored wings sprang forth from its body and the caterpillar became a beautiful butterfly. It never imagined that this could have happened. The caterpillar had believed its journey along the valley floor and then to the heights of the giant Oak were all that awaited him in life. It thought it would remain a caterpillar forever.

Spreading its wings, it flew back and forth above the valley. It could see the other caterpillars in the tall grass below but the bright sun and clouds above kept him from their view. The butterfly realized there was no way it could return to its brethren in the grass and that those below would never recognize such a beautiful creature as ever having been one of them.

Like the beautiful butterfly that flutters in the breeze above its brethren on the valley floor, those that the Lord Our God has called to his bosom patiently wait and watch over us until the day we, too, ascend to the heavens upon wings of our own.

A short while later with the words of Reverend Collins warming their fragile spirits, those gathered to celebrate the lives of the recently departed Reed family filed out of the small church and into the crisp November air. Their tears and condolences would continue at the cemetery. Among the mourners, and nearly unrecognizable without his uniform, stood Deputy Frank Griggs. He had spent the better part of the funeral service looking for guilt – as if the word murderer would be tattooed on somebody's forehead. But instead, he found himself struck by an odd little man in a black suit and his apparent fascination with the one person who held the answers, yet for now remained silent.

Chapter 3

CLARITY

Sheriff Buck Tanner had nothing but time on his hands and found himself putting it to use contemplating one of life's greatest mysteries; why do bad things happen to good people? While he wasn't what you would call a *religious man*, he did believe in a certain natural order to the universe, good things happened to good people and so on. That's what made it so difficult for him to wrap his head around why such a sleepy little town, by and large comprised of honest law-abiding citizens, could be such a magnet for brutality.

Long before his days in law enforcement, Tanner had seen his share of violence and death. As a young seaman he had watched from the deck of the USS Nevada as the Japanese pummeled the unsuspecting US fleet at Pearl Harbor. The battleship had been struck by at least one torpedo and six bombs before being beached shortly after it got underway to join the battle. The site of the charred bodies floating on the blood-red sea amid the twisted wreckage of the Pacific Fleet still haunted him.

And now, just under a month shy from the thirty-year anniversary of that fateful day, the cold hand of death had reached for him once again. The doctors had told him how lucky he was – both then and now. He survived Pearl Harbor with two broken and badly burned legs, among a variety of other less serious injuries, and would surly have drowned if not for the actions of his shipmates. As for the recent events and his bandaged head – the pain only reminded him that he was alive. If this is what it meant to be lucky then he could only hope that some of it had rubbed off on his son.

The good news – Johnny's condition had greatly improved. Of the twenty-three stab wounds throughout his upper body and face, the vast majority were shallow punctures. The most severe of them, however, had proven almost lethal -- missing his heart by mere centimeters. According to the doctors, the viciousness of that initial attack probably saved John's life. The wound was very deep and its location and angle caused the blade to wedge between his ribs. Although it had punctured his left lung, the fact that the blade had broken off during the attack had actually helped prevent major blood loss.

The bad news – the tumble down the basement stairs had left the young deputy with, among a variety of other injuries, a fractured skull. Doctors will tell you that the first twenty-four hours after any type of serious head injury are the most critical. Based on how a patient responds to certain stimuli doctors can place fairly accurate percentages on their chances for recovery. Some patients, however, remain completely unpredictable. Deputy John Tanner fell squarely into that category.

Buck wasn't a patient man, but the doctors and nurses had assured him that time was indeed his son's best friend. As the hours slipped into days the guilt of arriving too late at what they were now referring to as the death house weighed heavily on him. His broad shoulders slumped beneath the burden as he kept his bedside vigil.

He did find comfort in the fact that Laura wasn't here to see their son bandaged and broken. Just this past summer Buck had come home for a quick bite at lunch to find his bride of more than twenty-five years stretched out in the garden beneath her rose bushes. For most of that afternoon he sat in the garden, holding her in his arms for what would be the last time, and cried. He imagined her singing Patsy Kline beneath her wide-brimmed gardening hat with the late morning sun warming her arthritic bones when the clot finally made its way to her brain. Stroke, the doctors had explained – all completely painless and quite sudden. His luck, it seemed, hadn't rubbed off on Laura.

Making his way from his bedside roost, he moved to the window and looked out across the city. Under any other circumstance the view of dawn breaking over the skyline of Michigan's second largest city would be worth noting, yet Buck paid little attention. His quarry wasn't on the streets of Grand Rapids – of that he was sure. Beyond that certainty, however, were endless unanswered questions.

As he retraced the events of the past several days, his tired mind kept returning to a solitary word scrawled in blood and the realization that within those six letters was the answer.

After re-cataloging his thoughts for the thousandth time, the dots finally connected and a cold fist of fear closed itself around his insides Closing his eyes to the searing pain in his temples, Buck struggled to remember the details. It was 1958 and he was still fairly new to the department. He was at home when the call came in from the Sheriff. "Grab your camera and get your ass out to the Lake Hospital."

Buck had retrieved his Kodak Brownie and all the film he had from the hall closet and raced to the asylum – leaving an untouched meatloaf and his wife and young son at the dinner table. Although frustrated by the sound of his growling stomach, its emptiness would soon prove to be a blessing.

The faded memory flared to life inside his head in a series of black and white crime scene photos. From the lifeless bodies that littered the hallways and rooms to the blood-spattered walls and floors, each image was more grotesque than the last. With a final lurch, his racing mind settled on the final image. Traced in blood on a cinder-block wall deep in the bowels of the building, was a single word - REPENT. Was it a plea for forgiveness or a call for revenge?

Two brutal crimes, separated by less than ten miles but occurring more than a decade apart were connected by a single word written in blood. Standing at the hospital window, awash in the warmth of the morning sun, Sheriff Buck Tanner turned his gaze from the streets below to the bed that cradled his injured son and worried at the possibilities.

Only two minutes into the press conference and Deputy Frank Griggs already needed to change his shirt. The harsh lighting from the assembled cameras was searing, leaving the rattled deputy slick with sweat. It ran down his back and legs, leaving a soggy mess inside his steel-toed boots.

"Deputy Griggs – Ken Ritz from KATV-41 in Lansing -- what can you tell us about the wounds inflicted on the victims? Were they, as some are reporting, consistent with satanic rituals?" Ritz was tall and handsome with perfectly coiffed hair and a near blinding smile that positively gleamed beneath the lights and flashbulbs.

The question, although not unexpected, seemed to catch everyone more than a little off-guard. It was greeted with an uncomfortable silence as Griggs glared from behind the small wooden podium.

"Contrary to certain reports, there is no evidence of occult activity." Griggs delivered the answer exactly as he had practiced and just as Sheriff Tanner instructed. It was clear to everyone present just what the local law enforcement thought of KATV's unconfirmed reports of devil worshippers running amuck in the backwoods of northern Michigan.

Ritz countered quickly. "With all due respect deputy...what would you call the dismemberment and mutilation of the victim's bodies, removal of their organs, and," Ritz paused for dramatic effect, "the inscription of religious symbols in blood -- if not evidence of something satanic in nature?"

The reporter's smile widened in satisfaction as the reality of the bombshell he had just dropped settled over the room. The blood-scrawled message was one of the details not released by police. Someone, it seemed, was talking out of school.

Griggs' gaze moved from the smiling reporter and settled on the face of Lieutenant Jim Bowling of the Michigan State Police. Dressed in the standard issue blue uniform and cap, the trooper leaned casually against the wall chewing on the stub of a very fat cigar. Bowling's views on Bedlam's-finest were well known and the fact that Buck Tanner had retained jurisdiction had caused quite the shit storm between here and the state capital. He smiled at Griggs from beneath his mirrored sunglasses, dropped the still smoking cigar at his feet, and walked from the room, leaving the deputy with yet another mess to clean up.

Griggs turned his attention back to Ritz and continued. "This investigation goes where the evidence leads. And right now, there is no evidence of any occult or religious intent to these murders." Griggs paused to collected his thoughts -- his thick knuckles whitening as he gripped the podium. "As for what the wounds tell me about these crimes...it tells me there's a *sick son of a bitch* out there somewhere and with all due respect, I've got work to do."

Griggs stepped from the podium amidst a chorus of shouts and questions and made his way through the sea of reporters. Ritz moved forward to block the deputy's retreat. "You can't run from the truth, deputy. Your sick son of a bitch theory, while quaint, isn't getting anybody any closer to catching those responsible; and more importantly, might just end up getting more people hurt!"

And then, smirking one last time at the sweating deputy, Ritz turned to the rolling cameras, "In the meantime, rest assured KATV's investigation will continue. Tune in tonight at 11:00 for the latest."

Twenty minutes later, and with a fresh shirt neatly tucked into his brown uniform pants, Griggs was back at work sifting through the latest reports from the lab. The boys from the state had done a fairly thorough job with the crime-scene, and now, less than a week later, had everything organized into a tabbed three-ring binder complete with glossy photos.

As much as the reports revealed, and at just over 1,100 neatly typed pages it was quite a lot, investigators were still left with far more questions than answers. Chief among them was how and why young Lionel Collins was able to escape from that house of horrors unscathed.

The techs had come through with a handful of interesting details, however. Joanna Reed was very much alive when the hacksaw took her limbs. Thankfully, the twin's gruesome injuries were all post-mortem, having both been suffocated in their sleep before being dismembered in their cribs. And, finally, the suspect was small in stature, as evidenced by the angle of the wounds inflicted on Ken Reed, yet also strong enough to drag the lifeless body of Deputy Tanner from one end of the house to the other. Most assuredly, however, the devil was buried somewhere in the details.

Griggs tossed the binder on the desk where it landed atop a pile of newspapers. Press coverage of the investigation hadn't been kind. Although not all the reporting had labeled the acting Sheriff as Barney Fife revisited, most, if not all, were questioning the lack of any sort of official progress by law enforcement.

This investigative paralysis was more about where the evidence was leading than not having any evidence to work with. The house was thick with prints, footprints, blood spatter, and other items which lay neatly presented in that damn binder; two reams of paper -- at nearly five pounds in weight -- and all pointing in the one direction that nobody dared to look. Griggs' stare burned through its cover.

The ringing phone on the other side of the door reminded him of what a shitty day he had to look forward to. As if the torture of the press conference weren't enough, everybody and their brother was now calling to share suspicions, ask questions, and basically make the acting Sheriff's life a living hell. Fortunately, Maggie was doing her best to run interference. There was a small list of names that had access to him now. Frank considered scratching Jim Bowling's name from it but thought better of the idea.

"Frank," Maggie's voice echoed through the tinny-sounding intercom on his desk, "Sheriff's on the line."

"Thanks, love." The couple had dropped the formalities with both of the Tanner men out of the office. It would prove interesting once the Sheriff returned. Frank was hopeful for good news when he continued. "Put him right through."

Their conversation was brief and somewhat confusing for the young deputy. Using a dull pencil, Frank scratched notes onto a nearby piece of paper. A few short minutes later, Frank replaced the telephone receiver onto its cradle knowing little more than he had before picking it up. He scanned his chicken-scratched notes trying to piece together some kind of meaning. Johnny's prognosis hadn't changed. Buck hadn't shared whether this was a good sign or bad, and, as usual, Buck was limited with details and Frank knew from experience not to pepper the Sheriff with questions; simple "yes" and "no" responses were the elder law-man's preference.

His first act was to get Maggie down into the file room in the basement. The Sheriff demanded her full attention on an odd scavenger hunt for files from a crime committed more than a decade previous. Again, Frank thought better of asking the "whys" and "what fors" at this request.

Frank rose to his feet and for the first time since throwing himself into the Sheriff's cruiser a week before let out a big sigh of relief. Sheriff Buck Tanner was back. He wasn't sure what had changed but had the gut feeling that things were about to get interesting.

After only three minutes on the phone with the man, Griggs knew beyond a doubt that Buck Tanner sounded much more like himself; hard, determined, and pissed off at the world. And most importantly…was coming home.

From left to right across the AM dial, news of the homicides lit up the radio. Buck listened as he drove – the high beams from his old Ford slicing through the inky blackness of the northern Michigan night.

By day, autumn in northern Michigan was a lazy affair filled with color; trees showing and shedding their multicolored leaves for tourists, who in turn opened their wallets for eager shopkeepers. By sunset, with tourists packed safely into their cars, the warm fall colors were swapped out for long shadows that stretched eerily from the breeze-blown trees hanging over the winding roads and empty fields.

Buck passed beneath Bedlam's lone stoplight shortly after midnight. Snowflakes the size of quarters fell lazily across the windshield of his pickup as his tired eyes surveyed the deserted sidewalks and storefronts. He resisted the temptation to swing by the station and instead steered towards the lake... and home.

A short while later the sound of the crushed gravel road beneath the truck's oversized tires gave way to the dirt of his driveway. The flurries had stopped and the clearing clouds overhead brought a dramatic dip in temperatures – from just above freezing when he left Grand Rapids to down in the teens as he walked down the path towards the house. He paused briefly at the front door before dropping his bag and then continued walking down the path along the side of the house towards the lake.

The breeze grew stronger as Buck neared the water. He kicked his way through a maze of fallen leaves and branches that littered the pathway and yard. Stopping at the enormous maple that hugged the house and marked the path to the lake, he leaned his weary frame against the tree and drew in a deep breath of cold air. The slow exhale rattled from his throat in a puff of crisp white air.

Buck settled his gaze on the darkened asylum in the distance. From its hilltop perch on the far shore the remote hospital seemed small and altogether unimpressive.

Buck knew better, however. Surrounded by acres of farmland, the hospital had actually been a community onto itself. Small cottages and stately homes were spread across orchards, farms, and fields. All told, more than fifty-five hundred unfortunate souls had passed through its doors since they first opened in 1917.

At its prime, the Lake View Asylum for the Insane housed more than seven hundred patients and eighty staff. Together, they farmed, raised livestock, and even gave the Amish a run for their money in the furniture-making business. Hell, there wasn't a house in all of Bedlam County – or for miles beyond – that didn't have a table, headboard or other wooden furnishing stamped with the Lake View Furniture company logo. It seemed to make people feel good to have these pieces in their homes, as if they had helped those "poor patients," having no idea of the reality that they'd been crafted by some of the most dangerous, damaged, and genuinely sick people to ever walk the earth.

Yet standing on the shore, Buck's mind wasn't racing with thoughts of farms, furniture or even his injured son. Instead, the reports of desecrated graves had him wondering about the hundreds of small wooden crosses that dotted the rolling hills surrounding the hospital. He recalled driving through the iron gates and seeing those grave-markers; even pausing to snap a few photos. Upon reflection, he now could see an odd dichotomy – the serenity of the white crosses against the peaceful backdrop of the lush green hills mixed with the bloodshed he had captured on a half dozen other rolls of film inside the disturbing confines of the hospital's inner-most chambers.

Of course, it wasn't until much later that the meaning of the small wooden crosses truly sunk in. As he had watched the bodies of the hospital staff being zippered into plastic bags and ushered into waiting hearses for delivery to their grieving family members, Buck had noted with a pang of shame that the tattered remains of patients had been merely wheeled away on gurneys deep into the bowels of the building. Not even death, it had seemed seem, could grant a soul release from the Lake View Asylum.

Sighing, Buck turned from the lake and retreated along the path to the house. At the door he retrieved his bag and stepped into the empty house. He found his way up the stairs and into the guest room -- still avoiding the bed he had shared for so many years with his wife. Stripping down to his boxers, Sheriff Buck Tanner slid between the cool sheets and, despite the late hour and comfortable surroundings, waited unsuccessfully for sleep to grant him release from this living nightmare.

Chapter 9

CLEAN-UP IN AISLE FIVE

August 19, 2010
Bedlam Falls, Michigan

Man cannot live by pie alone. As much as Brady hated the thought of grocery shopping he knew the remnants of Maddie's apple pie wouldn't get him and Gruff through another day; nor would the half gallon of milk that the Griggs' had left for him in the fridge. Begrudgingly, he set out for Kroger's with Gruff riding shotgun.

He took the scenic route, driving past some of the landmarks and places he had frequented as a teenager. Everything looked smaller; buildings, parks, even the trees. Brady spied the shallow creek near the curve where Stewart Road hugged the train tracks, and smiled at the memory of hunting the murky waters for bullfrogs. The bike ride home, one-handed and cradling two of the largest frogs he had ever seen, had been quite the adventure. The real fun, however, began when his mother discovered the frogs in her bathtub.

The wind through the windows blew the worries free from Brady's cluttered mind – creating some breathing room. The last several months had proven nearly unbearable; a merry-go-round of emotions and activity that in many ways still had his head spinning.

As the Janie Pearce story grew legs it also grew teeth – eating into every waking moment of Brady's life. What started as a sad, but simple story about a soccer mom's unfortunate homicide quickly spiraled into a much larger project; ten column inches that would change his life forever.

It was around this same time that he and Karen had started trying to get pregnant. She was entering her final semester of law school and studying for the Bar Exam. Firms from across the country were courting her, yet Karen had her mind set on working for a small non-profit that provided free legal services to the disadvantaged. Even Karen had been surprised by her father's angry reaction. The announcement of her pregnancy only added fuel to the fire.

"You are throwing your life away, not to mention our family's reputation; and for what, this…pipe-dream?" Thomas Greene was pacing back and forth like a caged lion in the kitchen of Brady and Karen's tiny apartment. Her mother, Tess, sat quietly with Brady sipping at a glass of wine. What was supposed to be a happy occasion had taken its usual left turn into outrage.

"How much," he continued, drawing his checkbook from his breast pocket and laying it out on the table. "How much to make you forget this insanity?"

This was a Greene solution to every problem – throw money at it. But Karen would have none of it.

"You are unbelievable!" It was the first time Brady had witnessed his wife standing up to her father. From Greene's reaction, eyes wide open and mouth agape, it was his first time, too. "This is my life -- not yours! Not everything in this world revolves around you."

And then walking closer to him, "And as far as this family's reputation -- what have you done to foster that reputation? You've spent all of your life living off grandfather's name, grandfather's wealth. Your place in this world has nothing to do with your good works – your efforts. You sit where you are today, with your society friends and important connections, only because of the name you bear. Thomas Greene, as if it were a badge of honor. But I know you. I know the man you are…the father you are. And if grandfather were alive today he would not be honored by the son who bears his name, he would be disgraced!"

Karen had turned from him then, tears welling in her eyes, and retreated from the kitchen to the bedroom. The final realization of the man her father truly was overwhelmed her. Karen's sobs penetrated the apartment's paper-thin walls.

Thomas Greene's expression quickly changed from shock back to anger as he caught Brady's steely glare. Pen in hand, he scribbled something onto a check, tore it free from the book and then replaced the book in his jacket pocket.

"I believe that was our invitation to leave, dear," he said stiffly as he reached for his wife's elbow to help her from the chair. Tess withdrew from her husband's touch as if pained, and slowly stood on her own. Though small in stature, standing no more than five-foot-two-inches tall in her trademark heels, Tess Greene commanded a room. Brady could feel his father-in-law's overbearing personality shrink as Tess took control of the situation.

"Brady dear, if you would be so kind, could you fetch my things?"

Brady did as requested and helped his mother-in-law into her expensive cashmere overcoat. Thomas remained rooted in place, red-faced and silent.

Tess turned and wrapped her arms around Brady – the first real sign of affection she had ever shown him. Although never impolite, Brady hadn't exactly felt that he had won his mother-in-law over. Oddly, he sensed that something had now drastically changed.

"Take care of her, Brady," she whispered. "I'll be in touch." Releasing Brady, Tess Greene turned and walked to the door. "Thomas." The word slithered through her lips dripping with venom.

Thomas Greene straightened his tie and brushed by Brady to follow his wife from the apartment. He paused at the open door and then retraced his steps to stand before Brady.

"I left it blank," staring icily at his son-in-law as he shoved the check into Brady's chest. "You fill in the amount," his voice now thick with contempt. "Give it to charity. Hell, give yourself a raise, Tanner. With neither of you gainfully employed it looks like I'll be supporting you and your child, too." He stared down at Brady and added," We both know this is what you're after anyway."

Of course, months later, and in the solitude of his car, Brady could reflect on the occasion and think of a dozen razor-sharp retorts that would have cut the man to the bone. But at the time, he could only stare after the man in disbelief as Thomas Greene, the prick of all pricks, strutted through the open door, slamming it in his wake.

Brady hadn't mentioned the check to Karen; instead deciding to hide it away. Not that he had any plans for it. On the contrary, he wanted nothing to do with the man, let alone his father-in-law's money. But when an opportunity had presented itself, both to do some good and to finally take his own jab at Thomas Greene, Brady couldn't resist.

Thomas Greene's surprising $25,000 donation to Pride Chicago, a grass-roots gay and lesbian awareness organization, had been lauded publicly, yet derided privately – especially in the conservative circles in which he often traveled.

Thanks to Thomas Greene's generosity, Pride Chicago's president had proclaimed from the steps of city hall during the annual parade and rally, his organization's message of tolerance and understanding would be part of a new curriculum being implemented throughout the Windy City's public school system. The news had spread quickly and the memory of the coverage made Brady snicker.

So maybe the prick does have some cause to be pissy with me, Brady acknowledged as he drove. Regardless, he knew it wasn't a question of *if* the snake would call again, but of *when*, and Brady vowed the next time he would be ready.

Very few situations can leave a man feeling as helpless and lost as being turned loose and alone in an unfamiliar grocery store. It had taken every ounce of courage Brady could muster, but he had fought the urge to turn tail and run back to the car where Gruff was waiting. He knew from his passenger's hungry eyes that to come back empty-handed would not be tolerated.

Gruff was already a bit perplexed at being left alone in the car – even with the windows all partly down – and adding injury to that insult would surely result in some kind of backlash. The last thing Brady wanted were Gruff's little *surprise packages* scattered throughout the house. *Best to keep him happy,* Brady concluded as he pushed his rickety shopping cart aimlessly up and down the aisles.

He hadn't thought to make a list; that was his first mistake. Grocery lists had always been Karen's responsibility. Since Karen's death, the bulk of his shopping had been done via Chinese take-out menus. Sadly, Bedlam Falls was lacking in that department, thus he would be forced to resort to the dreaded grocery store. He could find the alcohol pretty easily in a grocery store – as for where the canned foods were in relation to the fruits and vegetables, Brady was at a complete loss.

His last solo excursion into a grocery store had been the worst shopping experience of his life. Shortly after they had been married Karen had sent him to the corner market for a box of tampons; Brady had been mortified. He only vaguely understood the mechanics involved in using a tampon and as he stood in front of the shelf, eyeing what appeared to be an endless sea of options; Brady could feel a growing wave of panic growing inside. There was regular, super, and super plus – whatever that meant. Add in the confusion of the pads – both maxi and mini – and some even with wings, and Brady was as close to a full blown panic attack as was humanly possible -- sweat pouring from him as he looked furtively over his shoulder at the imagined glares of the other women in the store.

His only other experience related to choosing a specific size of anything for Karen had not ended well. While they were dating Brady has picked out a sundress at a swank, over-priced boutique. He had wanted to surprise Karen for her birthday; and oh what a surprise it turned out to be. Brady had learned the hard way about the difference between a ladies size four and fourteen. Karen had been outraged that he would even consider her a size fourteen. Her reaction had flooded his thoughts as he stood in front of the tampons. Brady had cringed at the thought of what the reaction would be to the wrong size in this instance. Fortunately, he had grabbed the "regular" sized box and not a word beyond thank you had ever been mentioned.

Brady steered his squeaky cart towards the checkout. Beyond beer and dog food, he didn't know what else he had picked up, but the cart was nearly overflowing. He glanced at his watch, *twenty minutes – not too bad at all* – as if it were some kind of race.

The line was horribly long and it felt like an hour before Brady was able to start unloading his items onto the conveyor belt. As he watched the items make slow progress towards the register, he was struck by just how haphazard his shopping had been. Plus – it screamed bachelor. There were Funyons and beer, frozen pizza, ice cream and the assorted toppings, Cocoa Puffs cereal, pop tarts, and an odd mix of other items that he had no recollection of tossing into the cart. He was pondering this when a voice stirred him from his jumbled thoughts.

"I.D. please, sir."

Brady felt his face redden as he reached for his wallet to retrieve his driver's license. He handed it over and added sheepishly, "Sorry, I was just ….thinking."

The cashier took his license and studied it carefully. Brady raised his eyes from the groceries to the woman's face as she spoke.

"You forgot the bananas," she stated and then smiled. "I seem to recall that you always liked bananas with your ice cream."

Brady stared in puzzlement, unsure of how to respond. "I…uh…excuse me?"

The woman's smile widened as she continued. "Or have you outgrown the banana splits?"

In that instant Brady's eyes traveled from the woman's face to the name tag on her blue smock. Brady's already-reddened face flamed to an even deeper shade of crimson.

Of course, he told himself. Her blonde hair was shorter now – hanging loose above her shoulders, but the splash of freckles across her nose and cheeks marked her as *his* April.

They shared uncomfortable laugh followed by a nervous silence before Brady collected his thoughts and found his voice.

"So, uh…still in Bedlam Falls, huh?"

April cast her eyes back to the groceries and continued scanning the items. "Yeah, life doesn't always work out like you planned." She paused, and then added, "I'm sorry about your parents, Brady."

"Yeah," he replied, thinking about his own life over the past 18 months, "full of surprises."

The crackle of the overhead pager interrupted the conversation. "Clean-up in aisle five, April. We need clean-up in aisle five."

Brady laughed. "So what's in aisle five?"

"It's the breakfast aisle," April replied – and then muttering, "but something tells me it's not cereal I'll be cleaning up."

Brady chuckled as he paid for his groceries. "Better you than me."

April's frown eased into a loose smile. "Gotta run, but I'll be at Charlie's tonight about seven. First split is on me."

Brady watched her turn and walk towards aisle five. Wow, he thought as he wheeled his squeaky cart of groceries into the parking lot, *April Mayer all grown up.* And then it dawned on him, *and still taller than me!*

Chapter 10

CATCHING UP IS HARD TO DO

Brady arrived at Charlie's shortly after 6:30 and laid claim to a picnic table in the shade. Gruff sat at his feet panting in the evening heat. The pair had spent the better part of the day puttering around the *Up North House*; Brady had witnessed the Tigers get pounded by the Royals while Gruff kept watch. The usually lazy dog hadn't quite yet grown comfortable in his new surroundings. Truth be told, Brady wasn't entirely comfortable either.

He still found himself avoiding his parent's room; doing his best to keep those memories tucked neatly behind the closed door at the end of the hallway. The problem was, however, each and every room, piece of furniture, and knick-knack carried the weight of some memory. Fortunately, bumping into April had provided and unexpected bounce to his step ...and a pang of unforeseen guilt.

Brady played with his wedding ring; twirling it about his finger. It was a nervous habit he had picked up after Karen's death; a comforting reminder that he always carried a little piece of her heart with him. Today, it made his finger itch. *Guilt*, he thought, *and I haven't even done anything*. He was going to add *yet*, but reconsidered.

Instead, Brady turned his attention to what he was wearing. Although his cargo shorts, Pearl Jam concert t-shirt, and black Chuck Taylor's looked casual, it had taken way too much effort and energy to look this hip. He had felt like a teenager while trying on outfits in front of his mirror. Now, he felt like an old man trying to act young. Brady was so caught up with his tangled thoughts, not to mention trying to keep his stomach sucked in, that he didn't notice April's approach.

"You see honey, this is what a stranger looks like. You never ever want to talk to someone who looks like this."

Brady coughed nervously as he looked up from his sucked-in stomach to find April standing over him. Beside her was a child – a miniature version of the fetching woman that still, it would seem, could take his breath away.

Brady rose to his feet, trying his best to suppress his lopsided grin. "Yes, sweetie, it's true. This is indeed what a stranger looks like." Brady squatted down to be eye-level with the young girl, "But my name is Brady, and this here is my dog Gruff. And strangers are only strangers until you know their names." And then stealing a glance up at April, "Besides, I've known your mommy here for a very long time."

The girl responded with a toothless smile. "My name is Abby Mayer and I am five and a half years old and I have a goldfish at home because mom says dogs poop on the carpet."

Brady laughed, "Well, your mom is right. Gruff has had a couple accidents. But he's a really good dog. You can pet him if you want – especially behind his ears, he loves that."

With introductions over, Abby eagerly pounced on Gruff. He returned the attention with a very wet kiss and the two were quickly becoming acquainted.

"I see you brought your bodyguard," Brady teased as he stepped towards April. Dressed in a pale yellow sundress and chunky sandals, April returned his smile and nervously tucked her hair behind her ear.

"Yeah," she countered, "although I prefer to think of her as my man-repellant."

After an awkward silence, Brady invited her to the table to sit down. They sat quietly watching Abby and Gruff frolic in the grass.

"Let's see who gets tired first," Brady said. "My money is on Abby."

Laughing, "I'll take that bet, and your money. Abby doesn't get tired. Even as a baby she hardly ever slept."

Brady joined in her laughter. "She's beautiful," he added, "must get it from her dad."

Aprils smile softened as she turned away. "So did you decide on a banana split or are you trying something different?"

Brady cringed at what he had just said. Smooth, he berated himself.

"Um…I really hadn't given it much thought. Just know that Gruff wants a dish of vanilla."

Her smile returned, "You feed him ice cream?"

"We're roommates," Brady replied shrugging. "Split the tab right down the middle. He eats what I eat."

"Don't forget," April countered, "I saw first hand what your grocery shopping consists of – somebody should call PETA on you!"

"Then you should know that Funyons are all vegetable – potatoes for the fun and onions for the," Brady paused, "yons."

April's snorting laughter echoed across the picnic tables. Even Gruff stopped in mid-romp with Abby and cocked his head – his oversized yellow ears perking up.

April pressed her hands over her reddening face, as if hiding would make her annoying laugh less noticeable. She could feel the tears escape from her eyes as her shoulders rocked in a now silent laughter.

"Nothing to see here people, go about your business." Brady moved forward and placed his hand on her shoulder – guiding her towards the counter. "Let's get you some ice-cream."

They talked for hours as Gruff and Abby played; a lot can change in fifteen years – and for both of them it had. April had left Bedlam Falls right after high school, accepting a scholarship to Eastern Michigan University to study elementary education. She had wanted to put as much distance between herself and her hometown as possible. Like Brady, however, she was back in the one place she thought she would never be.

Her life couldn't be mapped in a straight line; instead it had been filled with peaks and valleys. After college she had settled in Ann Arbor and quickly found a job teaching kindergarten at a small Catholic school.

That was a peak.

The valley followed a year later when a positive pregnancy test abruptly ended what she had thought was a very promising and long-term relationship.

Abby's father -- April used that term only in the biological sense -- was completely uninvolved and provided absolutely no support. The juggling act of balancing a baby and a demanding job became too much, and with her pride fully swallowed, April found herself back in Bedlam Falls.

The tiny trailer she had grown up in was cramped, although less so now after her mother had passed away. April's father had been diagnosed with Alzheimer's and she now found herself spending most of her time caring for him. It wasn't the life she had planned for, but she was making the most of it – for herself and for Abby.

Brady hung on every word. He had known that April had always wanted to teach – something that he had never fully understood. Brady couldn't recall even one teacher that had made an impact on him. Besides, dealing with twenty-five screaming little kids just seemed more like torture. Now, however, as he watched Abby run and play, Brady could see just why April might enjoy children so much.

"How about you," April asked motioning towards Brady's ring. "I see the ring but have to doubt that there is a Mrs. Tanner at home eating Funyons right now?"

Brady didn't know how to respond. The subject of his wife's death had always been a difficult one for him to discuss. The wound was still very fresh, and somehow he felt that by sharing his hurt here, and with April, he would be soiling that memory.

"Peaks and valleys," he said looking away. "What do you say we save that topic for another day?"

April paused and nodded, "Sure thing."

A comfortable silence followed as they watched Abby and Gruff. Both appeared close to being at the end of their batteries. laid out perpendicularly on the grass using his soft fur as a pillow. Although unable to understand the words, Brady could hear Abby talking quietly and non-stop to the dog.

"Something tells me those two are going to be inseparable."

"Yeah," April agreed, reaching over and giving Brady's shoulder a soft punch. "Like long lost friends reunited."

Chapter 11

THE BEGINNING OF THE END

November 10, 1971
Bedlam Falls, Michgan

Sheriff Buck Tanner arrived at the station shortly before sunrise and parked his familiar truck around the block behind the library to mask his presence. He wasn't quite ready to be the official face of the investigation; *let Frank have a little more fun*, he thought as he entered the darkened station and put on a fresh pot of coffee.

As requested, Maddie had spent some time in the file room. A neatly organized mess greeted him on his desk. To the left was a very thick and somewhat intimidating appearing binder atop a stack of newspapers. Buck guessed at what was contained therein and quickly turned his attention to the small stack of files on the right side of his desk. Between the two piles rested a handwritten note.

Sheriff – Cupboard was left pretty bare. I'll keep digging.

Buck recognized Maddie's penmanship and set the note aside. He had expected as much. His predecessor's handling of the asylum affair had been less than thorough. Sheriff Rylan Walters had his deputies snap some photos, ask a few questions, and then basically wrote the whole thing off as though it was livestock merely thinning its own herd. Rumors had run wild but soon they, too, had died off from lack of interest.

Buck caught the scent of the cigar before he noticed Jim Bowling's shadow pass over his desk. "Morning, Jim."

State Police Lieutenant Jim Bowling stood in the open doorway and smiled down at the Sheriff.

"My, my, what do we have here? The long arm of the law finally come to save us simple folk?" Bowling snickered around the cigar clamped between his yellowed teeth. The Cheshire Cat should have envied the man's smile.

Buck looked up from his cluttered desk and locked eyes with the trooper. "You might call it that, Jim." The Sheriff's eyes glittered hungrily. He was in no mood for Bowling's bullshit. Buck had already heard enough from Deputy Griggs about how uncooperative the little prick had been; best to put him in his place right away. "Black, Jim, no sugar. How 'bout you go fetch me a cup?"

Bowling blew out a long slow plume of gray smoke and stepped into Buck's office, the trooper's beady little eyes full of instantaneous rage. "Excuse me?"

Subtlety wasn't one of Buck's strongest qualities – especially after recent events.

With his son bandaged and broken, a young family butchered, and a killer still roaming the streets, Sheriff Tanner didn't have time to mince words. Plus, having one's skull cracked open with a golf club tends to set a person in a foul mood.

"How long have your worn that badge, son? Five years? Certainly not much longer." Buck kept his voice calm and his eyes on the young trooper. "Now, you may be a big deal down in Lansing -- hell, maybe even outside the capital. But here, in Bedlam, you're a guest - my guest. And I don't take kindly to my guests pissing in my cheerios."

Buck paused, letting his words settle over his "guest." "You ever work a homicide, son? Not just string the yellow tape, but actually roll up your sleeves and work one?"

Buck could see the anger leaving the man as he continued. "Now I ain't saying you don't know shit, but dammit Jim, if you think running to channel forty-one with every last detail is gonna actually help in any way, then it's obvious – you don't know shit."

Bowling's face flushed with embarrassment. Buck held up a hand before the man could comment.

"I get it – you're pissed. You wanted this. Hell, maybe you even deserved it." Buck paused, and for the first time his calm demeanor and cool tone began to fray at the edges. "But this isn't about what you want…or what I think. This is about justice – for the Reed's, for my boy, and for Lord knows who else this sick son of a bitch has hurt."

Bowling stared across the desk at the Sheriff. The gray smoke hung heavy between them, but the tension had finally broken. "What can I do?"

"I need your help, Lieutenant. You have access to records, files…information that I could never lay my hands on. "

Bowling nodded, not fully understanding the request but suspecting he might be bending a few rules in obliging the man. "Done," he nodded, noting the seriousness in Tanner's eye. His hatred for Griggs' aside, the trooper had a modicum of respect for the aging sheriff.

Buck paused, reconsidering the man standing before him. He, too, had been young and brash once. Perhaps not the asshole that Jim Bowling had shown himself to be, but nonetheless there was no denying the kid had fire. That fire may just be the catalyst to nailing the murderer.

The file was marked **Lake View Asylum – 1958**. Inside were half a dozen sheets of handwritten notes and a few black and white photographs. Buck held it out to the state trooper.

Bowling opened the file and glanced briefly at its contents. The trooper's brow furrowed with puzzlement.

Buck removed a photo from the binder on his desk and held it up for Bowling. "Notice anything?"

The trooper's eyes moved from the file's contents to the photo Buck held. Bowling had seen the Reed's bathroom and quickly recognized the blood-scrawled word -- Repent. Bowling's eyes widened as he made the connection. His reaction was immediate.

"No fucking way!"

Buck smiled in spite of himself, "Yeah, my thoughts exactly. I'm not sure how or why -- but it's your job to find a 'fucking way.'

Bowling nodded, his mind spinning at the possibilities.

Buck rose to his feet, standing a full six inches taller than the young trooper, and extended his hand. "I'll talk to Griggs – let him know to give you a wide berth and all."

Lieutenant Jim Bowling accepted the offer and responded with a firm shake of the Sheriff's hand. Depositing the thin file on the Sheriff's desk, he left Buck's office with something to finally sink his teeth into. Walking to his car a few minutes later he had more than a passing suspicion that the elder lawman was grasping at straws. Yet the photos were eerily similar.

Maybe I should just take a look around, he thought, Pointing his cruiser east down Main Street. Placing his trademark mirrored sunglasses atop his nose, Lieutenant Jim Bowling drove towards the rising sun over the Lake Hospital. On that final drive, he never suspected how right Buck Tanner's hunch would turn out to be, or that, much like the countless souls before him who had ventured through the asylum's doors, he would never see the light of day again.

Lionel hadn't been to school since the incident. Instead, his father had thought it would be best if the boy took some time off – probably through the Thanksgiving break. By then, Collins hoped there would be some progress in the case and life would start looking more...normal.

While the elder Collins tended to his flock -- a task that considering recent events had been taking more and more of his time -- young Lionel was left pretty much to fend for himself. Fortunately for Lionel however, even when by himself he was never truly alone.

The soft and soothing tone to Ellis' voice had taken on a more pained and powerful tenor. Initially, this frightened the boy, but Lionel was quickly adapting to this stranger's voice inside his head. Oddly, this unseen companion provided him a sense of comfort.

It was also during this period of change with Ellis that Lionel noticed his own *loss of time*. There really was no other way to describe it. Entire portions of a day or night would be wiped from his memory. Once he had awakened to find himself standing over his father's bed as the man slept -- with no recollection of how or why he was there. It was only upon returning to his own bed that he noticed the kitchen knife in his hand. Another time he found himself alone walking along the wooded shore of Asylum Lake – a good six miles from his home – again with no recollection of how he had gotten there.

Today, however, was proving to be the most perplexing experience yet. Lionel could recall having breakfast with his father. If, by breakfast, a silent

glass of orange juice and dry toast qualified. His father had left shortly there-
after, mumbling something about visiting a church member; he would be back
by dinner.

And that was the last thing Lionel could recall – until now. Teeth chattering, Lionel slowly came to the realization that he was sitting on his front porch
swing dressed in only a bathrobe. His hair and skin were still damp from what
he assumed was a shower. Taking in a deep and cleansing breath of the cool air,
Lionel recognized the fresh scent of soap.

The strangest part of this awakening, however, was the feeling of utter and
complete fatigue that welled from deep inside his muscles and joints. That, and
the splintered pair of mirrored sunglasses he held tightly in his knuckle-scraped
hand. Specks of blood marked both the lenses and the white bracelet that encircled his thin wrist. A circular burn roughly the size of a quarter also throbbed
painfully on his forearm.

Exhaling a bitter plume of white vapor into the late afternoon chill, Lionel
rose from the swing and retreated to the warmth and solitude of his bedroom.
His father would be home soon and the voice was urging him to rest – for
strength would be needed before the night was through.

Buck had spent the better part of the day in the solitude of his office re-
viewing the case notes and lab reports from the Reed homicides. Much like
Griggs, the absence of certain evidence aroused more suspicion than what evidence they actually held. All things pointed to Lionel Collins.

The boy's prints and tracks were on everything. From the knives and
screwdrivers that had been used to puncture and slice the victims, to the golf
club that had taken a divot of the Sheriff's scalp. No other prints were found –
nor did it appear that any had been wiped away.

Most concerning was the boy's silence. All things considered, it was time
for Lionel to provide some answers, and Buck was confident that he would
know just how to pose the questions.

"Time to get to work, Maddie," Buck stated matter-of-factly on his way
out the door. "When Frank gets back have him meet me at the Collins' house,
would ya?"

"Sure thing, Sheriff," she responded reaching for the radio. "Snow is picking up – be safe out there."

Sheriff Buck Tanner's lips tightened into a thin smile. "And while you're at it, get Jim Bowling on the line. Have him join us, too."

Maddie watched the Sheriff turn and walk through the swinging door into the frigid November evening. How he kept that damn hat on in the wind was a mystery, she mused.

Always one to trust her women's intuition, she couldn't help but worry as a shudder of chills ran down her neck and shoulders. Snuggling deeper into the cardigan sweater she kept at her desk, she fidgeted nervously in her seat as she waited for State Police Lieutenant Jim Bowling to respond.

Chapter 12

AN OPEN DOOR IS AN INVITATION

The last time Buck Tanner had rolled up to a darkened house things had turned very ugly in a hurry. Removing his .44 from its holster, he vowed things would be far different this time. Of course, the good reverend and his son may just be out, but the tingling hair on the back of the Sheriff's neck told him differently.

Maddie's efforts to reach Lieutenant Bowling had proven unsuccessful, presenting the Sheriff with an altogether unsettling sense of déjà vu. *If that son of a bitch has done anything stupid I swear I'll kill him*, Buck fumed as he crept slowly up the porch steps.

Whether by force of wind or something much more sinister and likewise unseen, the door creaked open as the Sheriff placed his first booted foot onto the wood-planked porch. *An open door is an invitation*, Tanner mused, raising his gun to the ready position, *and the last thing I want is to be rude*.

Reverend James Collins couldn't decide which concerned him more -- driving up in his AMC Gremlin to find his house completely dark with the front door partially open, or the police cruiser parked in the driveway. Neither was tantamount to good news.

Not that he had expected good news. It seemed as if God's plan for him included a near-constant test of faith. Fortunately, James Collins had the patience of Job and a strong belief that in the end everything would work out exactly as it should. He pondered this as he left the relative warmth of his car and prepared for the biting chill of the wintry walk to the house.

Clutching his oversized bible in one ungloved hand and securing his unbuttoned coat against the wind with the other, he braced himself against the pummeling snow and walked gingerly through the ankle-deep drifts that blanketed his walkway and yard. Puzzled by the tracks that led from the police car and up the front steps to the open door, he followed them nonetheless. The creaking of the porch swing's movement in the wintry breeze echoed across the stillness.

The solitary tracks led into the darkened house. Collins stopped at the door and eased it the rest of the way open. Glancing back in the direction of the Police Cruiser, Collins' wrapped his frozen fingers around the worn leather of his bible and entered the shadowy confines of his disturbingly silent home.

Somewhere, in the hidden recesses of his subconscious, Lionel slept -- oblivious to the flurry of activity that his unwitting body was now undertaking. The boy's normally copper-colored eyes blazed like smoldering embers; their intensity surpassed only by the sinister smirk and hardened demeanor that now defined Lionel's once-delicate features. Transformation complete, Ellis Arkema's penetrating red gaze burned through the shadows. Fueled by vengeance and years of pent up hatred, Ellis spurred Lionel's unknowing body forward -- silently stalking his prey.

Slowly, Buck's vision adjusted to the dim interior of the unfamiliar surroundings. Even in the darkness his slow breath came out in visible white plumes; the house was bitterly cold.

The .44 felt like ice in his hand. Buck tightened his grip on the cold metal as he moved deeper into the shadows. Although he had never before been inside the Collins' home, the Sheriff had walked through enough of the old Colonial-style dwellings to know the basics of where everything was located. He moved easily from the foyer into the living room, brushing against the indiscernible furnishings.

The house was quiet -- too quiet. Buck trained his ear towards the kitchen and moved slowly in that general direction. The crunch of something beneath the Sheriff's steel-toed boot echoed across the stillness. *Fuck*, he cringed, freezing in place.

An eternity seemed to pass as Buck waited for something...anything to come leaping out from the darkness. Finally, he relaxed, easing his finger from the frosty trigger on his sidearm. Buck let out a long and steady breath as he contemplated his next move. Sadly, the press of cold steel against the back of the law man's head stirred him from his planning.

"My, my, my," came a whisper from the darkness. The warm breath on Buck's neck carried with it the scent of freshly turned earth. "Here for another golf lesson, Sheriff?"

The last time the good reverend had come home to such a peaceful house had been the worst moment in his entire life; finding his wife hanging from the bedroom rafters. The memory still haunted him. It had been the first domino in a series of events that were still tumbling out of control -- events that he still found himself struggling to find God's plan in.

Power's out, he surmised, flipping the switch on the wall as he closed the door to the winter chill. Stepping from his snow-covered boots, Collins started for the kitchen, to the cabinet where he kept the flashlight.

An unfamiliar voice in the darkness, thick with hatred and dripping with malice stopped him dead in his tracks and chilled him to the core. The reverend listened intently as the realization swept over him that God's hand played no role in this foul game.

"One should watch where one steps," the disembodied voice continued as the gun pressed harder into Buck's head. The sheriff could feel the distinct outline of a double-barrel just under the brim of his Stetson; enough firepower to spray his brains well into the next room – if not beyond.

"I believe those were your compatriot's sunglasses you just stomped to pieces. No worries, however, his days of requiring eye protection are passed."

Buck swallowed hard. In an instant his nerves of steel had crumbled. Neither his police training nor his years of experience had prepared him for the feeling of a shotgun to the back of his head. *Pretty sure this one's not in the manual,* his mind raced at the predicament. The .44 in his hand provided scant comfort.

"We've met before, you know – twice, if we're counting the golf lesson. Should we count the golf lesson?" the voice snickered. "of course, I don't expect you to remember. Our first encounter was years ago. As for the last time, you were…preoccupied. It's too bad there won't be a next time -- this time I plan to make a lasting impression."

The stranger was obviously enjoying himself – a fact that provided Buck a glimmer of hope. *Keep him talking.*

"I meet a lot of people," Buck replied dryly, "all part of the job. Don't take it personally. As for the golf lesson, it only reinforced my hatred of the game." Buck's pieced-together scalp itched beneath his hat at the memory.

The comment was met with silence. If not for the barrel of the shotgun pressed to his head, Buck would have thought for sure his attacker had reconsidered.

"Looks heavy," the voice replied – absent the previous traces of amusement, "the gun that is -- drop it."

Buck winced as he dropped his sidearm to the floor. If not for the .22 strapped to his ankle he would have been defenseless. Not that he stood a snowball's chance in hell of drawing it before the shotgun blast painted the walls red with his blood. Still, its presence kept hope alive.

"Turn around – slowly." The voice carried a certain don't fuck with me quality that Buck quickly obliged. Of course, reinforcing a demand with a shotgun tends to empower an individual. The Sheriff, mind ablaze with questions, was ill-prepared for the answers that awaited him as he turned to face his foe.

Standing before him, shotgun now trained at his chest, Sheriff Buck Tanner gazed down at young Lionel Collins. Even cloaked in darkness, Buck noted that the menacing voice wasn't the only change in the lad. Lionel's face was deathly pale with dark circles beneath each eye. His lips were drawn back into a snarling smile – revealing more teeth than Buck had thought humanly possible. Most startling, however, were the piercing red eyes that glowed from Lionel's sunken eye-sockets.

"You let them take her, Sheriff. Much of this could have been avoided... the hurt...the loss." For the briefest of moments the intensity of the voice wavered as it trailed off into silence. "The price for blood is blood, however, and I am here to collect."

Chapter 13

THE GOOD BOOK

For some, faith is a blanket that provides comfort in times of great distress or grief. For others, belief in a higher power provides a place to deflect responsibility – everything difficult is part of a master plan.

For Reverend James Collins, his faith had always been an anchor; a place of refuge during the storms of his life. Tonight, however, in the presence of what he could only describe as true evil, the reverend's faith became a weapon.

Buck started into the steel-eyed barrels of the shotgun and smiled. He had accepted long ago that any given day could be his last on earth – and had thought on at least a handful of occasions that his last day had finally come. But never had he considered that he would be taken down by a twelve-year-old boy.

Movement in the shadows behind the red-eyed figure caught the Sheriff's attention. "Promise me," Buck whispered in hopes of providing distraction, "it ends here...with me. Let my blood settle the debt."

The fire in Lionel's sunken red eyes blazed. "My good Sheriff, are you trying to bargain with me?" The hollow laughter that followed chilled Buck to the bone. "I'm afraid we are well beyond the point of negotiations." More laughter followed. "Besides, I do believe I have developed a taste for it."

The next few seconds were a blur of confusion. Unsure of what, if anything, the shadowy form behind Lionel could be, Sheriff Buck Tanner made the brash decision to reach for his .22. As the law man ducked for his weapon, a blast from the shotgun took the Stetson from atop Buck's head. He could feel the displacement of air as the buckshot slammed into the wall behind him. Pain from a thousand bee stings peppered his shoulder as Buck rolled to his feet with his back-up weapon in hand. His mind commanded his body to fire a salvo of shots, but not a single round left the barrel. His entire hand and arm was numb and immobile. Fear ran through his body, but when his eyes finally registered what he was seeing, Lionel's crumpled body lay unexpectedly sprawled across the floor.

Gripping what remained of his antique Bible, Reverend James Collins towered over the fallen boy.

The remnants of the family heirloom fell from his hands as he dropped to his knees beside his son. *"My God, my God, why have you forsaken me?"*

Buck's revolver fell to the floor as he collapsed. His eyelids became heavy as the sting in his shoulder intensified. Drifting into unconsciousness, the Sheriff could hear the reverend crying over his fallen son, as two smoldering red eyes waited for him in the darkness.

Chapter 14

THE COOKIE MONSTER

The power of a name is as ancient as the custom of naming itself. All throughout mythology, examples can be found of secret names, names that had the power to destroy, and names that had the power to bring great rewards.

Ken Ritz was hopeful that the great reward for his dubbing of Lionel Collins as *The Cookie Monster* would be a move to a larger market. Not that Lansing was small potatoes, but his sights had always been on something much bigger – and definitely more lucrative.

The highly popular children's television program Sesame Street had recently unveiled its latest Muppet – *The Cookie Monster*. The smug reporter saw the opportunity and ran with it -- nearly wetting himself with excitement when he saw his story picked up by the Associated Press and running in media outlets across the Midwest.

Ritz, it turned out, was privy to far more information than just the words written in blood above the bathtub inside the Reeds' bathroom. His unidentified source, acknowledged for his intimate knowledge of the investigation, had also revealed that the assailant was believed to have helped himself to a plate of freshly baked cookies before undertaking the vicious attacks that had ended with a family of five brutally murdered and the town gripped by fear. Sadly, Lieutenant Bowling had been unavailable for further comment, but Ritz ran with the unreleased details, and the clever moniker, nonetheless.

Ritz, much like the countless other members of the media present outside Bedlam Fall's small hospital, were camped out waiting for word from Sheriff Buck Tanner. Although the specifics had yet to be released, rumors were swirling that both the accused and the Sheriff had sustained what doctor's were calling non-life threatening injuries during the apprehension.

As the vultures circled outside, Buck sat quietly on the edge of the table in exam room one. A young doctor worked anxiously to remove the remnants of buckshot from his bloodied shoulder and arm. Beside him, an even younger-appearing nurse stood quietly with a syringe of morphine should the lawman finally decide to accept the offered painkillers. Buck Tanner needed a clear head, however, and declined.

Dressed for the second time in just over a week in an embarrassingly thin hospital gown, the Sheriff's thoughts vacillated between shock and anger. Most upsetting, however, was the loss of his cherished Stetson. *Damn it all*, he fumed, running an awkward hand through his thinning gray hair.

Task complete, the doctor exited with his nurse in tow -- encouraging his patient to get some rest. Alone at last, Buck Tanner was left to contemplate which was more frightening -- the small number of answers he now possessed or the multitude of questions that plagued his beleaguered soul.

Just down the hall from where the bandaged Sheriff sat in quiet contemplation, Deputy Frank Griggs stood guard outside Lionel Collins' room.

Again, the guilt-ridden deputy had been too late to respond to the call. This time, however, with good reason. Because of his efforts, a young child had been pulled free from the twisted wreckage of a fatal head-on collision. Griggs' quick thinking and brute strength had enabled him to literally pry the child from the back seat mere seconds before the vehicle burst into flames. Sadly, the child's parents had been killed upon impact.

Griggs had resisted the urge to pummel the driver of the other vehicle – a drunken teenager whose truck had crossed the center line and struck the unsuspecting family returning from vacation. The teenager had walked away unharmed – more concerned with the angry reaction of his parents to their damaged vehicle than with the devastation he had just caused. The angry deputy took a small amount of satisfaction when the teen's head "accidentally" slammed on the doorframe of the cruiser as he threw him into the back seat.

Just out of earshot stood a handful of State Police brass huddled together in hushed conversation. One of their own was unaccounted for, and they were fully unconvinced by the strange tale that was being spun by Sheriff Buck Tanner. Surely the man was rattled, Griggs overheard their whispers.

Griggs sighed in frustration drawing angry looks from the troopers. Battle lines were obviously being drawn and the pissing match over jurisdiction would soon begin anew.

As of now, however, Sheriff Buck Tanner was still in charge and his only order for the young deputy had been quite simple, "Nobody in. Nobody out." The smell of gasoline and charred metal clinging to him, Griggs folded his beefy arms across his barrel chest and with blazing eyes dared anyone to try to pass.

Chapter 15

METAMORPHOSIS

All things must change to something new, to something strange.
~ Henry Wadsworth Longfellow

Alone with his thoughts, the echoing silence in Lionel's mind was deafening – all but drowning out his father's incessant bedside recital of the Twenty-third Psalm. If not for his aching jaw and temple, the boy would have thought for sure he was merely dreaming.

Lionel knew he was in the hospital, and apparently in some sort of trouble; beyond that limited awareness, the lad was lost. The same deputy who had interviewed him after the incident at the Reed's was again lurking about; this time, however ,wearing a much more bitter expression on his already sour face. Lionel paid it little mind however and instead focused on what he did know – *something in him had changed.*

Resting amid the sterile bed linens, Lionel felt hollow; as if his soul had been carved out from its resting place within his core. The sound of the door opening didn't rouse him from his torment.

"Sheriff," Lionel heard his father mutter from his bedside. With the greeting, the patient turned his eyes toward his guest. Time seemed to freeze as they locked gazes. For the briefest of moments Lionel experienced an odd connection with the lawman; a passing sensation of the familiar that evaporated as the Sheriff broke his gaze.

"Reverend," Buck nodded as he slowly made his way forward. Nearing the bed, the Sheriff recast his attention on Lionel.

The man looked different without his hat, Lionel thought, smaller and far less imposing even. Maybe it was the way he was gingerly holding his arm or the slow and awkward measure to his usually determined walk.

"I've got some questions, son," Buck began. "But first, I need to explain a few things." The Sheriff looked down at the small form in the bed and drew in a deep breath before continuing. "You have the right to remain silent. Anything you say can, and will be used against you in a court of law…"

Three hours later, Buck left the hospital riding shotgun in Griggs' police cruiser. The deputy had retrieved the Sheriff's Stetson from the crime scene and had placed it strategically on the dash in front of the passenger seat. Without a word, Buck gently placed the shot-ridden hat atop his aching head.

Griggs drove without talking, knowing that the Sheriff would get around to it in his own time. It took all of fifteen minutes.

"Do you believe in God, Frank?"

Griggs hadn't known what, if anything, to expect from the man, but this question took the deputy by complete surprise.

"Ummm..yeah, I suppose I do." Like most small towns similar to Bedlam Falls, church membership was deemed almost mandatory. Rumors ran rampant about those who didn't at least grace the pews at one of the town's two small churches at least once in a blue came calling far too often. However, attending church and believing in God were two different things.

An uncomfortably long silence greeted Frank's reply; minutes passed before Buck continued. "I never cared either way – just did what I thought was right." Buck paused, collecting his muddled thoughts. "But I felt something tonight, Frank – something…evil. And it got me thinking -- if there is a God then it stands to reason that there is something else…something wicked and full of hate." Buck's words trailed off into silence.

Griggs' grip on the steering wheel tightened as he pondered his passenger's words. "Sheriff, I can't begin to imagine what it is you're feeling – what with Johnny and all -- but that Collins kid is just plain sick in the head; ain't nothing evil about that." It was the deputy's turn to pause. "You gonna head back to Grand Rapids now…check on Johnny?"

Griggs stared at the road ahead as he waited for the Sheriff's reply. When none was offered the deputy stole a quick glance at his passenger. Sheriff Buck Tanner sat motionless, staring straight ahead into the wintry night. "Sheriff?"

Buck recast his focus to the deputy. For the briefest of moments the Sheriff's tired eyes blazed red beneath the shadowed brim of his Stetson. Barely audible above the noise of the cruiser's tires crunching over the snow-capped road, Buck's reply sent chills down the deputy's spine. "Yes, Grand Rapids," the words dripped with vitriol from Buck's smiling lips. "I'll be taking care of Johnny in Grand Rapids."

Chapter 16

THE ROOM AT THE END OF THE HALL

August 30, 2010
Bedlam Falls, Michigan

The next two weeks breezed by as Brady and April rediscovered their teenage crush. Brady's anxiety over sharing the broken parts of himself slowly subsided – and in this sharing he found a degree of healing.

Sadly, as his days became filled with April, Brady's nights were plagued by strange dreams that left him shaken and beaded with cold sweat. Details of this reoccurring nightmare always remained at the periphery of his memory, although the icy blackness of the lake always seemed to be the setting. The lack of sleep, not to mention the anxiety of the nightmare itself, began to wear on him.

"Looks like somebody woke up under the bed this morning," April teased as she approached down the path from the driveway. Abby was at her side, struggling under the weight of an enormous picnic basket. Today's lunch by the lake had been her idea after all – the menu and everything. Gruff padded out to greet her.

Brady brushed his lips against April's cheek, gently encircling her fingers with his own. "Careful lady," he teased, giving her hand a squeeze. "You try sleeping with that great behemoth across your legs." Holding hands, they led Abby and Gruff down the path to the deck overlooking the lake.

April remained silent, knowing full well that it wasn't the dog causing Brady's sleepless nights. Just two days ago he had fallen asleep on the couch while watching television. It was 2:00 in the afternoon and April was watching Abby and Gruff splash along the shore in the warm lake water. With the latest issue of People Magazine spread across her lap and a Corona with lime within easy reach, April had just closed her eyes to enjoy the sunshine when a scream erupted from inside – sending nearby gulls into flight over the lake with echoing cries of their own.

April scooped Abby into her arms and sprinted up the back stairs, through the French doors and into the kitchen -- Gruff clawing at her heels.

She found Brady standing at the kitchen sink soaked in cold sweat and water from the running faucet. He was pale and stood motionless gripping the counter.

Setting Abby down, she approached him cautiously and placed a reassuring hand on his shoulder. "You okay?"

Brady's body quaked beneath her touch. He raised his eyes to briefly meet her questioning gaze as a forced smile tugged at the corners of this mouth. "Yeah, yeah – I'm fine," exhaling deeply, "just a dream."

April didn't ask for details and Brady didn't offer. Yet now, two days removed from that frightening event, Brady looked at her with bloodshot eyes ringed with dark circles. "Let's get some food in you," she said, leaning her head against his shoulder. "And maybe after we can see about finally getting this place organized?"

Brady smirked, "Organized? That just sounds like work."

"A little work will do you good, mister," another squeeze to his hand before she let it go and ran ahead to catch up with Abby and her over-filled picnic basket. "Besides," she said turning and smiling mischievously back at Brady, "after work there is always room for a little play."

"And that, Mr. Tanner, is how you organize a sock drawer."

Brady sat in stunned silence on the edge of his bed. The last three hours had been torture. From the kitchen pantry and linen closet to this – the dreaded sock drawer – he now felt like Martha Stewart had given his home a complete makeover.

"You do realize that the sock drawer is not meant to stay organized."

April glared in response.

"Don't blame me – socks get lost, even mismatched; before you know it the sock drawer is chaos. It's best to just let it be a mess and move on."

Brady tried to refrain from smiling, but couldn't resist. He rose to his feet pulling April into his arms and planting an easy kiss on her forehead. Their comfort level with one another was remarkably strong, especially given the hesitancy with which Brady had initially pursued his former crush.

April playfully drew away from his embrace. "Not play time yet, Mr. Tanner."

Brady collapsed back onto his twin bed and groaned. "Really? What could we possibly have left to organize?"

April extended her hand, inviting Brady to stand. He accepted, following her from his room and down to the closed door at the end of the hall. With each step towards his parent's bedroom his stomach tightened with worry.

They stood quietly, holding hands as Brady collected his thoughts... and his breath. "I don't know what you think this is going to accomplish." Brady muttered.

April turned to face Brady, gazing deeply into his hazel eyes. "Two things," she said. "First -- you have to face whatever it is you think is behind this door, Brady. And I promise you, it won't be as bad as you think."

Brady sighed in agreement as he reached for the doorknob. "Wait. You said this was going to accomplish two things. What's the other?"

April answered with a kiss – deep and passionate – rocking Brady to his core. "I thought tonight would be a great night for a sleepover," kissing him again on the lips. "But I am not sleeping in that sorry excuse you have for a bed, Mr. Tanner. This Amazon Woman needs room to stretch her legs."

Brady's erection was all the motivation he needed as he fumbled at the knob. April's giggle evaporated as quickly as his excitement as Brady opened the door.

"Houston, I think we have a problem."

As a young child, Brady had spent countless hours playing with his little green army men on the floor in his father's study. On rare occasions, and for reasons that were never explained, the room had been deemed off limits to him. On one such occasion he had taken the liberty of sneaking into the room while his parents were occupied elsewhere. The visit had left him with nightmares.

The room's walls had been covered with push-pins holding reports, hand-written notes, newspaper clippings, and what was obviously crime scene photos depicting a variety of different victims with battered, bloodied, and contorted bodies. Brady had run to his room feigning illness, where he remained for the next two days. The joy of waging make-believe war at his father's feet had been wrestled from him with that one ill-timed visit.

The memory came back in a flash as Brady stepped through the open doorway. He expected to see the room as he had remembered it – a neatly made bed topped with pillows, photographs and artwork from his childhood spread across chest of drawers in the corner accompanied by the familiar scent of his mother's perfume.

Instead, his parent's bedroom looked like it had been dressed by the same designers who had created the sets for NYPD Blue. The bed was gone, and the remaining furniture had been piled against the far wall beneath the blind-drawn windows. If not for the light filtering in from the open door the room would have been dark as night. Even still, it was replete with shadows.

Brady fumbled for the light-switch. A bare bulb hanging down from the center of the ceiling over a very small wooden desk sparked to life. Atop the desk rested his father's old PC. Brady instantly recognized the dinosaur.

"I like what you've done with the place," April snickered as she glanced passed Brady and into the room.

When the initial shock subsided, Brady entered and examined the room much more closely. Stacks of newspapers, some dating back decades, littered the floor. A large map covered the mirror that hung on the wall. Beside the map were blueprints of some sort pinned into the plaster. His father's easily-recognizable handwriting covered numerous legal-sized pads of yellow lined paper.

"Safe to say you're dad didn't take up interior design in his retirement."

Brady agreed with a chuckle. This made no sense. Although he had no idea what his father had been up to, especially after his mother's death, Brady had always assumed the old man's days consisted of puttering around in the garage, fishing for blue gill from the end of the dock, and watching his Tigers, Lions and Red Wings on TV. Maybe the old man had even mixed in an occasional beer or two down at The Hayloft with Frank Griggs.

If he didn't know better, Brady thought this room looked a lot like his father never really retired. He had been in enough precincts to see the trappings of an active police investigation – not to mention the memory of his last time inside his father's study at their home in Grand Rapids.

A cursory examination of the room, however, revealed little. Everything, from the newspapers to the notes and reports, appeared to be decades old – with some more than half a century.

Aside from the collection of papers, photographs, maps, and architectural renderings that occupied nearly every surface of the room, not to mention the relic of a computer on the desk, there sat two more personal items resting on a small shelf near the map.

Grandpa's hat, he recognized, reaching forward to touch the old Stetson that he had seen in so many old family photos. Although Buck Tanner had died in the line of duty long before his grandson was even a glimmer in his daddy's eye, the man whose name Brady carried had been discussed often, and with reverence, by those who had the fortune of making his acquaintance.

Brady's hand paused mere inches from his grandfather's hat; his attention momentarily diverted by a weather-beaten hospital bracelet that lay beside the tattered Stetson. His hand reached forward to pluck the bracelet from the shelf when April spoke.

"You're right," sighing her surrender, "we've done more than enough organizing for one day." Wrapping her arms around Brady's waist and leaning her head onto his shoulder, she continued, "Not even I have the energy for this."

Brady dropped his hand away from the shelf, turned and melted into April's arms. Taking her smiling face into his hands he leaned forward and pressed his lips to hers.

"I agree. Opening the door was a good first step." Brady led her from the room, turning once as he flipped the light off and closed the door. His gaze returned momentarily to the shelf as the room went dark. "Besides, I have a feeling you'll need your energy tonight."

Chapter 17

FIRST IMPRESSIONS

Buck awoke to find himself standing near the lake. The snow had finally ceased and the clouds overhead were breaking, raising temperatures into a much more comfortable twenty-degree range. A thin film of ice was just starting to form on the lake's surface, sealing its depths away for another winter.

Buck couldn't recall how he had ended up outside; his last vague memory was of climbing into Griggs' police cruiser. Instinctively, he reached for his hat and was pleased to find it resting on his aching head. He pulled it off to examine it under the moonlight, his fingers poking through its tattered brim.

Should have aimed about six inches lower.

Buck whirled around at the sound of the wind-swept whisper. The pathway leading from the house was deserted. Buck squinted his tired eyes into the darkness of the tree-line -- nothing.

Down here, Sheriff.

Buck dropped his vision from the winter-bare foliage to the shoreline at his feet. The moonlight overhead was reflecting off the thin layer of ice covering the lake. For the briefest of moments he saw something…a spark of light. Shaking his head, the confused Sheriff stared harder into the mirrored surface. Slowly his vision refocused. Staring back at him, from the haggard and unshaven face he knew so well, were two blistering red eyes.

And God said to Abraham, take your son, you're only son…go and sacrifice him as an offering onto me…

Buck Tanner's scream became laughter as his lips curled back into a sinister smile – a stranger's smile unrecognizable as his own. His last thought before succumbing to the darkness writhing inside his tired body was of Dr. Wesley Clovis, a man he had never met, moonlit walks along the lake in the company of a young woman, and the rancid stench of aged metal.

The old Ford was half way to Grand Rapids when Buck realized he was driving. The clock on the dash read 3:15 a.m. and the radio was tuned to static. It took a moment for Sheriff Tanner to orient himself to his surroundings.

Unfamiliar eyes looked on as unknown hands gripped the wheel of his Ford truck. Buck was a tourist in his own body; a feeling that made his stomach lurch and head spin with foggy thoughts.

Welcome back, Sheriff, the menacing voice echoed through the fog inside Buck's throbbing head. Although caught by surprise, the shock of hearing the disembodied voice had a far less rattling impact on Buck this time. The bewildered lawman did his best, however, to avoid stealing glances at his own reflection in the rearview mirror.

I must admit, Sheriff, you had me more than a bit worried back at the lake. For a moment I thought that old heart of yours had burst; left me wondering if the task of killing is something best left for the young.

The humming of the strange voice between Buck's temples suddenly ceased. In the deafening silence that lingered Buck sensed that for whatever reason he was at least temporarily alone with his thoughts and once again in control of his body. He slowly eased his foot off the accelerator to guide the truck off to the shoulder of the highway.

The absence of other vehicles on the road both relieved and frightened the law man. But at 3 a.m. what could one expect. Besides, Buck had a suspicion that he wasn't really alone. Although currently silent, he suspected that his passenger would return. In the meantime, Buck got his bearings.

Resting on the bench seat to his right lay a variety of items – each more disturbing than the last – and Buck had no memory of collecting them. A hand axe from his tool shed, meat cleaver from the kitchen, his .44 Magnum, and lastly his Springfield deer-hunting rifle. The powerful .30-06 had been overseas with Buck's father in World War One and would one day be passed down to Johnny. At the thought of his son, the humming inside Buck's head returned.

I also had the rifle in mind for your son; funny how great minds think alike – wouldn't you say, Sheriff?

Buck's insides turned to jelly as he watched his hand clumsily move to the gear shift and slide the truck back into drive. Once again, his trusty Ford was cruising uncontrollably down the highway. Buck's mind jumped from one possibility to the next as he tried to make sense of the madness that was engulfing him.

He looks a lot like you -- your son that is. The voice was taunting Buck now. *Of course, I saw him only briefly – and once covered in blood most people tend to look alike.*

Buck tried with every ounce of his fiber to stifle the voice in his head with a scream. It passed through his lips as more ghostly laughter.

The price of a memory, Sheriff, is the memory of the sorrow they bring.

He was running through the woods; small branches and overgrown foliage biting into his exposed flesh. To his right he heard the sound of breathing. Stealing a glance he saw a young woman struggling to keep up. He extended an unfamiliar hand to offer help. Pale white and porcelain smooth, the hand that was not Buck's burned under the filtered afternoon sun that fell through the trees overhead.

"Emily," the voice called. "Take my hand." Although absent of malice, Buck instantly recognized the voice as the unknown passenger inside his own mind. Now, it seemed, the Sheriff and the mad man had somehow switched roles.

Sightlessly, the woman groped for the offered hand. She's blind, Buck realized, struggling unsuccessfully to help.

"Ellis," she cried, "I can't." Her dirty cheeks ran wet with tears... and blood. "Run, Ellis. Run away."

As the figure glanced back into the trees, Buck could feel the indecision and fear growing inside his host. "We're close, my love – just a little further. The highway is just through that field."

Buck looked more closely at Emily's bulging belly, confirmation of a pregnancy. Six months or so, Buck reasoned. Ellis' frantic efforts led the law man to the certainty of parentage. Instantly, the Sheriff felt a sympathetic bond with Ellis and his struggles to save this woman and the unborn child she carried.

Effortlessly, Ellis lifted Emily into his arms and continued his trek towards the open field that lay beyond the tree covered bluff. The muscles across his back and legs burned with each stride.

Buck silently urged Ellis on, unaware of what he was fleeing from but sensing that it certainly couldn't be good.

The sun was blinding as Ellis emerged from the tree-line into the open field. The red winter wheat was lush and nearing time for harvest. Ellis waded through the waist-high crop as the sun's rays burned against his pale skin. Finally, after what seemed to be an endless sea of green, the pale man carrying the blind and bloodied woman emerged on the shoulder of Country Road 22 just outside the city limits.

Emily's blood was mixing with his own, running down his arms and leaving a trail along the pavement. Ellis trudged towards town, roasting beneath the afternoon sun as he hummed soothingly in Emily's ear.

Buck watched as Ellis struggled under the weight of Emily's unconscious form. Finally, over the horizon, an approaching vehicle came into view. Buck recognized the familiar rack of lights on the police cruiser. His excitement at the unexpected sight of help on its way turned instantly to fear as Sheriff Buck Tanner at last remembered his first encounter with Ellis Arkema.

Chapter

A SHOT IN THE DARK

"What in holy hell is that?"

Although relatively new to the force, Deputy Bradford "Buck" Tanner, fresh from a decade of service in the U.S. Navy, felt prepared for just about anything. The sight of the ghost-like figure, bathed in blood, and carrying a young girl in his arms, however, wasn't one of them.

He reached for the radio as he brought the cruiser to a skidding halt. "Dispatch – this is Tanner. I have…a situation. Country Road 22, three miles west of town. Get the Sheriff out here – pronto!"

Deputy Tanner eased the door open and stepped from the cruiser, hand placed on the gun at his side. With the black Stetson atop his head, the young lawman's hazel eyes were shadowed against the hot afternoon sun; Tanner looked like Wyatt Erp patrolling Tombstone. The .38 felt like a play-toy compared to the .44 he owned, but Sheriff Walters insisted on carrying the biggest gun, although he was now too fat to even carry one, -- a fact that Tanner was sure meant he was compensating for some other shortcoming.

"Sir," Tanner shouted as he stood at the front of the cruiser, a mere 20 yards in front of the approaching figure, "I need to see your hands. Please, put the woman down slowly and show me your hands."

The man was tall and slender. The girl in his arms was limp as a rag doll. Buck didn't know if the blood that covered them both was solely hers, but knew from the sinister tilt of her head that she was most assuredly in a very bad way.

"Please," the blood-covered figure mumbled, "help me."

Deputy Tanner noted the man's pale appearance and close-cropped snow white hair. Most striking, however, were the red eyes staring out from behind the exhausted and blood-soaked face. Drawing his gun, Tanner repeated, "Sir, I need you to stop and show me your hands."

The man's shuffling feet slowly came to a halt. "Please, she's hurt."

His knees buckled under the weight, spilling the girl onto the road. Deputy Tanner sprang forward using a precisely placed booted foot on the man's back to pin the stranger to the ground. "Don't move." Handcuffs were quickly clicked about his wrists. Tanner noted the plastic bracelet encircling the man's bloody arm – easily identifying him as a patient from the asylum. Although not common, patients sometimes wandered away from the hospital grounds.

"You have to help her," the stranger pleaded. "Please."

Deputy Tanner turned his attention to the girl, noting her delicate features beneath a tangle of blonde hair. She, too, was pale, but not like the man. The man was a ghost. A matching hospital bracelet encircled her thin wrist.

His quick inspection revealed that most of the blood was coming from under the woman's dress and running down her legs. The deputy dared not examine further. Her breathing was shallow and pulse almost non-existent.

"I promise you, help is on the way," Tanner reassured the man, releasing the pressure on his back – slightly. "What happened?"

The man was sobbing now, his thin frame convulsing on the road with each gasping breath. "They took her. I tried to save her...save the baby. Help me."

Deputy Bradford "Buck" Tanner looked up from the road to see the approaching police cruiser. Behind the car hurried an old white Studebaker. Relief swept through the young deputy as he recognized the hospital's ambulance. Neither sounded their siren as they rolled up to the scene.

"Rest easy, help is here." Tanner consoled the weeping man beneath his boot as he stole a glance in the direction of the young woman; the rise and fall of her chest was becoming fainter.

Sheriff Rylan Walters' heaved his corpulent form from the police cruiser, slick with sweat and gasping for air. His pants were cinched about his round waist by a length of rope. With short arms that could no longer reach down to his side, the man hadn't carried a gun for years.

Behind the rotund Sheriff, two men exited the ambulance, neither in much of a hurry. The driver was impishly small with a pencil thin mustache and greasy dark hair that he wore slicked back into a pony-tail. Pausing briefly to light a cigarette, the man exhaled a plume of gray smoke – with not a care in the world.

His passenger was equally disinterested in the events. A mountain of a man, the great lummox stood well above six feet tall with wide shoulders and the brow of a Neanderthal protruding from his flat face. The odd pair seemed perfect together.

"Dammit, Bradford," Walters panted as he approached the deputy, "tell me there's a good reason you have me out in this heat?"

Buck sighed and pushed his Stetson back, revealing eyes that carried little trace of sympathy. "Sir, they're injured. I'm not sure by who or what – but the woman especially is in pretty bad shape. The," Tanner paused, choosing his words carefully "...gentleman is more exhausted than injured."

Walters paused to catch his breath. Behind him the men from the ambulance approached, each sporting white jackets, trousers, and unaffected stares.

"Ellis, Ellis, Ellis," the smaller man stated sarcastically as he took a painfully long pull on his cigarette, "you know better than to run. Bill here," jerking a thumb in the direction of his oversized partner, "has that bum knee." The smoke poured from his nostrils as he spoke.

At the sound of the man's voice Ellis began to squirm under Tanner's softly-placed boot.

The greasy man laughed – a sniveling bark that brought forth the rest of the smoke from his lungs. "He's trying to run again, Bill – use of force authorized." The laughter amplified as the white-clad men drew nearer to Ellis and the deputy.

Buck removed his gently-placed boot from Ellis' back. Squaring his shoulders, the young lawman's eyes raged beneath his Stetson, stopping the approaching men dead in their tracks. Never one to stomach a bully, Buck shifted his gaze from the diminutive man with the bothersome laugh to the mountain named Bill that was lumbering at his heels. Buck's hands clenched into fists as he stood his ground.

"Stand down, Tanner," Walters bellowed. "Gettin' yerself all riled up – and for what?" The rotund Sheriff glanced in the direction of the escapees. "A blind half-wit and...and...what the hell is that anyways, Douglas?"

Douglas ran a nervous hand through his greasy hair as he giggled beneath his pencil-thin mustache, "Oh that's just Ellis, Sheriff. Funny lookin' fella, but harmless as they come."

Douglas took the Sheriff's conversation as an invitation to proceed and walked carefully by the deputy – raising his arms in mock surrender and grinning as he passed.

Ellis squealed as Douglas' shadow fell over his aching body. Mustering all of his strength, the injured man turned to face his would-be-captor as the hospital orderly squatted down beside him.

Douglas Wyatt, Lake View Asylum's most reviled orderly -- and unbeknownst to many also its most disturbed inhabitant -- smiled as he plucked the smoking cigarette from between his lips and blew the smoke into Ellis' pale face. The smile became a sneer as Wyatt pressed his face close to Ellis' ear.

"Dr. Clovis is very disappointed in you, Ellis -- very disappointed." The orderly's breath was stale and fell across Ellis' already burning flesh like a match-head catching flame. "He said perhaps it's time that I take a more vigorous interest in you." Wyatt drew closer, sliding his sweaty palm along Ellis's pale and blood-stained arm. "And I am so looking forward to it." Ellis cried in pain as Wyatt crushed his lit cigarette out onto the back of the injured man's hand.

Shaking with rage, Tanner stepped forward, prepared to snap the little man's neck with his bare hands. Bill, however, moved much more quickly than the deputy had thought possible and clamped his own iron hand onto Buck's shoulder. The Sheriff's plea for peace brought some sanity to the situation.

"Tanner, I believe these gentlemen have everything under control."

Buck paused, indecision eating away at his insides. He didn't know who these men were, but his instincts told him that they were far from medical professionals.

"With all due respect, sir," Tanner replied, shrugging free from Bill's grasp and turning to address the sheriff, "the woman needs medical attention…now."

"Son, did you not see these two gentlemen roll up in that ambulance?" Red-faced and dripping with sweat, Sheriff Walters looked as if he was on the verge of collapse from the heat. His sparsely populated head of hair was already turning pink under the blistering sun. "Now stand aside and let them tend to their business."

Bill mumbled something unintelligible as he brushed by the deputy. The man stank of sweat and booze. He effortlessly scooped the bloodied woman from the pavement and hefted her over his shoulder. A soft moan drifted from her open lips; giving Buck some degree of hope.

"Yes, yes," Wyatt's' nasally voice chimed in as he hefted Ellis to his feet. The pale-skinned man was mad with worry. His red eyes blazed as he looked to the Buck for help. "We'll definitely give them the… attention they deserve."

It took every ounce of self restraint Buck could muster, but he stood aside to let Wyatt lead Ellis to the back of the ambulance. The deputy's sharp eye caught the round cigarette burn on the back of the man's hand; his rage boiled over as he ran to the open door of the ambulance.

Emily lay on the floor of the darkened interior of the vehicle. The windows along each side had been blacked out with paint and there was absolutely no medical equipment in sight. The cabin smelled of urine…and death. Quietly, in the darkness, Ellis cradled Emily's head in his lap. The last thing Deputy Buck Tanner saw before Bill slammed the door shut were two red eyes, seething with rage, staring at him through the darkness.

Through the windshield, Buck noted the glow of oncoming headlights. He briefly recast his attention to the rearview mirror and was relieved to find his own hazel eyes staring back.

The memory of his brush with Ellis, fresh and vivid in his mind, was both alarming and at the same time very revealing. Buck could only imagine what fate the two lovers met upon their return to the hospital.

I see we have company, the voice startled the already shaken Sheriff. Buck resisted the urge to steal another glance into the rearview mirror. *Ever get the urge to just split the oncoming headlights, Sheriff?*

Buck shuddered as he watched his hand reach forward to switch the headlights off. The hand returned to the steering wheel and slowly began to guide the Ford across the center line and into the lane of oncoming traffic.

It's maddening to feel so powerless...so vulnerable. Buck could feel the anger rising within his uninvited guest. *You really should have done something.*

The lights from the oncoming car were drawing dangerously closer. Buck pushed with every ounce of energy against the unseen force inside his mind – trying to break free.

*The price for blood is blood, Sheriff...*more laughter.

The last statement, clearly a threat, gave Buck all of the motivation necessary to break through. His hand jerked forward and fell clumsily across the wheel – steering the truck from its forthcoming impact and off the road where it skidded from the pavement at more than sixty-miles-per-hour. The tires caught briefly in the loose gravel along the shoulder causing the truck to flip end to end several time before landing upside down in a nearby field.

The entire episode took mere seconds, yet time seemed to stand still as Buck was thrown around the cabin of his Ford. Ellis' collection of deadly items slammed again the glass and metal of the truck, the hand-axe biting deeply into Buck's shoulder as the truck finally came to a rest.

The cabin was crushed, pinning Buck's legs beneath the dashboard. He could feel the wet warmth of blood spilling down his face as the menacing laughter resumed inside his head.

As Tanner squirmed to free himself from the wreckage, the voice returned, an aching hum inside his foggy head.

I must say, Sheriff, you are full of surprises. This overreaction on your part is merely delaying the inevitable. I don't want you dead, sheriff, not yet, anyway. You've some business to take care of for me.

Buck closed his eyes to the voice and reached through the darkened wreck of the truck's cabin for something...anything to help him win his freedom. His outstretched fingers brushed against the familiar wooden grip of his .44 Magnum, sending a jolt of electricity through his aching arm. Instantly, the lawman knew that salvation lay in his hand.

Fighting against the laughter that was boiling up inside him, Sheriff Buck Tanner brought the weapon forth from where it lay and placed it beneath his bleeding chin. With a single squeeze of the trigger the Magnum burst forth a deafening flash of light; its echo bringing a welcoming silence to the darkness that had swallowed him.

Miles away, as the last flame of life winked out from Sheriff Buck Tanner's eyes, John Tanner awoke from his coma. He struggled briefly against the tubes and wires connecting him to the medical equipment at his bedside. Through the tumult of nurses and doctors prodding and poking him, the young deputy focused his cloudy gaze on the shadowy form at the foot of his bed; an unspoken shriek welling inside his arid throat as the figure's fiery eyes faded from view.

Chapter 19

SLEEPLESS NIGHTS

Brady awoke at 2:42 a.m. stifling a scream. April slept beside him in his tiny twin bed, wearing nothing but one of his Pearl Jam t-shirts. He carefully eased himself off the edge without disturbing her slumber and crept down the creaky steps to the house's main level.

Downstairs Abby slept on the couch in the family room amidst a sea of stuffed toys and coloring books. Gruff sat motionless, bathed in moonlight and staring out of the large window at the lake beyond. Tension filled the dog's body language as he stood watch over his sleeping friend.

You and me both, my friend, Brady thought as he drew near the windows. Gruff's tail began to wag at Brady's approach. The stars and moon in the cloudless sky overhead reflected off the lake's mirrored surface, creating the illusion of an endless galaxy -- a galaxy that in this universe included the asylum. Even the heavens seemed drawn to its shadowy outline.

Brady was both tempted and terrified by the thought of revisiting the puzzling collection of items gathering dust within his parent's bedroom upstairs. His journalistic instincts were sounding every bell and whistle imaginable; surely his father was up to something – something that Brady suspected the man would only share with his closest friend, if anyone at all.

The beginnings of a plan were just starting to take shape in Brady's tired mind as he turned from the window for a hasty retreat back to the comfort of April's arms. The unexpected sight of the scrabble board once again resting on the cluttered coffee table stopped him in his tracks. Gruff tucked his wagging tail between his legs, a motoring growl breaking the stillness of the moment.

Brady could recall quite vividly replacing the tiles and board in its box and setting the game back upon the built-in shelf in the den alongside the other games – cribbage, Risk, and Yahtzee, just to name a few. Letting his gaze drift to the moonlit coffee table, Brady's sixth sense warned him that the game board would not be vacant of tiles.

Like déjà vu, a series of tiles stared up from the center of the board. This time, however, Brady knew with certainty that no random act or fun-loving greeting from an old friend were responsible.

Brady could feel his face drain of color as needles of fright pierced his heart. *This cannot be happening.*

He nearly jumped out of his skin at the sound of Abby's voice. "Brady, is that you?"

Abby was sitting up on the couch, clutching a stuffed turtle to her breast and wiping the sleep from her eyes.

Brady sat beside her, taking her small hands and tucking her limp arms beneath the blanket as he eased her back onto her Dora the Explorer pillow. "It's just me sweetie...and Gruff. I just got up to get a glass of water. Can I get you one?"

Abby yawned and closed her eyes, snuggling back onto her side with her hands tucked under her cheek. "No, that's ok. Mom says if I drink too much before bed I'll wake up in a puddle."

Brady smiled and placed a gentle kiss on Abby's forehead. "Good night," he whispered.

Gruff jumped onto the couch and curled up protectively across Abby's legs. Brady gave the dog a quick scratch behind his ears and stood to make for a hasty retreat back into his bedroom.

"The man said not to be scared," Abby whispered through the moonlight filtering through the windows. "He'll take care of us."

Her voice trailed off as she once again fell into the sweet embrace of slumber. Brady was tempted to shake her awake and ask her about the man. Instead, he quickly plucked the scrabble board and tiles from the coffee table and walked to the kitchen where he reluctantly deposited them, box and all, into the trash.

Thank God mom refused to get me that Ouija Board I wanted so badly,

Brady mused with nervous trepidation as he retreated back up to the warmth of his bed…and April.

It wasn't until much later, as the first waves of sleep finally began to wash away his worried thoughts, that the faint memory of the white plastic bracelet encircling Abby's thin wrist jolted Brady awake. Trembling, he lay there in the darkness frightened by Abby's drowsy comments about the man, the scrabbled message he had found, and what answers may be waiting beyond the door at the end of hall.

The next morning, as Brady feigned sleep, April stole away to the privacy of the bathroom. It was still dark, sometime before sunrise, and all was quiet downstairs. Brady's mind, however, was an endless parade of thoughts – *few of them good.*

Never one to believe in the paranormal, he couldn't help but feel that something supernatural was at play. Or, Brady weighed, *I am simply losing my mind.* At this point, he didn't know which would be a more welcome option.

April returned a few moments later, fully dressed and smelling of minty-fresh mouthwash. Brady continued the pretense of sleep as she placed a gentle kiss on his head before quietly tip-toeing from the room. Ten minutes later Brady heard the familiar click of the front door closing downstairs followed by the sound of April's car backing out of the driveway. His feet were on the floor before its echo faded into the distance. Beside him on the bed lay a note.

Brady –
I told you your bed was too small for both of us! Let me make it up to you with dinner tonight, something besides Funyons - my place at 6:00.

April

p.s. I stole your dog. Abby insisted that Gruff come with us. He seemed pretty insistent on it, too. Ransom is a bottle of wine. Enjoy your day!

Brady smiled as he tossed the note back onto the bed. He wasn't sure if it was just his nervousness or truly the size of his bed, but their clumsy attempts at romance the night before had proven comical; just the type of ice-breaker that would definitely make their next encounter much more relaxed. As for Gruff, he was both relieved and troubled by the dog's absence.

Stepping into a pair of shorts, Brady retrieved what he hoped was a clean t-shirt from the foot of the bed; it passed the simple sniff test as he slid it over his head. Gone were the days of wrinkle-resistant khakis and uncomfortable ties knotted at his throat. Thanks to his Tigers' cap, even the chore of running a comb through his curly hair was no longer mandatory, and rarely, if ever, under-taken. Not that he was unkempt or slovenly, Brady just wasn't concerned with a little bit of stubble on his cheeks and chin or the dark circles shadowing his hazel eyes. Truth be told, however, the lack of sleep was wearing him down, ex-hausting him to the point where even such menial tasks were almost too much.

Brady emerged from his room to find the door at the end of the hall closed, exactly as he had left it the night before. He briefly mulled over just leaving the room and its mysterious contents undisturbed, but reconsidered. Maybe it was the lack of sleep that was starting to make him paranoid, and surely being back here with all of these memories played its part, but Brady couldn't shake the unsettling feeling that had been slowly overtaking him since his first day back at the Up North House.

He approached cautiously, as if sneaking up on the unsuspecting door would surprise whatever lay waiting for him on the other side. If not for the nervousness coursing through him he would have felt silly. Reaching an uneasy hand to the knob, Brady recoiled as the door slowly creaked open.

You've got to be fucking kidding me!

Gathering his courage with a series of slow and deep breaths, Brady eased the door open with his foot and was greeted by the stillness of a very empty room. *I am definitely going crazy*, he thought, reaching for the light switch.

The smile that had just begun to tug at the corners of his mouth van-ished as his uneasy gaze locked onto the small desk in the center of the room. Spread neatly across its surface, where just the night before his father's old computer had rested, laid the Scrabble board; its presence aroused both panic and curiosity.

Bracing himself against the impulse to flee, Brady instead did a cursory examination of the room from the relative safety of the doorway. Aside from the damn Scrabble Board everything else appeared untouched. His eyes came to rest on the shelf where his grandfather's Stetson rested. In the empty space next to the worn hat he noted the absence of the bracelet.

Carefully, he stepped across the threshold and into the room, noting the quick drop in temperature. Brady's arms instantly rippled with gooseflesh as his anxious breath wafted through the frosty air. Brady was not alone.

"Honey, where'd you get that pretty bracelet?"

April was smiling as she drove, her mind spinning with a million different thoughts…each more delicious than the last. She took note of the plastic band hanging loosely around Abby's wrist as she glanced back in the rearview mirror. Gruff's head lay cradled on Abby's lap, his eyes closed.

"The man gave it to me," Abby answered, running her tiny fingers through Gruff's fur.

"What man, sweetie," April countered, only half-paying attention.

Abby's matter-of-fact response caught her mother by complete surprise, "The man who lives with Brady, silly."

Puzzled, April hesitated to collect her thoughts before continuing. Kids are renowned for their imaginative storytelling, an exasperating skill that Abby had already mastered at the ripe age of five.

"I didn't know there was a man who lived with Brady," April stated as she rolled to a stop at the traffic light. "He must be awful good at hide-n-seek."

Abby rolled her sky-blue eyes and giggled, "Now you are being silly, mommy. He doesn't play hide-and-seek." Abby's childish laugh drifted into silence. "I don't think he plays games at all."

April's reply was interrupted by the sound of an impatient horn. Shifting her gaze in the rearview mirror from Abby to the SUV hovering precariously close to her car's rear bumper, April scowled at the driver before pressing her foot down on the accelerator.

Train of thought derailed, April's convoluted thoughts drifted from Abby's outlandish tale of a mysterious and unseen roommate and returned to planning the romantic evening ahead.

Chapter 20

A FRANK DISCUSSION

Frank Griggs sat in his leather recliner, clad in only a pair of boxers and a t-shirt, watching the morning news on television. The fresh-faced weather girl was doing her best to navigate the map, not stare too blindly into the camera, and maintain her balance atop ultra-high heels – all the while butchering the pronunciation of nearly every town and county in northern Michigan.

New to the station and fresh from college somewhere in Missouri, the re-tired lawman doubted that Miss Rhonda Fleming possessed any meteorological experience -- beyond the blond hair, spray-on-tan, and large chest that seemed to be the credential of choice these days when it came to local news. Frank grumbled his protests, but like most others in the important 35-65 male age demographic found himself tuning in each morning none-the-less.

This morning, as Miss Fleming promised continued sunshine and warm temperatures extending well into the following week, Griggs found himself massaging the stiffness from his knuckles. His rheumatoid arthritis was a much better weather predictor than the WTRC Weather Center Doppler Radar, and if the pain and swelling in his joints were any indication, a storm was brewing on the horizon – and it promised to be a bad one.

Maddie was in the kitchen paging through the Bedlam County Banner when Frank made his way in to freshen his coffee. Unlike himself, Mrs. Frank

Griggs preferred The Banner's coverage of church pot-lucks, friends of the library used book sales, and local high school sports over watching the beautiful people of the world perform voice-overs against "B-Roll" of car accidents, burglaries, and rising unemployment. Miss Fleming's *assets* held no sway over Maddie Griggs.

"Barn door's open," Maddie commented, looking up from her reading. "No worries, that pony went lame years ago and doesn't have the strength to run." She smiled from behind her own cup of coffee as Frank adjusted his underwear.

"I'll have you know, young lady," came Frank's quick reply, "Budweiser just contacted me for their next Super Bowl ad. Apparently one of their horses came up lame and they need a new Clydesdale; my name was first on their list."

Maddie rolled her eyes, sliding a plate heaped with bacon and scrambled eggs across the table. "Okay, Mr. Ed, eat up. You've got a busy day ahead."

Frank took a seat at the table and began shoveling the food into his mouth. At sixty-one, he still ate like a teenager – anything and everything – and was as healthy as a bear. After thirty-two years as one of Bedlam County's finest, the last fourteen of which he had worn the badge of Sheriff, Frank Griggs was a physical specimen. An avid outdoorsman, he remained fit with daily five-mile walks, fifty push ups each morning, and a shot of Jack – or two - at The Hayloft. Just sprinkle in a little fishing, hunting, and plenty of time with Maddie and Frank had the recipe for perfect health.

"Busy day?" he asked, gulping down his second cup of coffee. "We're not going to the flea market today, are we? I swear, woman, your fascination with looking at other people's junk is something that would have been a deal-breaker if I had known about it when we first met."

Maddie took the good-natured ribbing in stride – and with a smile. Managing her husband was a science which basically consisted of letting him talk until he wore himself out. His nervousness over today's plan was completely understandable, and if she were to be completely honest, shared, as well.

"Don't you think its time you pay Brady a visit? It's been two weeks, I'm sure he's settled in by now."

Frank grunted something unintelligible as he chewed on his last strip of bacon.

"Just go check on him," Maddie continued, setting the newspaper down on the table. "He's all alone in that house – probably bored to death. Take him fishing."

Frank smiled and nodded, unsure of how to share with his wife that despite the death of both of his parents, Brady was far from alone in the Up North House.

Brady walked from his parent's bedroom two hours later, arms laden with files, papers, and other miscellaneous items. Still puzzled, the one-time reporter now, at least, had some idea of what his father was doing with his retirement. As for the Scrabble Board's mysterious journey from the trash can to the room upstairs, Brady chalked it up to sleepwalking and did his best to put it out of his mind; no mysterious messages laid in waiting for him, this time. *For now, the board can stay right where it is,* Brady promised, *but if the damn thing shows up anywhere else or starts spitting out random messages again I'm torching it!*

The music from his phone, his standard selection -- Pearl Jam's *Wish List*, coursed through the empty house as he piled his research on the coffee table in the family room. The lyrics were the story of his life – every emotion he had ever felt condensed into three minutes and thirty-four seconds of pure genius, "I wish I was a neutron bomb, for once I could go off. I wish I were a sacrifice but somehow still lived on."

Fishing the phone from his pocket, he glanced at the caller ID and smiled. "Frank Griggs, I was just thinking about calling you."

"So what you're telling me is that my grandfather wasn't killed in the line of duty," Brady was shocked beyond belief as he listened to Frank's long and confusing story.

"I'm telling you what the State Police concluded, Brady, not what I believe." Frank was working on his fourth Pabst Blue Ribbon and was sweating profusely. The two men had spent the better part of the last four hours digging through his father's files and notes. Frank was proving invaluable in helping

Brady connect the dots, but much was still a mix of conjecture and in some instances complete insanity.

"The official report lists your grandfather's cause of death as suicide," Frank replied, holding up his hand to ward off Brady's protests. "But it's complete bullshit, Brady. You tell me how a man drives himself off the highway at sixty-five miles per then decides to take his own head off with a .44?" Frank winced as soon as the words left his mouth. "Sorry, son -- that was uncalled for."

Brady was stunned. His father's notes on the accident were vague and made no mention of the official State Police report. The thought of his own grandfather ending his life under such circumstances was disturbing to say the least.

"I'm confused, Frank. If what you say is true, and I have no reason to doubt you, what you describe sure as hell doesn't sound like suicide. Besides, I always thought he was killed in the line of duty?"

Frank took a long pull from his beer. In many ways he felt like he was betraying John by revealing family secrets. Some memories are *best forgotten*, he thought, mulling over where to start.

"Yer' daddy ever tell you how he got those scars?" Frank was staring out the window and across the lake. Never one to avoid eye contact, the man's body language did much to reveal his discomfort.

"Mmm....no, not really," Brady responded, trying to recall the brief conversations he had shared with his father about the scars that marked his chest and face. His father had laughed off Brady's questions with stories of shark attacks, rescuing kittens from trees, and even a wild story that involved cow tipping, a barbed-wire fence, and a bottle of Wild Turkey. Even his mother was no help.

"He didn't talk about them."

Frank remained silent. "I'm gonna grab another one," referring to the empty beer can in his hand, "something tells me we're both gonna need one.... or three."

Brady watched the old walk from the room and make his way toward the kitchen. A million different thoughts were rattling through his brain and he was pretty certain that another beer wouldn't help, but given the subject-matter it probably wouldn't hurt.

Frank returned a few minutes later carrying the rest of the case of PBR, a wide smile splitting his lips. "No sense trekking these old bones back and forth." He sat back on the sofa and handed Brady a beer. "You are so much like yer' old man that it's ridiculous," laughter followed a long swallow of beer. "You guys and that damn Scrabble Game. Spelling's not really my strong point. I much prefer cards. Give me a case of PBR and my cribbage board and I'm as happy as a pig in shit."

Brady smiled as he popped the top on his beer. "Yeah, we've always played Scrabble. Dad said mom taught him how to play back when they first met." Brady hesitated as the familiar tingle found its way up the back of his neck. "What made you think of Scrabble, Frank?"

Frank finished the rest of his beer and reached for another, letting out a long and arid belch. "Saw it on the counter in the kitchen. Who ya been playin with?"

Frank's hand froze in mid-reach as he saw the look of dread pass over Brady's face. "Son, you ok?"

Brady wasn't sure how to respond. Tomfoolery with the Scrabble Board aside, he had felt something in this house since the day he had arrived.

"Frank, you and Maddie come by here now and then, right – to check on things?" Brady rose to his feet and walked to the window. "And even before... mom and dad, ya know. You guys would visit, right?'

Frank's hand dove into the case of beer and returned with a fresh can. Popping its top he raised it to his lips and nodded. "Yeah, we've been here a time or two."

"Ever see or feel anything...strange?"

Frank laughed nervously, "Hell, son, when you get my age everything seems strange." After another long drink, he continued, "Did yer dad ever tell you about the time I shot that deer from my car..."

Brady interrupted, "Yeah, Frank, he did. It's hanging over the bar at The Hayloft. He told me all kinds of things...about you, about himself, and even about my grandpa; but what the fuck, Frank – how do I know what's true and what's not?"

Frank lurched to his feet, careful not to spill his beverage. At well over six-feet-tall he towered over Brady. The younger man didn't blink.

"What do you want me to tell you -- that your grandpa went crazy and blew his head off? How about I explain in excruciating detail how your dad was a certifiable loon who locked himself up in that room chasing after ghosts until he just happened to find one? Is that what you want to hear?"

Frank's raised voice boomed across the family room. "Ah, hell," he muttered, finishing another beer and tossing the empty can onto the coffee table.

"I want the truth, Frank," Brady urged. "I want to know why I wake up every night from nightmares I can't remember. Why my dog is afraid to be more than three feet away from me in this place. But mostly, I wanna know what the fuck is going on with that Scrabble Board!"

Frank stared long and hard into Brady's tired eyes. So *much like his father,* he thought. "Fine," Frank relented, "you want to know what I know or what I think I know?"

Brady returned Frank's stare, "I want to know everything."

"Grab the rest of the beers and take a walk with me," Frank added on his way to the kitchen and through the French doors leading outside before muttering under his breath, "I knew I should've brought more beer."

Chapter 21

THE TRUTH SHALL SET YOU FREE

Frank was right – one case of beer hadn't been nearly enough; a dire situation which had been rectified with a quick trip to the corner store. Brady had waited on the dock, feet dangling in the warm summer water, trying to piece together what had turned out to be a very complex and mystifying puzzle.

Sadly, Frank's *more-beer* prescription wasn't exactly what the doctor had ordered. The pair's rambling conversation drifted from Brady's past and current domestic and familial entanglements to the current price of gas and the sad state of Detroit athletics. All talk of things that go bump in the night – and sometimes during daylight hours, too – ended with that first case of beer. Everything after was a feeble attempt to put some distance, via alcohol, between that uncomfortable conversation and what would surely come next. Too many beers later, the afternoon ended with a phone call to Maddie. With Frank safely tucked inside, Brady stood at the end of the driveway and watched Maddie's dust-covered Cherokee disappear from view.

The ground rolled beneath Brady's feet as he made his way back to the relative comfort of the Up North House. For the time being, the alcohol outweighed the influence of whatever seemingly dark yet thankfully still unseen force that was trying desperately to fuck with his mind.

Brady's liquid bravado, however, soon evaporated. His search for something to help soak up the alcohol pooling in his empty stomach, drew him into the kitchen where atop the counter, exactly as Frank had described, rested the Scrabble Board. The damn piece of cardboard was quickly becoming the bane of his existence. Brady tried resisting the temptation to look, but his curiosity got the better of him. It took a moment for his drunken mind to focus, but the message spread neatly across the game board finally became clear.

Brady clung to the slippery walls as he stumbled from the kitchen, his uneasy mind clumsy from both beer and fright. Finding his way into the family room, he collapsed onto the couch. As his spinning head relented to the drunken blackness that awaited him, Brady heard the crying of the seagulls over the lake and for the briefest of moments felt the touch of an unseen, calloused yet comforting hand on his shoulder.

Brady was late for dinner. Not by much, but enough to make an already nervous April even more so.

"You and your damn fashionable entrances," she teased as she greeted him at the door. Again, she looked amazing. Her hair hung at to her shoulders in a pair of matching braids. A very comfortable pair of jeans and black tank top completed her style. It clung to her in all the right places.

The mobile home was smaller than Brady had imagined, but held a coziness that his own home, although much larger, severely lacked. "Had trouble choosing between white and red," Brady laughed, presenting the wine, "so I brought both." His PR smile camouflaged the nausea that was eating away at his insides. Frank and his damn Pabst Blue Ribbon had done quite the number on him.

At the sound of Brady's voice Gruff came galloping in from the next room, Abby trailing close behind. The dog paused a few feet from Brady, cocking his furry head to one side and giving his two-legged friend the once-over. Finally, Gruff's tail began to sway back and forth as he rushed forward to rub against Brady's legs.

"He likes you," Abby stated, as if this were Brady's first introduction to the dog, "Come on Gruff, let's go make a puddle." Gruff released himself from Brady's legs, emitting a soft whine, and followed Abby outside. Brady took note of the plastic band encircling the girl's wrist. It was all he could do to not rush forward and examine it more closely.

"That dog is amazing," April declared, taking the wine from Brady's hands and moving towards the kitchen. "I swear he puts up with way too much from her. Abby was literally putting ribbons and barrettes in his hair today and he just sat there like it was the most normal thing in the world."

Brady smiled as he followed, "Well, he did get his balls cut off about three months ago -- maybe he's finally discovering his inner-dog."

April's snorting laughter eased the throbbing in Brady's temples. "We've definitely go to do something about that laugh." He drew her into his arms, holding her tightly. April could feel him trembling.

"You alright," she whispered from his shoulder. "You look awful."

It was Brady's turn to laugh, "Yeah," he replied, planting a kiss atop her head. "I've just got a lot on my mind." Pausing, before shifting his embrace into a tickle, "And I will have you know, nine out of ten chicks agree, I rock this t-shirt."

April pushed him away playfully and continued into the kitchen with the wine. "The red will be perfect; I'm grilling ribs with caramel asparagus. And for desert…banana splits, of course!"

The thought of eating, let alone more alcohol, made Brady's stomach do somersaults. "Mmmmm, can't wait," he lied. "So where's your dad?"

"Out back manning the grill. He won't let anyone else handle the meat," April laughed again, cutting it just short from another snort. "Seriously, he's like Rain Man when it comes to the grill. Come on, let's go see how he's doing."

Brady followed April through the mobile home and out the sliding door leading off the den. The room had obviously been added on since his last visit and really provided a nice open area. He was surprised by the green grass and fence that greeted him outside.

"Daddy," April called, moving toward the grill where Henry Mayer stood brushing sauce onto a slab of ribs. "This is Brady Tanner. Do you remember me talking to you about him?"

Henry Mayer turned at the sound of his daughter's voice. Stooped-shouldered with red suspenders keeping his loose-fitting pants from pooling about his ankles, Mayer's bushy gray eyebrows framed his cloudy eyes. He looked like a muppet from a TV show Brady had watched as a child.

"Yes, yes, 'course I do." Henry's voice boomed from his frail body. Brady noticed the hearing aids encircling the man's oversized ears. Setting his jaw, and pointing the grilling tongs at Brady's chest, he continued. "You got a job, son?" Henry Mayer was ready to grill more than meat. "How 'bout drugs? I don't want my June Bug 'round no drugs."

April laughed, "Daddy, stop!" She grabbed Brady's hand and gave it a squeeze. "Brady is quite the fine and upstanding citizen. You probably remember his dad and grandpa – they worked for the Sheriff's Department." Turning to Brady, "Wasn't your grandpa the Sheriff for a while?"

Brady forced a smile, "Yeah, he was. Buck Tanner. It was a long time ago." He watched the rigid expression on Henry's face soften.

"Good man, Buck Tanner. Only man I ever knew who wore a Stetson. Looked like a real cowboy if you ask me." Henry lowered the tongs and nodded at Brady before turning his attention back to the grill. "Now move along, this meat ain't gonna cook itself."

April squeezed Brady's hand once more as she led him to the picnic table. "See, he likes you." She leaned over and gave him a peck on the cheek. "I've got you a surprise. Close your eyes."

Brady obliged, his world still spinning about from his liquid lunch with Frank.

"Ok, open them!"

Brady smiled. April held a bag of Funyons and an ice-cold Mountain Dew. "Hors 'devoures are served."

Hangover aside, the evening couldn't have been more enjoyable. Brady was able to nurse a single glass of wine, instead savoring his Mountain Dew and some ice water. The meal was delicious and helped settle his churning stomach. The real treat, however, was sitting back and watching April in her natural surroundings.

While Brady and Henry guarded the picnic table, the girls danced and played in the yard. Gruff kept a close watch on Abby, never wandering more than a few feet away and paying scarce attention to anyone or anything else.

Brady nearly laughed himself hoarse watching April teach Abby how to properly use a hula hoop. He was hypnotized by April's swaying hips and found himself wondering when Abby would finally call it a night. Next to him Henry was already snoring.

April must have been reading Brady's mind, "Okay missy," gathering Abby into her arms and hoisting her into the air, "I think it's about time we call it a night. Your grandfather is already sawing logs."

Abby giggled in her mother's arms. "I want Brady to read to me tonight."

"Now that's a deal, sweetie," Brady promised standing to his feet and taking Abby from April's outstretched arms. Gruff's low growl caught everyone off guard.

"Easy boy, you can come to," Brady joked, wondering what had gotten into his furry friend. "How about instead of reading you a book I tell you a story about the time I filled my mom's bathtub with frogs? Moms love when you do that, ya know!" He winked in April's direction, receiving a sarcastic grin in response.

Abby's cackle was magical, "Did you hear that Gruff – we're getting frog-gies tomorrow!"

The tiny trailer was finally quiet, except for Henry's snoring from the bedroom down the hall. It sounded like waves crashing on the beach. Brady stretched out on the fold-out sofa in the den nervously waiting for April. He felt like a teenager on prom night, minus the tux and bad haircut.

Abby had thoroughly enjoyed the frog story. Brady had secretly made plans with her to sneak off the following day to do a little frogging at the creek near Stewart Road. The thought of April discovering a bathtub full of frogs made Brady giggle as hard as Abby.

Gruff hadn't shared their enthusiasm. He had placed himself squarely be-tween Abby and Brady on her tiny bed, even going so far as to bare his teeth as Brady leaned in to place a kiss atop Abby's golden curls. Brady had enough on his mind and tried to just let his dog's behavior pass, but something kept tugging at the edge of his memory.

Enter April – minus the comfortable jeans. Her silky skin, coppery from time spent beneath the Michigan sun, practically glowed beneath the moon-light trickling in through the trailer's small window. The tank top, which so perfectly cradled her full breasts, was the only stitch of clothing that remained between them.

"Finally, Mr. Tanner," she purred, gliding forward to join him on the bed, "I have you all to myself."

Brady's erection was instant and enormous, pushing through the band on his boxers. Her lavender scent was intoxicating, and Brady felt his head begin to spin as he reached for her.

Their kiss was soft yet passionate, an introductory exploration of what was to come. His fingers traced the softness of her jaw-line and down her neck. Holding her face in his hands was like holding a small piece of the sun; the touch of April's lips heated Brady to his core.

Brady's kiss became hungrier as he rolled on top of her, holding her hands firmly against the sofa's thin mattress. Breaking the kiss, he stared deeply into her sparkling eyes.

"You do realize this could change everything," Brady teased, gently guiding himself inside her.

April responded with a breathless moan and raised hips. "Promise," she whispered, digging her fingers into Brady's back.

Her question hung in the air, a spoken response unnecessary. Everything was changing, in ways both magical and mysterious. Little did either realize, however, just what those changes would bring.

Chapter 22

THE
MORNING AFTER

Brady counted thirty-four ceiling tiles hanging over the pull-out sofa. April slept beside him, her naked form claiming most of the bed, yet Brady found himself counting ceiling tiles.

It's not that he was afraid of falling asleep, although lately his slumber had been plagued by nightmares. Instead, Brady found himself trying to find distraction from the guilt that was building inside. The tug of war between his heart and head over what he had just shared with April was both physically and emotionally painful. Brady tasted the salty tears before he realized he was even crying.

April stirred, raising her sleepy head from the pillow. "You still up?"

Brady turned his face to April's, the sting of tears fresh on his cheeks. "Yeah, trying to figure out what the use for algebra really is. I'm convinced it's merely the textbook industry trying to line their pockets." He paused, forcing a smile and raising a hand to brush the hair away from April's face. "Seriously, have you ever once had to figure out the whole two trains traveling in opposite directions thing?"

April found Brady's hand and brought it to her lips. "Tell me about Karen, Brady."

For the next hour Brady talked and April listened. He had met Karen while in college at Northwestern. For six weeks he had followed her around campus, not in a creepy stalker way, much more like a love-struck puppy. He knew her class schedule, where she had eaten lunch, and even her secret place in the library, tucked away behind the stacks of Medieval Literature, where she would steal away for naps and to nibble on carrot sticks while studying.

April listened as Brady described his life with Karen. Feeling the raw emotion pouring from the man with whom she was falling in love broke her heart, but also made her realize how deeply she cared for him -- and how damaged he truly was.

Fresh tears welled in Brady's eyes as he described the surreal experience of finding his brother-in-law waiting for him at the airport with the news of Karen's death.

"She was consumed with being healthy," he explained, fresh light brightening his reddened eyes, "especially during the pregnancy. Everything was about diet and exercise. Hell, I even lost ten pounds trying to keep up with her." Brady's voice was thick with adoration as he recalled his wife's little idiosyncrasies – the small details shared between only them.

His face darkened as he continued, "She was walking Gruff. Every day they would walk to the park near our apartment, a winding four mile loop that she insisted would keep her ass from growing out of control." Brady smiled in spite of himself. "According to the police report she was walking down Lexington, not two blocks from our apartment, when it happened."

April held her breath, unsure of where this memory was going, yet suspecting where it might end. She squeezed his hand in support.

"The kid was fourteen," for the first time a trace of anger entered Brady's shaking voice, "a fucking punk with nothing better to do than wave a gun around a liquor store."

April tensed; this was not exactly where she imagined this story would be leading.

"Funny thing is, the gun wasn't even loaded," Brady laughed; a heart wrenching sound that seemed misplaced with the tears now streaming down his face. "Kid got his money and bolted for the door. He almost made it, too." More silence. When Brady continued his voice was little more than a whisper. "His gun wasn't loaded, but the cashier's was. The place had been held up a dozen or so times. He emptied that .38, spraying bullets everywhere. He got the kid in the shoulder, a flesh wound that did little more than drop him to the ground. He laid there crying his eyes out until the police arrived."

April moved closer to Brady, wrapping her arm across his bare chest. His beating heart was working overtime.

"Wrong place at the wrong time," he continued. "She never even knew what was happening. One minute she's walking Gruff, probably thinking about paint colors for the nursery or how to celebrate the news of my book, and the next she's...gone. Sixty-eight bucks – that's the going rate for a life in Chicago these days. Hell, two for one at that price."

April's tears splashed onto Brady's chest. His pain, although agonizing to witness, was also a blessing to share. She felt helpless in easing it, however.

"Coroner said she didn't feel a thing – the bullet tore through her brain; she was dead before she hit the ground." He wiped the tears from his eyes and continued.

"Gruff went ballistic," Brady continued, smiling weakly at the thought of the young pup standing guard over his fallen wife. "Little guy wouldn't let anyone near her – not even the paramedics. Finally, one of the cops had to shoot the poor little fur-ball with his tazer," his fragile smile strengthened briefly, "Only dog on the planet that can charge cell phones by licking them."

Brady's last wall of defense finally crumbled, his sarcastic humor swept away by the rivers of grief flowing down his face, "I don't know how long the baby held on for; the coroner didn't say and I couldn't bring myself to ask." He hesitated, speaking aloud for the first time what he had always kept secret. "I named her Sara, after her grandmother. Karen was hoping for a girl."

The rest of the night was spent in silence. April had no words to soothe Brady's hurt. Brady had survived the last few months by making himself numb, to everything and everyone. Alone in the darkness, the couple clung to each other, knowing that Brady's promise of change had been fulfilled.

"Who the hell are you?"

Brady looked up from his bowl of Fruit Loops to find Henry Mayer standing over him. Wearing nothing more than a saggy pair of tighty whities and a coffee stained t-shirt, April's father looked every part the grizzled old man he was.

"Sir, um...Mr. Mayer, I, uh..." Panicking, Brady looked across the table for help from Abby. She smiled, lowering her half-filled bowl of cereal from the edge of the table for Gruff to share. Helpless, Brady did what any reasonable man in his situation would do, "April! April, you better get in here!

Clutching her robe at her breast and balancing a twisted bath towel on her head, his knight in shining armor stepped from the bathroom off the kitchen. "Daddy," she scolded, "this is my friend Brady Tanner. He had dinner with us last night."

Henry glared at Brady through his thick glasses and grunted something unintelligible before plopping down onto the seat directly across the table. April returned to her morning routine. Her shift at Kroger's started at nine.

"Where's my corn flakes," barked the half-dressed muppet.

Brady looked again to Abby. She rolled her eyes in response and skipped to the pantry, returning with the cereal, "Right here, grandpa -- bottom shelf next to the oatmeal." She wrinkled her nose at the mere thought that anyone would choose to eat the tasteless paste.

Henry busily poured his cereal and set to work heaping shaking spoonfuls into his mouth. Much of it spilled down his unshaven chin and onto the stained t-shirt. *What kind of bizarre world am I in*, Brady wondered, sipping the fruity milk from the bottom of his bowl.

"I knew a Tanner in school," He volunteered around mouthfuls of corn-flakes. "Johnny or Jimmy, maybe – hell'uva ball player."

Brady lowered the bowl from his lips. *This fossil went to high school with my dad?* Doing the quick math in his head, and recalling how frail his own father had looked during his last visit, Brady accepted Henry's statement as fact.

"John, it was John Tanner," Brady offered. Growing up, Brady had seen his father's old high school yearbooks. The man had been a four-year varsity player in baseball, football, and basketball, with plenty of offers to play at the college level. Instead, John Tanner had followed in his father's footsteps; something Brady was sure his own father had wished for him.

Henry returned to his corn flakes as Brady walked to the sink to rinse his bowl. Abby and Gruff had already vacated the kitchen, not even a good morning wag from his furry friend. *Something is definitely up with that dog.* Brady was pondering the possibilities when Henry's voice intruded.

"He came by, ya know -- yer dad, asking about the hospital." Henry had finished his corn flakes and was scooping sugar into his coffee. The elderly man's lack of coordination revealed the reason behind the stained t-shirt. The poor man winced with every sip as it dribbled from the corners of his mouth.

"Hospital," Brady asked, returning to the table with a cup of coffee of his own, and a paper towel for Henry. The man accepted the offering with a nod and wiped the coffee from his chin.

"Nut house is more like it," Henry continued. "Place gave me the creeps."

Brady hesitated. A million questions came to his racing mind, but Henry's fragile memory would surely fail under the weight of a heavy interrogation.

Instead, he let the silence do the work for him.

"Diggin' graves; two bucks a hole." Henry kept his eyes on his coffee. "I was just a kid, but my dad let me tag along. He did some work up there now and again." A pain-filled shadow passed over Henry's eyes. "A lot of holes."

April breezed into the kitchen, her blue Kroger vest doing little to distract from her casual style. Even without make-up she was breathtaking. "I'm late," she declared, digging through her purse for car keys. "It's just a three hour shift, I'll be home about noon." She smiled triumphantly, raising her ring of keys into the air. "Abby's fine here with dad, she'll watch Dora. Or, if you don't mind, let Gruff keep her company."

Brady's worries of being asked to baby-sit evaporated. As for Gruff, he wasn't sure he had a choice in the matter of whether the dog would be staying.

"Sounds good to me," Brady smiled. "I've got a few things to do. How about we connect later this afternoon?"

April stepped forward and kissed his cheek, her hand brushing against his arm. "Sounds like a date to me." She turned from Brady and playfully tussled her father's thinning hair. "I'll be home in a bit – behave yourself."

Brady watched her walk from the room, stopping briefly to give Abby a hug before leaving. Henry was lost in thought, staring into the bottom of his empty coffee cup. Brady cleared his throat, unsure of what to say. Henry nearly jumped out of his skin at the sound.

"Who the hell are you," he demanded, staring blankly up at Brady as if the man had magically appeared in his kitchen.

"Good grief," Brady muttered, running for the door. "April!"

Chapter

THE PRICE OF A MEMORY

Brady listened to his iPod as he drove. *Mrs. Potter's Lullaby* by Counting Crows was playing. He had never been much of a Crows fan, and couldn't recall having loaded to any of his play-lists, but with more than 10,000 songs at his immediate disposal, he wasn't completely surprised by the pleasant surprise. "If dreams are like movies, then memories are films about ghosts…" Brady connected with the words, thinking of his own recent bout of sleepless nights due to nightmares. The melody was contagious and Adam Duritz' voice was hypnotizing. "The price of a memory is the memory of the sorrow it brings…"

If my life were a movie what would the soundtrack be, he mused, scrolling mentally through the entire Pearl Jam catalog. He quickly realized that even Eddie Vedder had yet find word to describe the rambling wreck of a movie his life had become.

Brady's thoughts drifted from music to the tasks at hand. His mental checklist included connecting once again with Frank to hopefully learn more about his father's make-shift crime lab/work room/detective bureau upstairs – this time sans the PBR.

Good ol' Hank Mayer and his ramblings about Brady's father's visit to ask about digging graves at the hospital had planted the seeds of some fresh thoughts in the fertile soil of Brady's over-inquisitive mind.

And finally, Brady felt an odd pull to reconnect with his old pal Jeff Ryder. In the years since that terrifying night on the float, and beneath the waves, the two friends had spoken only once, briefly by telephone from Brady's bedside in Traverse City. It had been what the two boys had left unsaid that had bound them o closely together.

Mrs. Potter's Lullaby ended as Brady neared the Up North House. He could still smell April's lavender scent on his skin, and drank it in by holding his arm up and taking a big whiff. His iPhone skipped, which it never did, catching the next track in mid-song, as he pulled his Jetta in behind Frank's truck.

Yes, I understand
that every life must end, uh huh
As we sit alone,
I know someday we must go, uh huh
Oh, I'm a lucky man
to count on both hands, the ones I love
Some folks just have one
Yeah, others they got none, uh huh
Stay with me,
Oh, Let's just breathe

Just Breathe, Pearl Jam's haunting tale of loss, wasn't exactly one of Brady's favorites, but since Karen's death it had held a special, yet painful place in his fractured heart. So much so, that he had removed it from all of his play-lists; the lyrics chipped away at his unsteady resolve to just feel...nothing.

Brady pulled the buds from his ears, flinging them onto the passenger seat. It seemed his life did have a soundtrack, and for the time being at least, it was full of sad songs. Duritz had it right, Brady thought, stepping from the car. *The price of a memory really is the memory of the sorrow it brings.*

Frank's gravelly voice boomed from the direction of the house. "'Bout time you roll in."

The man looked no worse for wear after yesterday's heavy drinking. Wearing a black Harley Davidson t-shirt and a faded pair of jeans, he looked ready to kick someone's ass, "Only been sittin' here for an hour."

Brady smiled, knowing full well that Frank had been up since long before sunrise, anxious to walk his happy ass over four miles just for the chance to roust Brady from bed. "Yeah, you're not fooling anyone, old man. You get up at five every morning to watch your Murder She Wrote reruns; legalized porn for the elderly. "

Frank's bellowing laugh nearly shook the ground beneath Brady's feet, "You may not believe me, young man, but back in the day Angela Lansbury was one fine piece of ass."

Even when fully-rested and with no hangover, Brady would have been hard-pressed to find a worthy response to Frank's sense of humor. He shook his head and smile instead. "I'll just have to take your word for that one."

They met midway between the house and driveway, an odd showdown of sorts along the worn-out path; the one-time lawman and the son of the man he had once considered his best friend. "You do realize that we are both crazy as bat shit, right?"

Brady laughed, moving forward to embrace the man he had grown up referring to as Uncle Frank. "Certifiable bat shit, Frank. Certifiable."

"So tell me again about that night," Brady urged, leaning forward across the small table tucked into a darkened corner inside The Hayloft's cavernous interior. Third-shifter's from the local Ford plant, fewer in numbers since the lay-offs, filled the stools around the bar, filling their bellies with heaping plates of the famous "Haystack" breakfast – seasoned potatoes mixed with bacon, eggs, sausage and just about any other item requested. Tall draughts of ice cold beer were often the drink of choice to wash it all down.

Frank swirled the remaining swallow of water around in the bottom of his glass, keeping his eyes averted from Brady's. He glanced at the watch on his wrist, a gold Timex the County Commission had presented him with upon retirement. "Ah, hell," pushing the near-empty glass away, "I need a drink." Catching the arm of a passing waitress, Frank whispered something into her ear.

"I'm still reeling from last night," Brady pleaded unsuccessfully. He threw his arms in the air in surrender as the waitress reappeared with a bottle of Jack Daniels and two glasses. Smiling, she poured the first round and set the nearly-full bottle on the table between them.

Frank reached for his glass, wrapping it in his meaty paw and staring into the coppery-colored whiskey, "To Buck Tanner," raising the glass," the mean-est, hardest, toughest, orneriest son of a bitch I ever met," hesitating, "and the finest."

Brady clinked his glass onto Frank's before raising it to his lips. The mere thought, coupled with the smell of the liquor made his stomach twist, but he poured it down his throat nonetheless wishing he had something to chase the burning taste from his mouth. It was odd, toasting a man he had never met, especially given recent revelations; even so, Brady knew the words were justly deserved.

Frank was halfway into his second round before the words came to his lips. Like most people with a long tale to tell, he got to the meat of the story in a very roundabout way. "You deal much in what ifs, Brady?" He emptied the glass in one great swallow.

Brady considered the question, and the man asking it, before answering. The reporter knew a loaded question when he heard one, and Frank's query was definitely of the double-barrel variety. "Sure, I suppose," he replied, doing his best to keep the many *what ifs* associated with Karen's accident safely buried deep in his own subconscious.

"But my job isn't so much different than yours was," sipping his bitter drink, "As a reporter you go where the facts take you – whether you like the destination or not."

Frank laughed, "Bullshit," pouring his third drink and topping off Brady's, too. "You know as well as I do that sometimes it's not the answer that's important, it's having the fucking balls to ask the question." The former lawman's laughter trailed off as his gaze moved from Brady's face to settle on the half-empty bottle of whiskey.

After a moment, Brady broke the silence. "So that's the beast, huh – hanging over the bar?"

Frank craned his neck and nodded. "Yep, that's the beast." The giant buck hung prominently over the bar, yellow caution take draped across its enormous rack. If the mount was any indication, the beast had weighed well over two hundred and fifty pounds. He couldn't believe Frank had taken it down with his .38.

"So what's your what if, Frank; if you had to choose just one?" The question passed from Brady's lips before he realized what he was asking. He immediately wished he could take it back.

Frank shifted his focus from The Beast over the bar and back to the man seated across the table. "You don't fuck around, do ya?" His laughter brightened his eyes. "Big brass ones just like your grandpa."

Brady warmed at the complement, proud to hear he shared more than just a name with the man who had gained the respect of so many. He regretted never having known him.

"That's a long fucking list to choose just one from," Frank said solemnly, an uncomfortable silence falling over the table.

Brady interjected, saving Frank from his laundry list of what ifs. "Know what I wonder, Frank? I wonder what if my house is haunted. Yeah, I definitely think that's at the top of my what if list right now. Of course, that brings a million other questions to mind; like who and why – but it all starts with the what if, wouldn't you agree?" Brady emptied his glass with a long and uncomfortable swallow and poured another, doing his best to keep up.

Frank ran his age-spotted hands through his thinning gray hair. He leaned forward, lowering his voice, before continuing, "No need to wonder about that one, son. Something's been knocking 'round that house for some time." Shaking his head, "Maddie's nervous as a long-tailed cat in a room full of rocking chairs every time she goes in there."

Brady exhaled. "So, I'm not crazy?"

Frank's laugh filled air, drawing looks from the patrons clear across the other side of the bar. "Son, I can neither confirm nor deny your sanity, but I can tell you that I had this same conversation with your daddy not four years ago. He thought he was going crazy, too; hell, I had my own suspicions about the man. Even a blind man could see that something fairly strange was going on – and had been for years." Frank paused and poured them each another round. Raising his glass in toast, he smiled, a smile not unlike Brady's own mischievous grin, "But like I said, sometimes it's not the answer that's so important."

Frank downed his Jack in one gulp before he continued, "Now if those truly are brass balls yer packin', quit sipping at that drink and let's get the fuck out of here. People are goanna start thinking we're dating with all this whispering." Frank stood, peeling two twenties from a wad of bills he pulled from his front pocket. He tossed them onto the table as Brady finished his drink. "I think it's about time we start asking some fucking questions."

Chapter 24

THUMBING IT

The argument over who would drive was both contentious and comical. They had arrived at The Hayloft in Brady's Jetta, with Frank complaining the entire way about the cramped space of a foreign car and Brady doing his best to explain how the entire vehicle was built right in the good old USA. The generational gap couldn't have been more evident.

"Toss me the keys," Frank barked as they stepped from the dim confines of the bar into the late morning sun.

"No way, old man," Brady scoffed, knowing full well that Frank had been at least two up on him in the drink column, but also suspecting that he shouldn't be driving, either. "Where the hell are we going, anyway?"

Frank's grin widened, "Good question. The answer costs you the keys to this Nazi death trap."

Brady sighed, knowing full well that there was no winning this argument. "You do know how to drive a stick, right? I mean, this isn't your father's Oldsmobile we're talking about here. It's a machine built for driving." Brady could feel the mischievous grin spreading across his drunken face as he tossed the keys over the hood of the car.

Frank snatched them from the air and smiled. It took a minute, but he eventually had the seat adjusted to his exact specifications. Brady winced with every slam of the seat on its sliding rails. "Easy there, Frank. I think you've tried just about every available position – plus a few that don't come standard."

Frank turned to his passenger and winked. "Lighten up, Mr. Tanner. Your precious car is in the hands of a trained professional." He inserted the key into the ignition, smiling at the sound of the engine purring under the hood. He slid the stick into neutral and revved the engine. "Not bad – for a foreign car."

The professional stalled the care twice before he had even left the parking lot. The Jetta disappeared from view around the bend of the sweeping country road, the sound of grinding gears echoing in the distance.

Abby and Gruff were playing fetch when it happened. Over and over she tossed the stick from one end of the yard to the other. For most people, especially those over the age of five, the small patch of grass in a trailer park advertised as a yard really isn't much more than a half dozen or so passes with a lawn mower. For Abby, however, the small, fenced-in area was her playground. Grandpa would sit in his chair, reading a newspaper – never a recent one – and complain about last week's or last months headlines as if it were breaking news. He did, however, keep a very watchful eye on his little *junebug*.

Gruff had just chased the stick for what seemed like the hundredth time, showing no signs of tiring, when Abby first complained of the headache. "Grandpa, my head feels funny."

The morning sun was blistering, the promise of a near-record temperature hanging warm and moist in the air. "Let's get you a drink," Henry replied as he stood. He had added a pair of blue work pants over his briefs. They were hiked up to his armpits and fell nearly four inches from the tops of his slippers. "And you too, my good sir," he added, pointing a gnarled finger in Gruff's direction.

He shuffled to the garden hose that lay coiled near the trailer's rusted skirting. His once-thriving grass was riddled with dandelions and other assorted weeds. His wife had managed the yard-work, and the small vegetable garden; tomatoes and cucumbers mostly. Many an afternoon had been spent sitting on the bench swing eating freshly peeled cucumbers sprinkled with salt. The swing, much like his beautiful wife of forty-two years, had succumbed to age, leaving the patchwork lawn and overgrown garden as a memorial.

The hose dribbled to life, the rust-colored water clearing as it flowed. They took turns at the hose, Abby and then Gruff, both wearing more than drinking. The cold water did little to dampen their spirits and soon both were running through the yard at full speed again.

Henry settled back into his chair, his mind drifting back over last week's news. His memory was hit or miss, and today he had leafed through the same newspaper four times without realizing it. His recollection of more distant events, however, remained razor-sharp, and today he couldn't help but think about digging holes at the asylum; the pungent smell of freshly turned earth filling his nostrils. With it, came the uncomfortable memory of a man with a mustache; his hands touching and grabbing in places that no man's hand should ever venture. Henry shivered beneath the sweltering sun as he reminisced.

The pained wailing of an animal shook him from his thoughts. His eyes darted from one corner of the small yard to the next, coming to rest on his grand-daughter. His muddled thoughts couldn't comprehend what his tired eyes were seeing. Backed into a corner, Gruff lay in a ball, his piercing yelps shattering what had been a quiet morning. Standing over the dog, with a strength Henry could not fathom, was Abby, raining blows down upon the dog; the stick once used for fetching turned weapon.

Henry sprinted across the yard, wrapping his arms around his grand-daughter; her hammering blows ceasing in his firm embrace. She trembled as tears filled her eyes, her grandfather's calming whispers drowned out by her own sobs.

Gruff stood on three wobbly legs, his right front paw held against his body, unable to bear weight. Hobbling forward, he placed his wet nose against Abby's tear-stained cheek and began to lick the tears from her face.

The bracelet which had once hung so loosely about Abby's delicate wrist, had tightened its grip; her pale flesh reddening from its bite.

"Trust me, I know what I'm doing." No words in human history preceded stupidity more than those seven. In this case, they were uttered by Brady as he instructed the former Sheriff on how to drive while slightly inebriated.

"Just remember to keep your hands at eleven o'clock and one o'clock on the wheel, not ten and two like they teach in driver's training" Brady's words were slurring slightly. "Now raise your thumbs."

Frank did as he was told, positioning his hands on the steering wheel and raising his thumbs into the air.

"Now just keep the road between your thumbs," Brady explained. "Pretty fucking cool, huh?"

Frank laughed. The road did seem much easier to navigate via thumb. "I'll be damned," he admitted, "son, you just might be a genius."

Brady beamed with pride. "Not me, Frank – Beaver's the genius. He was a fraternity brother in college – Sigma Phi Epsilon." Brady smiled from ear to ear as he recalled his Sig Ep days. "Damned if I can remember his real name," laughing now, "but Beaver taught me that little trick - works every time."

Frank glanced at his passenger. He had a hard time thinking of the kid as more than just that – a kid. *The boy who was too afraid of worms to fish with anything but lures, teaching this old dog a new trick. So much like his father, he thought.*

"You know he was proud of you, right – 'yer dad. He was real proud of you."

Brady's grin vanished. This was not the conversation he wanted to have, especially loaded with Jack Daniels. He changed the subject, watching Frank drive with his thumbs.

"So where the hell are we going anyway?"

Frank scoffed at the question, as if it were the most ridiculous thing he had ever heard. Pressing his foot down on the accelerator and staring between his thumbs, he answered, "Where everyone turns for answers – church."

Chapter 25

SINS OF THE FATHER

Sterling State Park - Brady read the sign as they drove through the entrance. He recalled fishing from the pier with his father, too afraid to touch the worms; instead using small pieces of bologna as bait. His fear of worms remained, especially on rainy mornings when they would crawl from the earth and stretch out on the sidewalks and pavement.

"I think we should've taken a left turn at Albuquerque, Frank," Brady joked as the Jetta rolled deeper into the park. He still found humor in the old Bugs Bunny cartoons on DVD; nothing like a Looney Toon to brighten one's day. Sadly, Gruff was much more of a Foghorn Leghorn fan and didn't appreciate the rabbit's appeal.

"Seriously, what the hell are we doing here?

Frank guided the Jetta into a parking spot near the campground. He pulled the keys from the ignition and let out a long whiskey-scented breath.

"Your grandpa asked me once if I believed in God. Seemed like a silly question at the time. Hell, it stills seems silly when you ask it out loud." Frank fell silent as he collected his thoughts. "Not ten hours later he was dead."

Brady sat in silence, allowing Frank's words to settle over him. Beyond the door at the end of the hall, his father's makeshift office had contained piles of handwritten notes, police files, and other items. Brady had found the article from The Banner mourning the loss of Sheriff Buck Tanner among the stacks. . The clipping had been light on details, and Brady wasn't able to glean much from the six inches of copy. His father's hand-scribbled notes did little to connect the dots. In fact, if anything, Brady worried that his father's seemingly illogical attempts to connect the old asylum with his grandfather's death – not to mention the Lionel Collins affair – seemed more than a bit far-fetched; it was downright crazy. And given his own recent experiences, Brady didn't need doubts about his father's sanity to start him down the path of questioning his own.

"Are you serious?" The last thing Brady wanted was a deep theological discussion with Frank Griggs. The mere mention of the topic had him hearing the sound of those damn silverware chimes.

"Listen, Frank, I appreciate this whole Jedi Master vibe you got going, I really do. And it's been a blast drinking with you and teaching you how to drive drunk with your thumbs, but you didn't really bring me all the way out here to *save me* did ya?" Brady laughed, "Trust me, it's been tried before and I am beyond saving."

Brady's grin melted under Frank's steaming glare. "We can sit here and jerk off all day long, son. Hell, I can do that with the best of 'em." The old man was getting riled. "Or, we can quit the bullshit and finally do something. Personally, I'm sick of all the foreplay."

They locked eyes across the Jetta's small interior. Brady knew the man was right – running from whatever was happening wasn't the solution. He had been running for fourteen years, trying to put distance between himself and the painful memories that plagued his sleep. The memories, he was learning, were always waiting around the next corner and he was exhausted from the chase.

"Fine, no more foreplay," he muttered, shaking the clouds from his groggy head.

Frank reached over and patted Brady's shoulder. "Good. Now get yer ass in gear, it's time for church.

Abby was asleep on the couch when April walked through the door. Gruff sat uncomfortably on the floor near the couch, licking his front paw and whining. The dog's movement pulled her eyes from Abby's sleeping form. She took note of her father, newspaper spread across his chest, asleep in the recliner, legs out and snoring.

April dropped her purse to the floor, an oversized bag that looked more useful for overnight travel purposes than daily transport, and approached the couch. Gruff's whine intensified.

"What's wrong, boy? Everybody go to sleep on you?" She reached forward and stroked the dog behind his ears. She, too, had learned Gruff's sweet spot. The dog trembled beneath her touch. Her eyes traced down from his head to rest on the matted hair on his front paw. He was holding it close, in the air, and it was bent in all the wrong places.

April's first instinct was to reach for the injured limb, but thought better of it as the dog's whimper intensified as her hand left his ears. Instead she retreated for her purse and found her cell phone. She nervously dialed the phone, her attention momentarily diverted from the inactivity of the living room."

"Mommy," the odd tenor of Abby's sleepy voice added to April's anxiety. She turned to find her daughter sitting up on the couch, rubbing the sleep from her eyes. "My head hurts, mommy."

Phone pressed to her ear, April stepped forward. Instantly, she froze, her skin rippling with gooseflesh. Gruff's had raised himself to an unstable standing position, curling his injured paw to his chest. His soft whimper was replaced with a low and steady growl revealing sharp teeth. He positioned himself protectively between April and the couch.

The phone pressed to her ear emitted an unfamiliar ringback tone; Brady's usual *The Waiting* by Tom Petty and the Heartbreakers had been changed. April glanced down at the phone to double-check that she had the right number.

Brady's name appeared on the screen. She placed the phone back to her ear, returning her gaze to Abby. Even in the noon-time sun creeping through the trailer's windows, the eerie red glow flickering from her daughter's blue eyes was unmistakable. The phone fell from April's shaking hand, landing on the floor with a thud; the lyrics from the Guns 'N Roses classic *Used to Love Her* echoing through the room.

I used to love her, Oo, yeah
But I had to kill her
I used to love her, Oo, yeah
But I had to kill her
I knew I'd miss her
So I had to keep her
She's buried right in my backyard

Frank trudged through the overgrown foliage and into the woods; Brady followed. The jovial conversation from their car ride had been replaced with an unspoken trepidation. Sterling State Park was enormous, and Brady had the uneasy feeling that their journey would take them to its very heart. The sunlight overhead crept through the leafy branches. Brady was more than a bit surprised when they emerged into a clearing on a small stretch of beach.

"Wait, the lake is in the other direction. Where the hell are we?"

Frank answered by pointing across the water. No more than two hundred yards away, Brady could see an old building; a series of them actually. It took a moment for his brain to process what he was looking at. His gaze swept from the building across the water, tracing the shoreline before returning to the tall stone structure.

"That's the asylum, right? And over there," pointing across the lake, "that's the *Up North House*. Where the hell are we?"

Frank laughed. "Technically, we are at the boundary. Not my word, the state's; this clearing right here is officially where the State Park ends and the hospital grounds begin. Beyond those trees," he pointed to the north, "hospital grounds. There's hundreds of small wooden crosses peppering the hills; one right on top of the next. Not all laid out and orderly like you see at Arlington, either. Kinda spooky when you think about it."

Brady furrowed his brow, "You mean, like a cemetery or something?"

Frank nodded, "Yeah...or something."

Brady had no desire to go traipsing through a cemetery. "Please, tell me you didn't bring me out here to go rob graves or anything, Frank." Brady's attempt at humor failed to mask his nervousness.

Frank shook his head and smiled. "No, no grave robbing - not yet, anyway." Frank moved forward and placed his hand on Brady's shoulder. "I wanted you to meet someone. Thought maybe we could all have a good long conversation about things; hopefully shed some light on....recent events."

Brady was confused. *Who the hell could I possibly meet out here?* The answer came with the snapping of twigs, warning him of the approach of someone or something through the trees. What emerged was completely unexpected.

"Brady Tanner," came Frank's introduction, "I'd like to introduce you to Reverend James Collins." The silence that settled over the clearing was deafening. Brady stared at the man, trying to place where he had seen him. Like a match catching flame the memory finally flared to life. *Santa strung out on crack.*

Below a tangle of gray hair, and masked by a beard that would make ZZ Top jealous, the man smiled and offered a dirty hand. "Mr. Tanner, I believe we have something in common." He nodded in the direction of the asylum. They collectively peered in its direction, sharing a moment of quiet introspection as each reminisced about how and why the abandoned building had brought them each together. When Collins continued, his voice was barely above a whisper.

"Your grandfather was a wonderful man, Mr. Tanner; yer father, too. I hope you'll accept my deepest sympathies for your loss." His offered hand remained unaccepted

Brady's shifted his gaze from the asylum to the man standing before him, allowing the apology to truly settle over him. *What a burden to carry all these years.* Brady accepted the offered hand, and its accompanying apology, with a nod of his own.

""Lionel and I would fish here," sweeping his arm towards the crystal waters of Asylum Lake. "It was our secret spot; well of the beaten path, as I am sure you noticed on your journey through the trees." The reverent was speaking more to himself than Brady; reminiscing out loud. Brady remained a silent, yet attentive audience.

"The waters are deep here, almost straight down once you get out passed the sandbar. On a good day you can tire yourself out before the perch stop biting." Collins' voice broke as he continued. "On a bad one...who knows what ya might hook."

The phone in Brady's pocket began to vibrate. He had silenced it while at April's, not wanting anything to disturb his time with her. He slid a hand into his pocket and with a simple press of a button sent the call to voicemail.

"Lionel didn't know, but I saw him hook it. He thought I had drifted off - I usually do, especially when the perch are sleeping," he smiled at the memory. "Just resting my eyes..." His voice trailed off again.

Brady had no idea what the man was rambling on about, but felt compelled to listen. He glanced in Frank's direction and found the man listening intently to the ragged reverend. It was obvious that Frank knew more than he had let on. *Bastard*, Brady thought, returning his attention to Collins.

"Sunken treasure, that's all I thought it was. Merely something rescued from the bottom of the lake." He tore his gaze from the lake and directed it back to Brady. "But like the fairy tales I used to read, some treasures come with curses and are best left undisturbed."

Frank cleared his voice, the reverend's rambling story obviously falling directly under the foreplay category. "What was Lionel hooked that day?"

Collins blinked several times before answering, clearing his mind from the painful memories. "A bracelet, of course," pointing towards the hospital, "from there."

Brady was confused. The whole affair was reminiscent of an episode of The Twilight Zone. "Okay, obviously I am missing something here. Would either of you care to clue me into whatever it is we're talking about?"

Collins stepped forward, much more quickly than Brady would have guessed was possible, and grabbed Brady's arm. "He was just a boy, he didn't know. He didn't know!" The boney fingers were digging into Brady's flesh.

Frank stepped between them, his vice-like grip breaking Collin's hold on Brady's arm. "We're not here to place blame, reverend. We're here for answers – same as you." Frank paused, his voice taking on a much more serious tone. "I was there, sir. I saw...them; their bodies." He stole a quick glance in Brady's direction before continuing, "And I saw Buck after his...interview with Lionel. Now I don't know what happened in that hospital room, or exactly how things went down at your house. You're the only one who can shed light on that, but ten hours after walking out that door Buck Tanner was dead...and for thirty-plus years I've had a bitch of a time trying to convince myself that it's not all related."

Collins stepped toward the water, staring out across its sparkling surface at the asylum on the hill. "It was little things at first, he just seemed...distant. Lionel had always been such a fun child, full of life and laughter. He didn't smile much after that day...the day he brought forth that foul bracelet from its resting place. His moods became darker. He constantly argued with his mother. She would argue with me. It was a vicious cycle...one that I selfishly excused myself from." Collins carried the guilt on his frail shoulders; its weight crippling him.

"Your wife...it wasn't suicide." Franks words were more statement than question.

Collins nodded. "I wasn't sure what to believe. By then Lionel was acting so strangely, and Melody had become so angry; as if it were all my fault." He turned to Frank, tears welling from his eyes. "Never underestimate the power of denial."

Brady's mind was doing back flips as he tried to follow the conversation. He had read about Lionel's conviction in his father's notes and had learned from Frank many of the more grizzly details. How it played any part in his grandfather's death or even what was currently happening he still had not figured out, but somehow it all seemed to come back to that damn bracelet. His racing thoughts finally settled on a very disturbing image – the thin band of plastic wrapped about Abby's wrist, and her sleepy comment about an imaginary man in the house. *The bracelet...Abby has the bracelet!*

Chapter **26**

THE EXORCIST

Their trip to church had proven quite sobering, and Brady drove without a word of argument from Frank. The good reverend, full of mystery and not lacking in the odor department, sat in the backseat of Brady's car. Without his trademark cardboard sign, he sat clutching an oversized bible -- the family heirloom held together by duct tape. Things just seemed to be getting increasingly bizarre for Brady.

His leg vibrated with three quick bursts, signaling a new voicemail on his phone. He fished it from the pocket of his cargo shorts, and pressed it to his ear. As April's voice drifted from the phone, the color drained from his face listening to the frantic message. Frank noted the change.

"What is it, son? What's wrong?"

Brady's responded with silence, pressing his foot down on the accelerator and gripping the wheel.

'Aw, shit!" Frank swore, buckling the seat belt over his chest as he recalled the last time he had rode shotgun with a speeding member of the Tanner family. "Here we go again."

If not for the seriousness of the situation, not to mention the supernatural elements, April may have laughed. As Gruff's barking intensified, so did her father's snoring. The mixture of sounds, despite its oddity, did little to distract her from Abby's glowing gaze.

"Mommy, my head hurts," she repeated, extending her arms for a hug.

April stepped forward, only to be met by more barking from Gruff. Her motherly instincts were in full blown panic-mode now. "Honey, come here." April motioned, fearful of what Gruff may do if she were to advance any further.

Abby smiled, sliding off the edge of the couch, and advancing toward her mother. Gruff's growl intensified. Meanwhile, Henry Mayer continued to snore.

Abby paused, glancing down at the dog with a menacing expression drifting across her small face. Gruff recoiled beneath her gaze, whimpering to the ground.

A threatening smile, unlike any April has seen her daughter wear, spread across the child's lips. Abby looked from the cowering dog to her mother, eyes suddenly seething with rage. The next words spoken, although falling from the child's lips, carried the tone of a frightfully different voice.

"Come to me...mother," the voice that wasn't Abby's hissed, dripping with sarcasm as she brought forth the oversized kitchen knife she held behind her back. "Surely your kiss will ease this ache."

Fucking speed bumps, Brady fumed, racing recklessly down the winding streets of the trailer park, heedless of the fact that every twenty yards or so the mechanical crunch of the undercarriage slamming against the concrete mounds guaranteed increasing damage to his Jetta.

"Oooh," Frank winced, "I'm afraid that one left a mark."

Brady shot the former Sheriff a brief look of irritation as he skidded to a halt in front of April's trailer. Frank was out of the passenger door before Brady had turned off the ignition. The good reverend sat calmly in the back seat leafing through his tattered bible as if preparing a Sunday sermon.

The retired lawman raced the one-time reporter up the rickety steps and to the trailer door. Frank's bulky frame filled the doorway as he barged through, Brady shadowing his every move. The noise of Gruff's hysteric barking warned of dark tidings on the other side.

"It's Abby," Brady's breathless words were barely audible, "she's got the bracelet."

The door opened into the living room and Brady rushed in past the former sheriff, his adrenaline outpacing his nerves. April lay on the floor, her back pressed against the carpet, clutching at its fibers in panicked retreat. Between her kicking legs stood Gruff, wobbly atop three legs, and snarling in protection. Crimson gashes lined the dog's face and shoulders; fresh drips and drabs of blood pooling beneath him.

"Holy shit!" Frank exclaimed.

Abby, at little more than three feet tall, towered menacingly over Gruff. Dressed in a pink princess tank-top and tiny white shorts spattered with blood, she teasingly waved the enormous knife in front of her, encouraging deeper snarls from the dog and ever-more frightening shrieks from her mother. At Brady's entrance, she shifted her red gaze from the dog to Brady's hazel eyes.

The ghostly voice emanating from Abby's delicate form chilled Brady's blood. "Ahh, yes…it would seem our guests have arrived."

Brady stopped short, blocking Frank's approach. April clawed her way to Brady's legs, wrapping her trembling arms around him and burying her tear-streaked face into the comfort of his cargo shorts.

Brady broke the crimson gaze and quickly scanned the room. Gruff blocked Abby's path with a snarl that could wake the dead – although apparently not the sleeping; Henry snored loudly, oblivious to the sinister events transpiring around him.

The sound of Frank's voice over his shoulder startled him. "The power of Christ compels you. The Power of Christ compels you." Frank moved around Brady, index fingers in the sign of the cross and shouted the incantation with a surprisingly strong and confident tone.

Brady pulled April up from the floor and drew her into his arms checking her for injuries. Physically, she appeared fine – emotionally she was a wreck. Her vacant eyes darted about the small trailer as her chest heaved with labored sobbing.

Brady ushered her out the door. "Go!" he screamed, shoving her from the trailer and nodding in the direction of his car. "And tell that old man to get his ass in here!"

Frank's familiar incantation continued, though Brady's reeling thoughts couldn't place it. Its impact on Abby, or at least whatever currently inhabited her, was instantaneous.

It laughed; a vile sound reminiscent of the scratching of fingernails down a chalkboard. The noise echoed through the small trailer, causing Gruff's protective snarl to trail off into a defeated whimper.

Frank raised his arms in mock surrender and took a cautious step back. "OK, son, 'yer up."

"What do you mean, I'm up?" Brady countered, "and what the hell was that all about anyway?"

"Exorcist," Frank answered anxiously, shrugging his wide shoulders. "Now that I think about it, didn't work too well in the movie either."

Brady fought the urge to flee from the trailer. Gruff's nose was pressed firmly to the floor and his whimpering had ceased. If not for the dog's labored breathing Brady would have thought for sure his four-legged friend was dead.

"P-p-pl-lease," Brady stammered, staring between Abby's glowing eyes, fearful of what actually locking its gaze could do to him. "You don't have to do this."

The laughter intensified. "Yes, yes, you are definitely right." Trailing off into a prolonged silence, the memory of its dark laughter still hanging in the air, the disembodied voice continued, "Much like your grandfather, I could choose to do nothing."

This reference to the past meant nothing to Brady. His ignorance was proving very frustrating. He had gleaned just enough from his father's notes and drunken talks with Frank, to be more dangerous than helpful. Brady's best guess was that whatever malevolent power was at play had been set free from behind the locked doors of the abandoned asylum years before, and like most wounds left untreated, had festered and was now quickly spreading.

"She's just a child," Brady pleaded, wracking his brain for any detail that may prove helpful. His gaze fell to the bracelet on Abby's wrist. "Ellis…Ellis Arkema, right." Brady's said; more statement of fact than question. "Let me help you, Ellis. Please, tell me what it is that you want…what you need."

Abby's small lips curled back revealing the innocence of baby teeth, causing Brady to recoil in fear. She raised her delicate arm in the air, placing the sharp blade at her own throat. "What I want? You want to know what I need?" The voice's rage boiled over into silence. "I want that which you cannot give -- only that which can be taken; vengeance for the lives that were destroyed." The ethereal voice hardened once more. "The price for blood is blood, Tanner. Your grandfather understood this. Even your father, near the end, understood." The flaming orbs gleamed beneath Abby's blonde bangs, as the laughter resumed.

What happened next unfolded in a matter of seconds yet seemed to occur in slow motion. From the corner of his eye, Brady noticed movement and watched in dismay as Henry Mayer lurched from his recliner and with two uneasy strides reached Abby. The confused old man clamped his age-spotted hand firmly onto his granddaughter's wrist, twisting the knife from her grasp. Instantly, the malevolent presence which had hung so thick in the air vanished, shaking the trailer on its flimsy foundation.

Abby's once glowing eyes rolled back white. She momentarily swayed on her tiny feet before collapsing to the floor unconscious, a faint scratch of blood marring the curve of her small neck. Gruff sprang forward, his wet nose surveying his fallen friend.

Mayer stood motionless in the center of the room staring down into his hand at a twisted piece of plastic wrapped around the heavy handle of the knife; the bracelet had apparently torn free from Abby's delicate wrist during the brief struggle for the blade.

"Little girls don't play with knives," Henry stated matter-of-factly, letting his gaze travel from the knife and down to his granddaughter on the floor. "Somebody's apt to get hurt." He paused, hiking his blue pants higher onto his hips. When he looked up he found Brady and Frank cowering in the doorway.

"Who the hell are you," the old man barked at Brady for the third time since meeting him the night before. "And where the hell is my newspaper?"

Chapter **27**

REVELATIONS

It was a disparate collection of souls seated around Frank's kitchen table; the retired lawman and his wife of nearly forty years, a deeply disturbed preacher lacking faith, three generations of the Mayer family, and finally -- a young man and his dog.

"Let me see if I have this right," Brady began, trying to rub some understanding into his throbbing temples. "Somehow you," tracing his finger in the air from where Frank sat at the head of the large oak table to the far end where Reverend James Collins stood, staring out the window into the afternoon sun, "think what happened to me," glancing in April's direction, "in the lake has something to do with what your son did thirty years ago. Not to mention why my grandfather supposedly killed himself? And – that it all leads back to that damned hospital?" Brady shook his head as he turned to April's father. "What do you think about all this, Henry?"

Brady expected a nonsensical response from the forgetful old man, perhaps even another *who the hell are you!* At this point, he was hoping for something – anything – to lighten the mood. When Henry finally spoke, however, Brady was amazed by the clarity of the man's usually-muddled thoughts.

"A lot of people dying up there," he stated, more as a thought out loud than in response to Brady's question. "A lot of holes..." His voice trailed off. "

"Nine hundred and thirty-three to be exact," added Collins, turning his attention from the window and back to the conversation at hand. "And that's just counting the ones marked with crosses. There are others, too – mounds of dirt, some ringed with stones and some not."

Henry nodded, adding quietly. "Not to mention ones the lake swallowed up."

Six heads swiveled in Henry's direction at his mention of the lake – seven if you count Gruff. He lay under the table, patched up courtesy of Maddie Griggs and her first aid kit. His leg would need to be checked by a vet, but it was surely broken; just how badly was anybody's guess. For now, he was comfortably laying at Brady's feet, resting his aching bones with one eye open, just in case his help was required.

Frank nearly choked on his beer. "Swallowed? Did you say swallowed by the lake?"

April interjected before her father could respond. "Mr. Griggs, you should know that my father was diagnosed with Alzheimer's three years ago. His memory isn't exactly what I would call...reliable." She reached over and gently patted her father's hand.

Henry waved his hand in irritation, withdrawing it from April's touch and raising his own can of beer. Unlike the others, the old man had done little more than take disinterested sips at the Pabst Blue Ribbon. Frank and Brady, however, had already knocked back a twelve-pack between them; the others gathered at the table drank glasses of water from the tap.

"I know what I saw," Henry said stubbornly, the hollow sound of the empty beer can echoing through the kitchen as he slammed in onto the table. "Greasy little bastard." The man paused to collect his thoughts. "Never trust a man with a ponytail – that's what my pa always said. You can tell everything about a man by the cut of his hair." He stole a glance in Brady's direction and offered a teasing wink.

"He and that big fella would walk 'em right to the drop-off and then just," Henry illustrated by walking his fingers off the edge of the table, "send 'em right down. Hell, they didn't know what was what. Big fella would always carry the block of cement."

A hush of disbelief fell over the room as confused looks passed amongst the make-shift congregation. Henry reached for another beer and popped it open.

Collins broke the silence, "That's where we fished, Lionel and me, the drop-off; always thick with perch." He looked down at the large bible clutched in his hands. They had placed the plastic bracelet inside for safe-keeping; Frank's idea. Brady had wanted to burn it.

Brady noted the reverend's diverted attention and surmised his thoughts. *That fucking bracelet! It all comes back to that thin piece of plastic -- or did it?*

"Okay," Brady began, trying to analyze the situation logically, "so this Ellis guy takes a dive into the lake. Years later, your son," pointing at Collins, "hooks Ellis' hospital bracelet while fishing in the aforementioned lake. Makes for an interesting story, but still doesn't explain why the boy butchered that family." Brady knew his tone was harsh, but somebody needed to grab this situation by the balls before it got out of hand. Before Collins could protest, he continued, "But I honestly don't see how any of this has to do with me, my family, and whatever the hell is happening right now." Brady's frustration boiled over, "It's a fucking piece of plastic!"

> *Someone told me long ago,*
> *There's a calm before the storm*
> *I know*
> *It's been coming for some time*
> *I wanna know – have you ever seen the rain*
> *Comin' down on a sunny day*

The ring from Brady's phone caught everyone by surprise. He stood, reaching into the pocket of his cargo shorts to retrieve it. Scanning the display, the blood drained from his face and the phone fell from his trembling fingers. It landed on the table with a thud. Brady backed away, knocking his chair to the ground.

Frank leaned across the table and plucked the phone from the tabletop; Credence Clearwater Revival's song of dark and gloomy times pulsing from the iPhone's small speaker. He couldn't help but think of The Death House and Brady's father every time he heard the tune. He looked up from the phone and found Brady's unsteady gaze.

"Up North House," he stated, projecting a much calmer tone than he felt, "I thought the land line was disconnected when your dad passed."

Brady nodded, "Yeah, me too."

Chapter **28**

GETTING THE BAND BACK TOGETHER

The decision was made without conversation. The men, minus Henry, would venture back to the Up North House. Mr. Mayer would stay with the girls, and Gruff, safely tucked away with at the Grigg's modest home. Besides, April's memory-disadvantaged father had already forgotten where he was and why.

The drive to the *Up North House* was uneventful. Frank drove the Cherokee with Brady riding shotgun. The good reverend climbed into the backseat, paging aimlessly through the oversized tome. Brady noted with mild interest that newspaper clippings and handwritten notes were stuffed between the pages of the bible.

Ramblings of a mad man, Brady mused, looking back at Collins' haggard face and natty beard; *even the Unabomber would be jealous*. Brady raised a hand to his own whiskered chin, wondering how far away he was from joining the good reverend on the long walk of insanity. *My own thoughts* haven't exactly been clear lately, he admitted begrudgingly to himself.

"Reverend," Brady began, "I want to apologize to you for what I said... about your son." Brady hesitated as Collins looked up from his bible. The man's eyes were brimming with tears.

"Lionel was always a good boy – a better son to me than I ever was a father to him." The reverend's thoughtful expression hardened as he continued. "My son did not do those things, Mr. Tanner. He was merely…a vessel by which they were done."

If not for what Brady had recently witnessed with Abby, he would have laughed in Collins' face and called him crazy. A vessel, he agreed. Indeed, someone or something had definitely overtaken the girl – *who's to say it couldn't have happened the same way with Lionel? Almost easier to wrap one's head around that thought than the alternative.*

Brady extended his hand over the console and into the backseat. Collins stared at it a moment, surprised by the gesture. Events seemed to be spiraling forward en route toward some sort of end; Collins was unsure what and where that end may be, but felt relieved to have company for the first time in decades.

Brady was surprised by the strength of the old man's grip; even more so when Collins drew him closer. The man's stale breath turned Brady's already-nervous stomach.

"I heard its voice," the reverend's grip tightened painfully around Brady's hand, "the night your grandfather came for Lionel. They had met before, you know, your grandfather and…him – Ellis."

Brady tried unsuccessfully to free his hand from the old man's grip. "Tell me Tanner," craziness returning to Collins' eyes, "how do you kill something that is already dead?"

Brady never had a chance to respond. "Well, we're here," Frank cut in, the rumbling of the Jeep dying as he turned the ignition off, "now if you two lovebirds can wrap up whatever it is yer doing, we got work to do."

The house appeared to be exactly as Brady had left it, except for one very important detail – the temperature inside the log home had dropped fifty degrees. Their breath came out in white plumes as soon as they crossed the threshold.

"Somebody leave the fridge open?" Frank joked, rubbing some warmth into his arms.

Brady brushed passed Frank, letting the reverend bring up the rear. Collins left the door open; praying some of the heat from the mid-afternoon sun would penetrate the frosty air of the house.

Brady's cursory glance around the main floor revealed nothing out of place. He mounted the stairs taking them two at a time, rushing ahead toward the room at the end of the hall. Frank caught Brady's arm in his vice-like grip, spinning him around. Brady's was surprised by the older man's agility.

"Hold yer horses there, son," he gasped through the chill. "Ever consider that we may not like what we find on the other side of that door?"

Brady hesitated, looking from Frank's worried face to the door at the end of the hall. The reverend had finally joined them on the stair. He, too, looked frightened and frail behind Frank's massive frame.

"Given the situation, I've decided its best not to think too much or too hard," Brady answered with his mischievous smile. "You can wait here on the steps if you want," he offered, turning towards the door. "But my presence has been requested."

Brady crept down the hallway, walking deeper into the frozen house; ice crystals coated the walls and doorframe. Even the brass doorknob was iced over. The door creaked open as he raised his hand to the knob. Brady peered nervously over his shoulder before stepping into the room. Frank waited on the step, leaving him alone to accept to the invitation.

Abby tossed and turned on the Griggs' sofa, her troubled sleep plagued by dark and terrible nightmares. Gruff stood watch over his friend, calming her with the occasional brush of his cold nose against her cheek. Although relieved to see the bracelet removed from Abby's thin wrist, the dog's instincts were sharper than his human counterparts. Something had changed within his sleeping friend. Although the ominous scent had drifted away, an underlying odor of something unseen and as yet unknown remained.

Maddie and April sipped iced tea in the kitchen. In an odd way, Frank's wife reminded April of her own mother; exhibiting the quiet confidence that comes with age. Little did she know however, Maddie was merely more experienced at masking her anxiety. Inside, her stomach was doing somersaults.

"Brady seems quite taken with you," she stated, smiling over her drink. "You two were close back...before, right?"

April blushed, "Yeah, we were...are quite close." April chewed nervously on a small bit of ice. She had been doing her best to not think about how hard she had fallen for Brady. Present circumstances aside, they each had enough baggage in their personal lives to fill the cargo hold of a very large airliner. April smiled and changed the subject. "How long have you and Frank been together?"

"Too long," she laughed. "Next month will be forty-one years since our first kiss," blushing at the memory, "not that a woman keeps track of such things."

The women shared a nervous giggle. No matter their ages, two women discussing the men in their lives always led to laughter. The ice was officially broken.

"You know about Karen," April asked, "about what happened?"

Maddie looked down into her iced-tea and nodded. "We read about it in the papers. Brady's father got Frank hooked on reading The Tribune when Brady started working there. John collected his son's clippings like a kid does baseball cards," Maddie's brief smile vanished. "Terrible what happened."

April shifted her gaze to the floor, and her silent response affirmed for Maddie that Brady had already revealed the details of his wife's death. His new friend wasn't merely fishing for details – she was feeling the pain of the situation. The weight of Brady's past rested heavily on her shoulders.

She reached forward and grabbed April's hand, giving it a reassuring squeeze. "Come with me," she stated, leading April from the kitchen and into the family room where Abby rested. Gruff acknowledged their entrance with a casual glance before returning his attention to Abby.

The room was dominated by Frank's passion for the outdoors. Mounted deer and elk racks hung over the mantle of the great stone fireplace and some of the largest fish April had ever seen decorated the walls. Maddie noticed April's sweeping gaze and squeezed her hand again, "Not exactly my choice of decoration, but we women have to choose our battles."

April nodded and followed Maddie to the fireplace. The mantle was lined with framed photos, most taken before April had even been born. Maddie reached forward to retrieves a silver-framed photo from its resting place, passing it to April.

"Their wedding photo," Maddie explained. "They were such a beautiful couple."

April softly traced a finger across the framed photo, seeing for the first time the woman who had once filled all of the empty places in Brady's heart; places that she was not trying to fill.

Maddie drifted away, leaving April alone with her thoughts. Karen was beautiful -- in ways that April could never be. Small and delicate with dark hair and striking brown eyes, Karen Tanner a natural beauty. April's height and athleticism had always made her feel less womanly and awkward.

April was distracted from her musings by the scratchy sound of music. She recognized the tune but not the voice. It took a moment for the lyrics to sink in, but by the second verse April's nerves were eased.

I still want you by my side
just to help me dry the tears that I've cried
cause I'm sure gonna give you a try
and if you want, I'll try to love again
but baby, I'll try to love again, but I know

The first cut is the deepest, baby I know
The first cut is the deepest

Maddie held the album cover in her hand as Cat Steven's voice drifted from the small speakers. She smiled at April and winked, an unspoken understanding of the inner-turmoil she was facing with her rediscovered feelings for Brady. April smiled back, replacing the photo on the mantle and stealing one last glimpse at the former Mrs. Brady Tanner.

The lone bulb hanging over the small desk lit the entire room. Brady entered cautiously, unsure of what, if anything was waiting for him. As was the case with his last visit into the room, Brady sensed the presence of something or someone. He knew without a doubt that he was not alone.

Although he had taken a fair amount of what he had determined to be the most interesting of the notes and files from the room to review with Frank, Brady was certain he was being called back into this house...into this room to find something. It didn't take him long to discover what it was.

Spread across the desk, atop the God-forsaken Scrabble Board, was a se-ries of tiles. At first glance, Brady could make no sense from their order.

H E W A I T S F O R U T O S E T T H E M F R E

Ever-so-slowly Brady deciphered the cryptic message. *He waits for you to set them free.*

"Who waits for me?" he whispered to the frosty air. "Set who free?"

Brady watched in wonder as the tiles began to move, rearranging their order with old ones being traded-out for new.

E L L I S W A I T S U M U S T F I N D H E R

Again, Brady read the message. He sighed in relief, *One mystery solved – you're not Ellis.* "Find who? Who does Ellis want me to find?"

The tiles did their slow dance across the board once again.

J E F F W I L K N O W W H E R E S H E R E S T S

"Jeff," Brady wondered aloud. He paused, letting the name settle over him. "Jeff Ryder? How the hell will he know anything about this? I don't even know where Jeff is."

The answer came not from the board this time, but from the doorway. "I do," Frank said gravely to Brady. "I know where your friend is."

Brady had turned from the game board at the unexpected sound of Frank's voice. He could see the frigid plumes of breath as the man spoke. "Yer dad and I tracked him down."

Brady's confusion was evident as he recast his focus to the Scrabble Board. His mind was spinning with thoughts and questions, but only one came to his lips. "Who are you?" he pleaded.

The tiles remained still. "Please, tell me who you are?" Brady's raised voiced echoed throughout the icy room.

The room warmed noticeably; the frosty air no longer evident from Brady's anxious breathing. The Scrabble pieces remained in place. Even the dim bulb seemed to brighten over the desk. Brady hung his head in exhausted disappointment; whatever presence he had been communicating with had now departed.

A ruffled thump across the room drew his attention. On the floor beneath the wall where the blueprints for the asylum were stapled into the drywall lay his grandfather's Stetson; resting gently on the floor after its tumble from the shelf

Brady stepped forward, standing over the black hat that had been his grandfather's trademark. He knelt down and traced his fingers along its woolen brim and through the small holes that peppered the worn material. *Buckshot*, he recalled, standing to his feet with the hat held in his grip.

Taking the Tiger's cap from his head and dropping it to the dusty floor at his feet, Brady was struck by how heavy the Stetson felt in his hand, both in the weight of the wool and in the responsibility it had carried. Brady placed it atop his head, pleased by the perfection of the fit, and turned to Frank.

"I think you've got some explaining to do."

Chapter 29

COOKING SCHOOL

"I didn't know why yer dad was looking for Jeff. He didn't say and I never thought to ask," Frank was back-peddling as he drove. "Towards the end, he wasn't exactly thinking too clearly."

Brady leveled his gaze at the man. Frank looked over once and quickly turned away. From beneath his grandfather's hat Brady looked far more intimidating; not so different from his namesake.

"Spill it, Frank. All of it."

Frank's knuckles whitened on the steering wheel. "Honestly, I don't know what to tell you. We've been through this." He hesitated, shaking his head. "After your mom passed your dad became consumed with that asylum. Hell, he even contacted some professor at Michigan State University to discuss urban exploration," Frank enunciated the words as if it were in a foreign language. "I think he was planning on going into that wreck of a place and digging around."

Reverend James Collins had been sitting quietly in the back seat of the jeep. Silent since entering the Up North House, Frank and Brady both jumped at the sound of his voice.

"He did go in – about a week before he died." The revelation settled over the SUV's interior like an invisible fog. "That's when he brought it out…the bracelet."

Brady's eyes moved from Frank and settled on the backseat passenger. "Brought it out? What do you mean? What happened to the bracelet after your son was arrested?"

Collins shrugged, looking away from Brady's glare. "Lionel kept it. He wore the wretched thing throughout the trial." Collins' hesitated, "I didn't know what it was…not then. Hell, I still don't know what exactly it is."

Frank remained silent as Brady considered the reverend's comments. "Ok," trying to keep his voice under control, "so if your son was wearing the bracelet when he was convicted, how the hell did my father find it thirty-odd years later back inside that damn hospital?"

It was a rhetorical question, Brady wasn't expecting a response. But much like Frank had indicated, *sometimes simply knowing the questions to ask makes the unanswerable questions easier to bear.*

"Reverend," Brady continued, "where did they send Lionel after he was convicted – surely not to prison?"

Collins hesitated, "Out of state," he answered. "With so much press coverage the courts worked out a deal to send him to a psychiatric hospital in Indiana."

Brady nodded, understanding the benefit of hiding the boy away somewhere out of sight until his brutal crimes became old news. "And then, I assume he was incarcerated until the age of twenty-one, unless they found reason to keep him longer?"

Frank grunted in agreement. As a law enforcement officer he had intimate knowledge as to how the system worked and knew where Brady's thoughts were leading.

Collins shook his head, "I don't know. They lost him."

"Lost him," Frank and Brady responded in unison.

"You can't just lose someone," Frank added, "not very easily anyway, especially not in a prison or nut house."

Brady agreed. "They actually told you they lost your son?"

Again, Collins shook his head, "No, no…of course not. He was transferred from their facility just six months after being admitted. At whose request was always very uncertain. Regardless, a fire in their records room destroyed all of the paperwork. It's as if Lionel Collins was never there at all." The reverend's tone was calm, as if he had long ago resigned himself to the fact that Lionel's whereabouts would remain another small piece in this grand puzzle.

Brady didn't believe in coincidence. "So you have no idea where he is today? He's never once tried to contact you?"

"No," Collins answered. "Only Dr. Clovis would know that. His signature on the sign-out sheet was the only record of the transfer. I have found no record of a Dr. Clovis, first name unknown, practicing anywhere in the state of Indiana. It's as if he fell off the face of the earth."

The name sounded alarms in Brady's head. He reached for the bible, ripping it free of Collins' grasp. Frank looked on, keeping one eye on the road and the other on Brady as he flipped through the loose pages. When it fell open on the 23rd Psalm, Brady stopped, looking down at the bracelet.

"Here, don't you see," Brady declared, pointing at the broken band of plastic. Etched onto its worn surface, beneath the smears of dried blood, was the answer. Listed among Ellis Arkema's patient information was the name of his doctor --W. Clovis.

Collins reached forward at the sight of the exposed bracelet, slamming the bible closed and wrenching it from Brady's hands. "Must we look upon it?" he pleaded.

The uncomfortable silence that followed the outcry was broken only by the sound of the reverend's muttering, "Yea, though I walk through the valley of the shadow of death, I will fear no evil: For thou art with me..."

The revelation of the connection between the old asylum and the fate of Lionel Collins created a quiet calm in the cabin of the Jeep's interior; each occupant alone with their thoughts.

Lionel's father finally slept. After years of sleeping in the wooded areas of the State Park, keeping a watchful eye on the darkened asylum, the comfort of the Jeep's backseat overtook his frail bones.

Brady's thoughts rolled through his tired head like the metal ball in a pinball machine; his logic centers were flippers batting at the ball resulting in a great deal of noise, intermittent flashes of light, and eventual disappointment.

As for Frank, he tried not to think. Reacting without forethought had gotten him through sixty-one years fairly unscathed; no sense trying to change things up now. Although for the life of him he couldn't understand this fascination with Jeff Ryder. *The dude was plain trouble any way you sliced it.* Frank glanced over at Brady's furrowed brow and wondered what the boy was thinking. *Nothing good, I'm sure.*

"Alright," Frank announced to the cabin, waking Collins from his slumber and pulling Brady back from his thoughts. "We'll be taking the next left up here. Officially we're leaving the good ol' U. S. of A. This is Indian land, the smallest reservation ever settled. Hell, it's not even on the maps." Frank hesitated, letting his words settle over his anxious passengers. "It's twenty-five square miles of trees, poverty, and drugs. Locals know me a bit, from my days wearing the badge. We should be just fine." Frank's grin wasn't comforting.

The turnoff came as promised; little more than a washout of a road leading into the dense woods. Brady' scanned the trees, unsure of what he was looking for, but curious nonetheless. This was officially his first time off U.S. soil; not exactly the tropical beaches he had in mind.

The Jeep bounced and churned along the road. Several times Brady could see what appeared to be small, dilapidated wooden shacks within the trees. "Houses," Frank answered Brady's unspoken question. "Not exactly the three-bedroom two bath variety, either."

Even Brady, accustomed to stepping over the homeless living on Chicago's busy sidewalks, was shocked by the squalor.

"At one time this whole mitten of a state belonged to them," this time it was the reverend who spoke, "bands of them, actually – different tribes."

Brady felt like he was in fourth grade learning about Michigan history. He was about to speak up when Collins' said something very interesting.

"In fact, an offshoot of the Chippewa's who had claimed much of northern-lower Michigan actually settled right here in what we now call Bedlam County," Collins' voice was gaining strength as his lecture continued.

"Long before there was an asylum on that hill, the natives had established a thriving community," Collins hesitated. "Until they disappeared -- the entire tribe just vanished; *ga-da-wa-hi tsu-ga-sa-wo-dv* or Lake of Tears is what the natives refer to the area now."

Collins fell silent as he fell once again into a deep sleep. It seemed that nothing good had ever come from the lake.

"We're here," Frank announced a short while later, his gravelly voice shattering the silence. Brady looked through the dusty windshield into a small clearing that opened beneath a canopy of trees. Dominating the space was quite possibly the oldest Winnebago to ever roll the earth. It's rusted exterior and flattened tires revealed much about the owner.

Brady glanced into the backseat at the reverend's sleeping form. "How about we just let the old guy get rest?"

Frank nodded in agreement, "Three's a crowd anyway." Turning to Brady, "You ready, son?"

Brady nodded, "Don't suppose I really have a choice now, do I?"

They exited the Jeep, Brady allowing Frank to take the lead. He couldn't help but notice the butt of the .38 sticking out from Frank's jeans. "Hey," he called out in a hushed whisper, "What the hell is that?"

Frank turned to Brady, casually hiding the exposed gun once again under his Harley t-shirt and then holding up three fingers on his right hand, he recited the Boy Scout motto, "Be prepared."

Brady groaned and said nothing. Sometimes it's best to just let *Frank be Frank*.

The Winnebago's appearance only worsened as they drew closer -- as did the smell. The overwhelming scent of fingernail polish mixed with cat urine burned Brady's nostrils. He buried his nose in the crook of his arm, gagging against the stench.

Frank turned back once again and smiled. He drew in a deep breath and let it out slowly, "Nothing clears the sinuses better than the smell of meth in the morning."

Brady had known that methamphetamine was the new drug of choice in many rural areas. It was relatively easy to manufacture and provided a high un-matched by most other narcotics. He couldn't imagine how or why Jeff would be mixed up with the drug. *A lot must have changed in the last fourteen years.*

The barking of a very angry dog shook Brady from his reverie. Frank had his .38 drawn instantly. From the shadows at the rear of the Winnebago lumbered the largest dog Brady had ever seen. The beast of a Rottweiler easily weighed over two-hundred pounds and apparently had the temperament of a grizzly bear being poked with a very short stick.

"Manson, heel!"

The dog froze in place, snarling his protest, yet obeying the order. Frank kept his gun trained on the dog as he glanced at the trailer. Brady very coura-geously cowered behind Frank, unsure just how well-trained the dog truly was.

Manson, Brady nervously acknowledged the irony of the dog's name, *why not just call him death or killer and be done with it.*

"Afternoon, sheriff, can't say I recall sending you an invitation." Standing in the trailer's open doorway, beer held firmly in one dirty hand, was a man of indeterminate age. His voice was vigorous, but his body was aged. Open sores and scabs marked his ripened face, and he smiled with sporadic, rotted teeth. "And I see you've brought company."

Brady stepped out from behind Frank, looking hard at the stranger. Although the voice seemed familiar, Brady could not place the broken man standing at the Winnebago's open door.

"Don't suppose you've got a warrant," the man continued, swilling the rest of his beer and tossing the can to the ground. "Oh hell, come on in," turning and disappearing into the Winnebago, "Just don't forget to wipe yer feet."

Brady exchanged a nervous glance with Frank as the retired lawman tucked the .38 into the back of his jeans. "After you," Frank indicated, sweeping his arm out in a formal gesture, "this is your party, son."

Brady smiled weakly, brushing passed Frank as he approached the trailer. The dog traced Brady's movement across the clearing with beady eyes and salivating jaws. The stink became nearly overpowering as he neared the doorway. Taking a deep breath, he mounted the steps and entered the Winnebago, leaving Frank outside to bond with Manson.

Aside from the nauseating fumes, Brady found the Winnebago's interior to be strangely free of clutter and mostly unsoiled. He stepped into the cramped quarters of the kitchen area and easily found the 'cooking" area. The fold-out table was a maze of glass tubing, and liquids of varying colors boiled over heated Bunsen-burners. The whole thing looked like a junior high science experiment gone wrong.

"You might wanna stand back – give it some room to breathe," the stranger called from Brady's right. He turned to find the man seated on a small slip of couch. "Contact buzz can be nasty for the uninitiated." The man's rotted smile flashed from behind his chapped lips.

Brady returned a nervous nod as he stepped furtively away from the table. His eyes scanned the trailer, noting the impressive array of LCD screens and computer gadgetry. *Business must be good*, he thought, returning his gaze to the man on the couch.

"DEA? State Police?" the amateur chemist prodded. "I know you're not local." He paused, squinting his red-rimmed eyes in consternation. "Ah, hell," the smile returned, "Brady Tanner!"

Brady nodded, allowing the surprising sight of his childhood friend to slowly sink in. The Jeff Ryder he remembered had been smart and funny, not the lazy and uneducated type of person Brady had always associated with the drug world. This man's bone thin frame and scarred appearance looked nothing like the vibrant teenager Brady had last seen.

"I see that the career in gay-porn you had always dreamed of didn't quite pan out," Brady teased his one-time friend, allowing a brief smile to play across his face as he motioned to a chair next to the couch. "Mind if I take a seat, I think the fumes are starting to get to me."

Jeff sprang to his feet; every movement exaggerated and energized, and brushed the litter from the chair. "Of course, please, please sit down."

Brady collapsed into the offered chair, his head spinning from the vapors of the cooking meth. Jeff grabbed a can of Oust and sprayed it into the air above Brady's head. The addition of deodorizer into the ripened air had little effect.

Brady closed his eyes and tried to quiet the room's spinning. After a few moments he felt the rush of wind blowing over him and opened his eyes to find an oscillating fan pointing directly at him.

"Luke, I am your father," Jeff's voice echoed through the spinning blades in his best Darth Vader impersonation.

Brady laughed. This was the Jeff Ryder he remembered - the practical jokes and dry humor of his best friend was still there - hidden beneath the scabs and scars. "Thanks," he offered, shaking the rest of the haze from his clearing head, "that's much better."

Jeff returned to the couch, leaving the fan to blow the fumes away from his guest. "What are you and Barney Fife up to?" nodding in the direction of the open door. His lack of respect for Frank was evident in both his tone and expression..

"Frank?" Brady replied, slow to recognize the Mayberry reference. "Come on, man – Frank's good people."

Jeff shrugged beneath his wrinkled clothes, "If you say so, man."

Silence settled over them – each collecting their thoughts.

"Heard about your parents," Jeff finally announced, "sorry, man."

Brady nodded, "Yeah, thanks. That's kinda why I'm here – heard my dad came to see you before he passed."

Jeff leaned forward on the couch, "Should have known." He reached across to a small shelf and brought forth a small wooden cutting board. Sprinkled across its surface were several parallel lines of glass-like powder. Producing a rolled up bill from seemingly out of nowhere, Jeff bent forward and snorted an inch-long line, closing his eyes against the sudden rush and wiping the residue from his nostrils.

Brady looked on in disgust. *God, what happened to you?*

After a moment, Jeff's eyes fluttered open and he rubbed his hands together vigorously before replacing the cutting board on the shelf.

"I'll tell you the same thing I told him – I don't remember!" Jeff's light-hearted tone changed to irritation. "Hell, what's it even matter."

Brady didn't allow his own ignorance to derail his train of thought, "What exactly is it that you don't remember, Jeff? What did my dad want to talk to you about?"

Jeff's unblinking eyes locked onto Brady's. The meth was already in full effect now - his friend's dilated pupils staring back at him. "The past, man – he wanted to talk about the past."

Brady could feel his frustration bubbling to the surface. He did his best to remain calm, but the irritation in his voice was undeniable. "Something tells me you can be a little more specific."

Jeff laughed – a maniacal sound that echoed through the Winnebago's crowded interior. "You want specifics, Brady. I can give you specifics. But first – tell me something," he paused, the crazed laughter leaving his voice. "How you been sleeping lately?"

June 29, 1996
Bedlam Falls, Michigan

Brady's awkward fall into the lake was met with a chorus of laughs. As much as the group of friends had dreaded the thought of the swim back to shore, the spray from Brady's splash reminded each of them that the water would be far warmer than the chilly air. When he didn't reappear above the waves their laughter turned to concern.

Finally, after what seemed an eternity, Jeff spotted his friend in the distance, the sweeping current from the storm dragging Brady further out into the darkness of the lake. The rush of the wind across the waves drowned out his cries for help and the rain made it nearly impossible to keep him in sight. Jeff looked nervously beyond his friend's head bobbing along the surface of the choppy lake to a distant point on the horizon to identify a landmark and, without a word to either of the girls, dove off the float into the water.

Jeff was an above average swimmer, yet even he struggled against the odd current. It almost felt as if he were caught in a swirling vortex that carried him not only out further into the lake, but also weighed him down as he fought to the surface. The air rushed into his burning lungs as he finally broke free, emerging above the waves and back into the stormy night.

He could see Tammy and April in the distance through the sheets of rain, rocking back and forth on the small wooden float. They clung to each other in fright. Jeff felt torn -- unsure of which was a better option – swimming through the blinding rain into the depths of the lake to search for his friend, or returning to the relative safety of the float to ride out the storm with the girls. In the end, the decision was simple – staring into the distance, Jeff spotted the outline of the menacing building in the distance and started out in search of Brady.

Each stroke carried Jeff further away from his goal -- the current's vice-like grip tightening around his burning muscles. In the distance, roughly twenty yards away, he spotted Brady's head breaking the surface. As quickly as he had appeared Brady was once again swallowed by the dark water. Jeff dove beneath the waves, kicking his tiring legs in Brady's direction.

The repeated flashes of lightning from the storm above created a strobe-light affect below the waves, providing Jeff short-lived glimpses of his friend's limp body falling into the depths of the lake. Ignoring the burning pain in his chest, Jeff coaxed his air-deprived body deeper and deeper. Finally, after what seemed an eternity, his outstretched arms found something fleshy in the darkness. He dug his fingers into the flesh, relieved to have finally found his friend.

Another flash of lightning from above, this one much more powerful than any of the bolts which had burst before, confirmed his grip on Brady. But the ghost light that illuminated Brady's slack body also penetrated further into the lake—revealing a vision that would haunt Jeff Ryder for the rest of his life.

Brady's pale and lifeless body rested on the rocky lakebed amidst an unearthly graveyard of scattered bones and cement blocks. The bleached bones were clad in rags, with most festooned in heavy chains. Jeff's reeling mind couldn't register the overwhelming number of skulls littering the bottom of Asylum Lake.

Numb fingers digging deeper into the flesh of Brady's arm, Jeff raised his eyes to the surface. *Too far*, he thought, recasting his gaze to the underwater graveyard where Brady's body rested among the heap of skeletal remains.

Glancing downward, something began to move. In sheer terror, Jeff screamed—stupidly sacrificing his last dredges of breath. As his lungs filled with a mouthful of stagnant water, a glowing ethereal figure rose, gliding toward him. The rush of water into his already burning lungs overtook him. He looked one last time from the glowing form and up to the surface – the display of lightning intensifying above the waves.

Jeff felt his grip on Brady's shoulder begin to weaken as his mind became foggy and chest burned in pain and screamed for oxygen. Redirecting his attention to the glowing form, he was shocked to see the once skeletal figure transformed; blonde hair rippled through the water behind her, revealing unblinking eyes and a soft, yet calming smile on her delicate face. The once-ragged clothes hanging from the bones had been replaced with what appeared to be a hospital gown.

The burning in Jeff's lungs ceased as the fog of panic cleared from his mind. The ghostly figure extended her hand. Jeff took note of the white plastic bracelet clutched in her thin fingers.

Go, an ethereal voice echoed through the water, *you do not belong here among the dead. The veil has been parted. You have been warned.*

Brady sat in stunned silence, no longer even aware of the noxious fumes. Jeff's wild-eyed expression hadn't softened; if anything it had intensified as he shared the story of what happened beneath the waves that night.

"So what happened – you just pulled me up? I don't recall any of it."

Jeff shook his head, "Man, I don't know what happened." He drew his arm across his face, wiping at his nose. "That's the last thing I remember. Hell, probably just a hallucination from the lack of oxygen to my brain."

Brady collected his thoughts. Although math was never his strong suit, it did appear as though things were starting to add up. Everything was coming back to that godforsaken lake and the hospital looming over its northern shore.

"Your dad finally came out in the pontoon boat," Jeff continued. "I don't even remember swimming back to the float. The girls were freaking out – well, Tammy was anyway. April started CPR on you right away – probably saved your life. You were blue, Brady. We thought for sure you were dead."

The frustration playing across Brady's face was evident. He remembered none of this – yet knew with an unexplained certainty that his friend's unbelievable tale was indeed true.

Jeff leaned forward once again, his fingers dancing across the keyboard. Instantly, the LCD screens came to life.

"There's a reason I asked you how you were sleeping, Brady." His tone was slow and deliberate. "Same reason I keep up on my little science experiment," gesturing towards the beakers and tubing on the table. "Something happened that night – we were touched by something." Jeff paused, reaching forward and swiveling the monitor in Brady's direction. "And I don't think it's done with us yet."

Brady's eyes drifted from Jeff's gaunt face to the computer screen. His Google search had revealed thousands of listings. It took a moment for the subject of the search to register. Parting the Veil.

"It's a term as old as mankind itself," Jeff instructed, "from Christians to Jews, Buddhists to Muslims, even Satanists talk about death being merely a veil drawn across the eyes of the living."

Brady's brow furrowed as he listened, his eyes still glued to the screen. Jeff's scrolled through the search results and eventually clicked on a link. It appeared to be a research paper of sorts, not a religious dissertation at all. Brady scanned the first few lines before stumbling across a familiar name.

The paper was titled simply, Parting the Veil – The Thin Line Between Life and Death. It was the author's name that sounded the alarms in Brady's overworked mind - Dr. Wesley W. Clovis.

"Holy shit," Brady exclaimed. "I think I'm gonna need you to print that off for me."

Chapter **30**

PARTING THE VEIL

Collins' refusal to exit the jeep made bringing everyone up to speed cumbersome. Exacerbating the situation was Jeff's agoraphobia. He hadn't left the small patch of earth surrounding his trailer in more than two years, instead relying on "business associates" to bring him groceries and other essentials. If not for the seriousness of the subject matter Brady would have just thrown his hands up in surrender. Instead, he wore a path between the jeep and the Winnebago.

"Reverend, what can you tell me about any biblical reference to *Parting the Veil or the Veil of Death?*" Brady was leaning through the open window of the Jeep's backseat, grilling Collin's for any information that could shed light on what was going on.

"The term veil is used widely in both the old and new testaments," Collins offered, flipping through his ancient Bible. "The most familiar passage is from the gospel of St. Matthew, describing Christ's crucifixion – *"And Jesus cried out again with a loud voice, and yielded up His spirit. Then, behold, the veil of the temple was torn in two from top to bottom."*

Brady stared at the reverend in confusion. Again, his lack of interest in religion left him ignorant to what any of what Collins' words meant. "OK, how about you give me the Cliff Notes version?"

Collins smiled, enjoying the opportunity to share a bit of scripture. "The veil in the temple signifies sin – the separation of man from God." He paused, waiting for Brady to acknowledge the connection. Brady's blank stare did little to reassure Collins, but he continued nonetheless.

"God deliberately tore this curtain to make a point -that mankind's sins, which had cut us off from Him, could now be forgiven through Jesus Christ's shed blood."

Brady nodded, understanding the passage's meaning, but not how it fit with what was currently happening.

Collins smiled, laying a dirty hand on Brady's arm. "Without the parting of that veil, man would have no promise of eternal life – heaven. The price was paid in the blood of Jesus."

The price for blood is blood, the words pounded back into Brady's thoughts. *What the hell was Dr. Clovis doing in that hospital? And how was Ellis mixed up with it?*

"He died for you, Brady," Collins squeezed the younger man's arm sincerely.

"Um, yeah," Brady replied uncomfortably removing his arm from the man's grasp. The reverend's words rang like the silverware chimes from Bible Camp. "I think I read that somewhere…died for us all, I believe."

Collins smiled, "Yes, Jesus did die for us all. But it's not of the Son of God that I refer." Collins returned his gaze to the worn bible, searching among its torn pages. Finally, he removed a folded news clipping and passed it through the window to Brady.

Brady accepted the offer, slowly unfolding the yellowed newsprint. He immediately recognized the article from The Banner announcing his grandfather's death. He had discovered a copy among his father's notes and files.

"Your grandfather thought he understood, Brady. He offered his life – his blood – as payment for the sins of others." Collins paused, closing the Bible on his lap. "That's sound Old Testament teaching straight from Leviticus - *Breach for breach, eye for eye, tooth for tooth: as he hath caused a blemish in a man, so shall it be done to him again.*"

A fresh trickle of tears fell from the reverend's weary eyes. "Sadly, Brady, the price for blood isn't more blood. I refer you now to the New Testament and the words of Matthew - *Ye have heard that it hath been said, an eye for an eye, and a tooth for a tooth: But I say unto you, whosoever shall smite thee on thy right cheek, turn to him the other also."* Collins' smile returned, "The price for blood isn't blood -- it's forgiveness."

Frank's conversation with Jeff was far less touchy-feely than Brady's had been with the good reverend. The retired law man stood in the open doorway of the Winnebago marveling at Jeff's handiwork with the Meth lab.

"Son, you obviously got some brains – or at least did at one time. Why the hell throw it all away messing with this bullshit?"

Jeff smirked, snorting another thin crystal line from the dirty cutting board. He wiped the back of his grubby arm across his reddened nose and stared up at the man. "You asking me as a concerned friend now, sheriff?" He laughed, "Or maybe doing some research for some law enforcement training seminar?"

Frank's patience was wearing thin. Stepping towards Jeff he took the cutting board from the man's filthy hands and tossed it across the Winnebago where it crashed into one of the computer monitors – knocking it to the floor.

"What the fuck, man!" Jeff began to stand. Frank's forced him back down onto the soiled couch with a finely placed push into the man's chest.

"I don't give a shit about you, son. Snort your brain away – blow yourself up with this home-made easy bake oven – no skin off my nose." Frank glanced outside, "But he does," jerking his thumb in Brady's direction. "For some reason I'll never understand, he gives a shit. A big juicy one."

Jeff eyes fell away from Frank's angry glare. "Have you ever been afraid, sheriff – truly afraid?"

Frank's anger faded away as he considered the question, "Sure, fear is a natural instinct – right up there with hunger and the need to fuck." He laughed nervously, unsure of where Jeff's question was leading.

Jeff returned his smile, and nodded, "Yeah, right up there with fucking." He paused. "You see, sheriff – what keeps me up at night," motioning at his self-styled Easy Bake Oven on the foldout table, "aside from the devil's dust I've become so adept at cooking, is that…crazy as it sounds, I'm afraid to sleep. I'm afraid of what happens when I close my eyes - what I see - and even more frightened by what sees me." Jeff's last words whispered across his chapped, peeling lips as his eyes glazed over looking past anything physically in the trailer.

Frank considered the addict's comments. "Yeah, there's been a touch of that going around," he muttered, moving forward to the monitor on the floor. He bent down and picked it up, brushing it off before setting it back on the small table.

The uncomfortable silence that settled over the Winnebago was broken by Brady's appearance in the doorway. "What are the chances this death trap is actually drivable," he asked, out of breath and pale with worry. "Something tells me its time for a road trip."

Jeff and Frank exchanged a brief glance and nodded – truce officially called. "No worries," Jeff stated with his yellow-toothed grin, "I got a couple of tires in the back with just a trace of tread left on them. If the good sheriff here doesn't mind working a jack, I believe we can get *Chef Jeff's Mobile Meth Lab* street legal in no time."

Chapter 31

STRANGE BEDFELLOWS

After a fair bit of coaxing, the group made two very important decisions; the good reverend would indeed join them on their Winnebago road trip – but only after assurances that he wouldn't be required to "smoke any drugs," as he so poetically put it. The second decision, just as ridiculous, was made only after a fairly contentious argument - Frank got to drive.

The one-time lawman beamed as he slid into the driver's seat and placed his greedy hands on the oversized steering wheel. "A man could get used to this," he muttered to himself.

The repairs to the ancient Winnebago had been fairly minor – two new tires and a couple quarts of oil. The beast started on the first turn of the key – great plumes of black smoke spewing from its tailpipe. Jeff even tossed his science fair project out the door, watching it shatter into a million pieces on the dusty ground. Brady shared a proud moment of silence with his friend before retreating with him into the RV.

The good reverend rode shotgun, keeping as much distance from the addict, his drug paraphernalia, and Manson -- the monster of a dog that had also joined them on the journey – as possible. Brady and Jeff huddled together in the small living area of the RV -- their whispered planning drowned out by the sound of the Winnebago's exhaust scraping against the road.

"I need you to dig up every bit of information you can find on this Dr. Wesley Clovis," Brady instructed as he surveyed the high-tech gadgetry at Jeff's disposal. "Do I even want to know what you do with all of...this?"

Jeff grinned, his fingers dancing across the wireless keyboard. "Let's just say I am an associate of a certain prince in Nigeria who needs your help to gain access to his inheritance."

Brady groaned, rolling his eyes. "I should have known. Regardless, it's about time we start using your powers for good instead of evil – Wesley Clovis, get on it."

Brady moved from the research wing of his self-described Air Force One and into the cockpit. He arrived just in time to hear the tail end of yet another Frank story.

"So there I am on Beaver Island, completely shit-faced," Brady had listened to enough of the man's stories over the last few days to know that this was Frank's standard introduction to a tale that would assuredly include some form of debauchery. Reverend Collins stared through the windshield, searching for any distraction he could find beyond the words pouring from Frank's mouth.

"Sorry to barge in," Brady interrupted, smiling at Collins' look of relief. "I've got Jeff trying to find the last known whereabouts of Dr. Clovis – thank god for the internet." He paused, choosing his words carefully. "Up until this point we haven't done anything illegal or immoral -- and although I would like to keep it that way – I think we may soon find ourselves bending the rules here just a bit."

Frank exchanged a quick glance with the reverend – sharing a smile with the grizzled old man. "Ah hell, son," Frank laughed. "You got both the law and God on your side here, what kind of trouble could we possibly get into?"

The gathering clouds overhead added a much-needed dramatic effect to the situation – as if the work at hand wasn't gloomy enough. By the time the Winnebago rolled up to the gates of the Lake View Asylum a light drizzle had started to fall.

During their hour-long drive, Jeff had collected what little information he could find on the mysterious Dr. Wesley Clovis. The addict's investment in satellite internet was finally being put to good use. The limited details left far too much unanswered.

"Basically, we have two references to Dr. Wesley Clovis," Jeff announced, fanning out his collection of printed papers on the small table. "The first," pointing at the article he had shared with Brady previously, "is some kind of research he had submitted for publication. As you can see from the title -- *Parting the Veil: The Thin Line Between Life and Death* – the good doctor had a certain fascination with the afterlife."

The article was passed around the table, Frank barely glancing at it before handing it off to Reverend Collins. As usual, the retired sheriff was a man of action, not words – especially the printed variety. Collins accepted the paper and excused himself from the table to give it a more thorough read-through.

Jeff continued, shuffling through the papers. "Dr. Clovis is mentioned only one other time – courtesy of The Bedlam County Banner. It's dated just a week after the asylum closed."

Jeff cleared his throat before reading aloud, "The Lake View Asylum for the Insane unexpectedly closed it doors this week following rumors of a possible assault. The Bedlam County Sheriff's Department has confirmed that it was called out to the hospital two days ago in response to a reported *disturbance*.

When pressed, Sheriff's Rylan Walters would not elaborate on what prompted the call and did not provide details on what, if anything, investigators had discovered. Closure of the facility comes just eighteen months after Dr. Wesley Clovis assumed responsibilities as Hospital Superintendent. Clovis, from Indiana, replaced longtime Superintendent Clarence J. Withers, who had been the driving force behind construction of the lunatic asylum. Withers disappeared in 1956 under unusual circumstances.

The Lake View Asylum was the state's second-largest psychiatric hospital and has housed more than 4,100 patients and staff since opening in 1917."

A collective hush fell over the table as each of the assembled guests digested the vague details. It was Frank who eventually spoke up.

"That's it? That's all you got? Hell, son, I thought this internet thing was supposed to change the world – give you everything you want right at yer fingertips." Frank stood, shaking his head, "Just another passing fad – kinda like those fuckin' pet rocks."

Jeff laughed. "Easy there, grandpa. I said that was all I could find on Dr. Wesley Clovis – I was able to find a few other interesting details that may help us connect a few dots."

Jeff handed the remaining papers to Brady. The former reporter quickly scanned through the pages. If what he was reading had any connection with what he had found himself mixed up with, it made very little sense, yet opened up a whole new set of worries.

Jeff had used what few leads the article in The Banner had contained -- a vague reference to Clovis being from Indiana – and was able to uncover some interesting details.

Gray's Crossing, Indiana was home to The Clovis Brother's Mortuary – a family owned business which had opened its doors sometime in the late 1800's. Wesley Clovis was listed as one of the proprietors on the deed.

"Let me see if I follow this," Brady stated, talking himself through his jumbled thoughts. "Dr. Wesley Clovis wasn't a real doctor at all – he was an undertaker?"

Jeff nodded, "That's what I gathered, too." He turned back to his computer and scrolled once again through the pages.

"I'm not sure how an undertaker gets a job running a nut house," Frank interjected himself into the conversation, "but it sure explains all of those graves."

Brady hadn't considered that, but found an uncomfortable truth in Frank's statement. He mentally reviewed the field full of white crosses against the supposed 4,100 residents of the asylum. As for how an undertaker was able to play himself off as a doctor – not only to the folks in Bedlam Falls but also to the hospital staff in Indiana where Lionel Collins was signed-out into his care – Brady hadn't a clue.

Jeff continued to scroll through the pages on the computer screen as Brady's thoughts drifted from one possibility to the next. Frank waited patiently for direction, offering Manson the occasional scratch behind his clipped ears. None of them were prepared for Reverend Collins' re-introduction back into the conversation.

The man's shaking voice startled the assembled group. Even Manson let out a concerned whine. "If any of what this Dr. Clovis proposes is truly possible," he stated, waving the unpublished report in front of him, "I fear that we may have bigger issues to deal with than simply a demented spirit."

The padlock was rusted and snapped easily under the weight of the swinging hammer. Frank grinned as it fell to the rain-soaked ground.

"My first breaking and entering," he beamed, "can't wait to write about it in my diary."

Brady groaned, shoving Frank aside and pushing the massive gate open, its iron hinges squeaking beneath years of rust and weather. "You really do need to get a life – you know that, right?"

Frank laughed, his eyes moving from Brady to the Winnebago; the RV's headlights slicing through the now pouring rain. "Yeah, not the first time I've heard that." He paused, the seldom-used wheels turning inside his worried head. "Quite a crew you've put together here, son. You sure any of us know what the hell we're doing?"

Brady hesitated, raising his face to the clouds overhead and letting the rain wash over him. After a few moments, his gaze returned to Frank. "Not a clue," he admitted, "but I know without a doubt that not doing anything isn't the answer either."

Frank nodded, "Yep, I concur with that sentiment."

If even half of what Collins had shared about Clovis' wild theories concerning the afterlife were possible, the self-described undertaker turned doctor had already spent years practicing his dark arts – with countless victims at his disposal. The mess with Ellis Arkema and the bracelet, although connected in some way to Clovis, was merely the tip of a much bigger iceberg – an iceberg that chilled Brady to his core.

Motioning the Winnebago through the now open gate, Brady wondered what laid in waiting for them in the darkness beyond. Following Frank up the stairs into the RV, he paused once; directing his eyes to the building perched on the horizon.

Ellis waits -- you must find her, recalling his Grandfather's cryptic message on the Scrabble Board. Brady entered the Winnebago the beginnings of an outrageous plan taking shape.

Chapter 32

CONFESSIONS

The somber drive through the winding road leading to the massive stone structure was uneventful. The sight of the small wooden crosses brought an odd sense of reality and responsibility to the undertaking. *So many holes*, Henry Mayer had said.

Frank parked the Winnebago near the crumbling front steps of the asylum. Fortunately, Jeff has an assortment of flashlights - for what purpose Frank didn't bother to ask, afraid that their planned use would be to MacGyver together something illicit...and illegal.

"OK, Jeff – I need you to stay here," Brady had assumed control of the small group and was eager to dole out assignments. "Depending on what we find inside, I may need your assistance," pointing in the general direction of the computers, "or, as a last resort, it's your job to call 911 in case something goes to hell."

Jeff nodded, relieved that he and Manson would remain inside the RV. He had already started Googling exorcisms and the supernatural, unaware that Frank already had that ground covered with his extensive horror movie knowledge.

"Frank, I need you and the reverend to come with me," Brady continued, handing out the flashlights. "We're looking for anything we can find on Ellis Arkema - Clovis, too - files, photos, social security numbers. Hell, at this point I'd be happy with just about anything that pointed us in the right direction."

Brady dug his phone out from the pocket of his shorts -- *half-charged*, he noted. "Jeff, you have my number and I have yours – stay in touch."

Brady scanned the faces before him. *A preacher, a sheriff, and a reporter all walk into an asylum*, he laughed, thinking it all sounded much more like a joke than a plan.

They stepped from the Winnebago, armed with flashlights, a .38, and an oversized Bible – not exactly ready to kick ass, but definitely prepared to take some names.

They mounted the steps together, careful to avoid the areas of loose mortar. The place was eerily quiet – even with the wind and rain. The sound of the front door exploding beneath Frank's booted foot boomed through the stillness.

"Subtle, Frank – real subtle," Brady chastised the retired lawman. "Next time why not just send them flowers to announce our arrival."

Frank laughed, "Announce our arrival to who, son? Place is empty, right?" He paused, removing his pistol from the waistband of his jeans. "Besides, I think the very talented Ray Parker Junior said it best, and I quote – *I ain't afraid of no ghosts.*"

Brady cringed, dropping his head to his chest as he smiled. "Fine, Frank - fine. If playing this like Ghostbusters is what it takes to get you through then go ahead and run with that."

Brady turned his attention to the somber reverend. "How about you?" he asked, acknowledging his quiet companion. "You ready for this?"

Collins nodded. "Even though I walk through the valley of the shadow of death, I fear no evil; for thou art with me; thy rod and thy staff, they comfort me."

"Amen," Brady responded, laying a comforting hand on the reverend's frail shoulder. Their eyes met briefly through the darkness, "forgiveness, not blood, is the answer, right?"

Collins smiled.

Brady turned, leading them through the shattered doorway and into the darkened hospital. Once safely inside, he raised the phone to his face. "Alright Jeff, we're in. You got the blueprints pulled up?"

Brady could hear the familiar rattle of his friend's fingers dancing across the keyboard. "Sure do. The place is a rat's nest, Brady – not just the hospital. It's all connected with tunnels. Looks like some crazy shit."

"Thanks for the commentary, pal, but what I really need right now are some general directions. Anything on those maps that look like a central office or records room?"

More rattling before Jeff responded. "Yeah, to the left and down the hall is the registration area – looks like office space behind that. It's really hard to tell from these renderings – they're ancient."

"Just do the best you can," Brady responded with disappointment. He turned to his companions, "Let's start this way," sweeping his flashlight to the left, "Jeff says there's some kind of office down the hall."

They stepped carefully across the exposed flooring. Plaster from the walls and ceilings littered the hallway. Their progress was met by the sounds of tiny scurrying feet and high-pitched squeals.

"Fucking rats!" Frank stated the obvious. "I didn't sign on for rats, Brady."

"Suck it up, old man," Brady teased. "You've hunted and killed far more dangerous beasts than rats." He paused, shining his flashlight across Frank's pale face, "wanna bag one and take it back to The Hayloft for another trophy?"

Frank raised his middle finger in front of his squinted eyes in response.

"Gentleman," Collins called from down the hallway. "I think you need to see this?" The reverend stood in an open doorway, the beam from his flashlight filling the room beyond.

Brady led Frank down the hall to the doorway, carefully stepping over debris. Collins stepped aside to allow for an unobstructed view. The reverend had definitely found the main office. A dust-covered brass plaque hung on the wall near the door – REGISTRATION.

So far - so good, Brady thought, relieved that Jeff's directions were for the time being reliable. The subtle relaxation of his nerves didn't last long, however. Rounding the corner and peering into the office he was completely unprepared for the sight that greeted him.

The office was a ramshackle reminder of what it had once been. Wooden desks and chairs lay scattered on the floor among other rubble. It looked as if a tornado had whipped through the space – leaving nothing but destruction in its wake. The blood-spattered walls were what drew Brady's attention, however.

Discolored from age and dried nearly to dust, the bloody show indicated signs of an immense struggle. Looking closer at the floor, Brady could see the stained floorboards marking where the crimson liquid had once puddled.

"Frank, you care to shed any light on what the hell happened here?"

Frank paused, shining his light around the room – revealing even more stains and gore.

"Wish I could, son," he added dryly. "Wish I could."

Brady turned his gaze from the room to Frank, "Well, let's start with what you know and go from there."

Nodding, Frank entered the room, kicking at the rubble. "Way before my time, son -- why, I was just getting the first batch of short and curlies down below when this all went down."

Brady waited patiently, knowing the retired lawman was building up courage with each word.

"Yer grandpa was still green behind the ears, I believe." Frank's flashlight continued to probe the darkness. Collins waited in the hallway, unwilling to enter the office.

"My daddy told me there was some kind of riot – patients killing one another, even some staff. Maybe it was the storm – the big one they had back in fifty-eight...maybe not. Something definitely went haywire up here."

Brady pressed for more details, searching for connections to pull his frayed thoughts together. "Right, people say a lot of things...daddy's included," Brady stated, thinking of his fathers own wild stories about the scars that had marked his chest and face, "but what did the law say happened here?"

Frank laughed softly, shaking his head. "The law? The law said nuthin," he admitted weakly. "Different times, Brady. Sheriff Walters wasn't like your grandpa."

Frank paused again, stealing a nervous glance into the hallway at the reverend. When he spoke his voice was barely a whisper. "Hell, son, when Lionel butchered that family I had binders full of reports, boxes of files, and every asshole with a camera or microphone stickin' their fingers in the cookie jar. People cared. They were angry."

Frank turned and considered the wreckage of the room again. "But here, these people, what happened – nobody cared. Seventeen dead, mostly patients – some staff, and the town didn't bat an eye. Maybe the storm had grabbed their attention...maybe not. Either way, they boarded this place up, shipped the rest of 'em off, and washed their hands of the place."

Brady was furious. This couldn't be true. "There was no investigation? No arrests?"

Frank shook his head. "Not a one. Walters did his dog and pony show --had yer grandpa snap a few photos -- but no real investigation."

Brady looked from Frank to Collins, hoping the reverend would have something to add. The man's silence spoke volumes.

Brady's thoughts were interrupted by the vibration of his phone. Jeff's nervous voice filled the empty office.

"You guys may want to hurry things up in there. We got weather out here...bad weather. As of two hours ago they were reporting twisters across Wisconsin and it's all heading across Lake Michigan."

"Yeah, we're hurrying," Brady responded, before a spark of a smile lit his tired face. "Jeff, you know those boxes of files Frank and I brought along?"

The sound of Jeff moving through the cluttered trailer greeted Brady's question. "Yeah, yeah --they're right here." More papers shuffling on the line, "Damn some of this shit is ancient."

"We're looking for anything on the asylum – would be dated back in the fifties. I know I saw something when I was rifling through that stuff." Brady looked to Frank as he continued. "It's a file...a thin one. Can you find it?"

Jeff searched through the box, humming a tune that Brady quickly recognized. "Yellow Ledbetter?" Brady noted, laughing.

"What? Oh, yeah – damned if I know the words, though."

"Yeah," Brady replied to no one in particular, trying to think of the Pearl Jam lyrics, "leave it to Eddie Vedder to make mumbling sound so righteous."

It took a few moments, but Jeff finally found what he had been searching for. "Got it," he said, "not sure what good it's gonna do you. I got ten maybe twelve photos here and some scribbled notes."

Brady recalled the file and its contents. "Forget the photos, Jeff, I'm looking for names. I seem to remember a couple different lists." Brady gaze shifted briefly to the two men before him. "The first is labeled victims – the other, I believe, unaccounted for."

Jeff scanned the handwritten notes. "Yeah, two columns – the first has," Jeff counted them aloud, "seventeen names -- the other column only three."

"We just need the three," Brady instructed.

"Sure, we got Douglas Wyatt, noted as staff, Dr. Wesley Clovis, also noted as staff, and Ellis Arkema – no staff note on him."

Brady's thin smile widened. "Good work, Jeff. Now I just need two more things. First, I'm looking for the private offices that the doctors would have worked from – or whoever would have been in charge." He looked to Frank for help.

"Superintendent's office," Frank offered. "That's what the boss man would have been called."

"Okay," Jeff replied, "and the second thing?"

"Time," Brady laughed. "Keep us up to date on the storms."

"Will do," Jeff agreed. "Umm..by the way, not that I want to be like his best friend and start texting him all the time or anything, but does Frank have a phone, too -- maybe one of those Jitterbug things with the really big numbers?"

Frank's face reddened at the comment.

"I just think it makes sense in case something happens for me to have his number."

Brady smiled as he provided Frank's cell number and ended the call with Jeff.

"Real smartass of a friend you got there, son," Frank complained, "Real smartass."

Brady nodded, sliding the phone into the pocket of his cargo shorts, and patting Frank gently on the back, "I tend to attract those, Frank."

The older man nodded -- the gist of Brady's response slow to settle over him. Soon he was laughing, a deep baritone of a howl that that seemed almost fitting as it echoed through the empty asylum.

From the shadows of the doorway, Collins smiled, watching the two men share a moment of levity. His voice broke the moment. His words without thought, yet left all in deep contemplation.

"Definitely no place for a baby," gazing around the shadowy recesses of the old building, "Lionel drew his first breaths here…somewhere – amongst this wickedness."

Brady exchanged a puzzled glance with Frank. "Come again, reverend?"

Collins dropped his eyes, stepping into the office for the first time, balancing the weight of the oversized bible as he navigated the rubble. "Seems that list of yours isn't quite as complete as it should be," he stated dryly. The reverend paused, standing across a large pile of debris from the two men; he slowly raised his weary eyes from the floor to their faces.

"The place was quite a mess – literally and figuratively." He chuckled nervously, his graze growing distant as the memory drew closer. "Junior pastors don't get to choose their flocks. In those days I was little more than a teenager with a bible – but I was strong in the lord."

Again, Brady glanced at Frank. The brief shrug of his friend's massive shoulders convinced Brady that he, too, was unsure what the strange old man was talking about.

"I had been at the asylum just two days – not even enough time for formal introductions, when it happened. They had Melody and I bunking at one of the farm cottages, not here in the hospital itself." The man's tone and pace were gaining strength. "I was the one who found the….remains."

Collins' dirty knuckles whitened around the bible as he continued. "His birth had been a miracle of course – a blessing swathed in bloody rags." He looked directly into their faces, "We took him – made him our own."

Brady couldn't keep his thoughts silent any longer. "You stole a baby!" It was more accusation than question.

Frank interjected, placing himself between Brady and Collins. A deep roll of thunder shook the very walls around them. "Listen, all things being considered, we have enough shit to deal with right now without adding to it." Glancing uncomfortably at Collins, "now unless there's anything else you have to tell us

– anything that might actually be helpful to the task at hand, I say we get back to work."

Collins said nothing, dropping his gaze once again to the floor. Brady nodded in agreement; aware that time was already working against them. "Wait," he suddenly reconsidered, lurching over the rubble toward Collins. "You found a newborn alive and unharmed…here, among the dead?"

Collins nodded.

Brady looked from the haggard old man to Frank, "No women were listed among the dead, Frank – all men." More thunder greeted his comments. "How does a mother, sane or not, give birth amidst this chaos, allow her child to be taken, and then not say or do anything once help arrives?"

Chapter  33

SEPARATE WAYS

Ellis cradled Emily in his arms, the stench of death thick in the rear of the ambulance. He could hear them laughing in the cabin of the old Packard; a sound that tied his stomach in knots.

His eyes, always sensitive to light, slowly grew accustomed to the blackness, allowing him to barely discern the shadowy form of the woman he held in his blood-soaked arms.

"My love," he whispered gently, leaning down and placing his trembling lips upon her forehead. At his touch, she stirred, sending a momentarily jolt of elation through his tired body. *She lives.*

"Emily," he whispered through the darkness, "I am here."

The laughter from beyond ceased as the Packard roared to life; he could feel the vibrating mass of metal lumber down the road, surely back to the hospital from which they had just fled.

Emily groaned, arching her back against a bursting dam of pain. Her shallow breathing became deeper. "The baby, Ellis...the baby is coming."

Ellis looked from Emily's tear-streaked face to her bulging belly. *No, no...not here, not now!* Removing his torn and soiled shirt he balled it into a rumpled pillow and laid Emily back. The windows on the rear doors of the Packard had been painted over. Ellis dug at the paint with his nails, each fleck allowing sunlight to filter through.

Emily's pained moaning drew his attention from the windows. "Ellis, please. Promise me, Ellis – promise me that you will run."

Ellis ran a gentle hand through her sweaty hair, combing the hair away from her face with his shaking fingers. "No time to run, my love," he whispered with a soothing smile. "We're about to have a baby."

For the briefest of moments Ellis' smile lifted the weight of worry from her shoulders. Emily closed her eyes, drew in a deep breath, and pushed with every ounce of energy she could muster. Ellis knelt between her spread legs, eyes trained on the crown of hair budding from Emily's tired body, and waited.

The baby's delicate shoulders emerged with a gush of blood. Reaching forward, Ellis scooped the newborn into his arms, pulling it from the mess of the Packard's floor. In the excitement of the moment the proud papa had not felt the Packard stagger to a halt. Holding the newborn in his arms, he called for Emily. "My love, it's a boy – a beautiful healthy boy."

Emily raised herself onto wobbly elbows, eager to greet her new son. Instead, the rear doors of the old ambulance were torn open; blinding sunlight filling the dim interior.

"My, my, my," Douglas Wyatt sneered from the open hatch. "What do we have here?"

Ellis's cradled the baby protectively, turning his body to the open doors and raising an arm to shield his sensitive eyes from the burning light.

"Clovis said to bring you back…preferably alive, but dead would be acceptable." The orderly paused, turning to the bulky figure beside him. "Get the girl, Bill," Wyatt ordered with a smile, "doctor didn't say what to do with her – thought I'm sure you'll think of something."

A shadowed arm reached into the Packard and grabbed Emily by the hair. Her scream filled the metal cabin, echoing into the sunlight beyond. A lone gull cried in response.

Ellis reached for her, his hand slick with blood. "Nooo!" he screamed, clutching the crying baby to his chest. Her fingernails bit into the flesh of his forearm, tracing deep gashes across his pale skin as Bill hauled her violently from the ambulance. Her last frantic efforts for help from the man she had loved yet never seen would leave her with his bloodied hospital bracelet clutched between her fingers.

The baby, still connected to its screaming mother, was nearly wrenched from Ellis tiring arms. Ellis held on, gripping the child like a football, and bracing his feet against the Packard's slick floor.

"Dammit, Bill," Wyatt complained with a laugh, "let me give you a hand."

The Packard's rear doors slammed, catching the umbilical cord in its metal teeth. Ellis felt a stiff tug on the bundle in his arms. Panicked, he pulled against the strain, wrapping his free hand around the slick cord and jerking it towards him.

The door opened, Wyatt's face haloed in a burst of sunlight. Instantly, the door slammed again – over and over. Finally, the tug of the cord ceased and Ellis fell back into the darkness of the Packard's interior.

The overpowering sound of his beating heart drowned out the baby's shrill wail, but not Emily's last agonized scream. That sound, Ellis would take to his grave.

Brady led them deeper into the building, questions of Lionel's parentage weighing heavily on him. Frank had grown quiet, a fact that was both a relief and a worry. The man's incessant banter, although tiring, had also proven to be a welcome reprieve from the serious work at hand. Without it, Brady was left to continue his reckless planning in silence.

Jeff's directions led them down winding staircases deep into the bowels of the forsaken structure. The beams from their flashlights provided terrifyingly brief and mysterious glimpses of rusted bed frames with tattered linens, rotted furniture, and crumbling walls. Up and down the hallways they walked, through vacant rooms and offices.

The dripping sound of water echoed through the barren tunnel as they emerged into the basement of the asylum. According to Jeff, the tunnel to the left ended with the morgue and furnace room. To the right waited a series of small offices and one large space labeled simply – TREATMENT.

Brady's phone buzzed. "Talk to me, Jeff," he answered nervously.

"National Weather Service is reporting heavy rotational activity in the storms coming in through Kent City, Brady. That's about 25 miles south and heading this way fast. Wind gusts as high as seventy-five miles per hour. Power is out from Muskegon down to South Haven."

"Great," Brady replied. "We've just reached the basement. Keep us posted."

Brady turned to Frank, "Running out of time. Why don't you and the good reverend head down to the treatment room and offices. I'll take a peak in the morgue. Something tells me that may be where an undertaker would be doing the majority of his business."

Frank shook his head, "No way, son. I'm not sure splitting up is the right idea. You heard your friend – we got weather coming down hard on us."

Brady disagreed, "That's exactly why we need to split up, Frank. Come on, I'm a big boy, and Jeff's got your number now too, in case you get scared." Brady smiled at the retired lawman.

Frank puffed his barrel chest out and snickered, "Fine – you got ten minutes and then we meet back here." He paused, a look of concern passing over his otherwise stoic face. "Don't make me come looking for you."

Brady smiled, "Never. Ten minutes, Frank." He brushed by the older man, pointing his light down the pitch-black hallway. Collins remained a step behind the former sheriff, waiting for Brady to pass.

Brady stepped clumsily around the rubble on the floor and fell awkwardly against the frail reverend. Collins' flashlight and bible clattered to the ground.

"Pardon me, reverend," Brady said, kneeling down to help gather the scattered papers. "Nerves," he explained.

Collins returned Brady's anxious smile and nodded. Tattered bible once again intact and flashlight in hand, Brady watched the old man turn and follow Frank down the empty corridor. He waited until their lights disappeared from view before opening his closed fist. Lying across his sweaty palm, beneath the pale beam of his flashlight, was Ellis' bracelet.

"Okay, Mr. Arkema," Brady challenged the darkness ahead as his fingers closed once again around the cold plastic, "let's dance."

Jeff sat in front of his bank of computer monitors and danced his fingers across two separate keyboards. Doppler Radar colored the screen to his right – a splotch of greens and reds covering nearly half of Michigan's lower peninsula. The screen in front of him was finalizing an additional search on Clovis. This search was a bit more...elaborate, and included hacking into several law enforcement and governmental databases; something Jeff had grown quite proficient at. The screen to the right was tuned to C-SPAN. Manson lay in a heap across his feet.

Already, he could feel the familiar itch that came from withdrawal. It started behind his eyes and worked its way throughout his body. Jeff chewed four Motrin and tried to ignore the ache.

What a fucking day, he thought, stretching his arms out above his head. Never in a million years would have ever dreamed he'd be parked outside the old nut house while Brady Tanner and his merry band of fools paraded through its wreckage.

"Not exactly our first rodeo, hey Manson," Jeff stated, rubbing his bare feet across the course hair of the Rottweiller's stomach. "Remember the time we partied with that roller derby team?" Jeff's hoarse laughter whistled from between his rotted teeth. "We kinda learned the hard way about that Jammer being a transvestite."

Jeff's laughter was interrupted by the unmistakable wail of emergency sirens in the distance. Their cries drowned out the howling wind and rain that had battered the aged Winnebago for the last forty-minutes.

"Shit," Jeff muttered, turning his attention back to the radar as he reached for the phone. "Things are about to get a little hairy, Manson."

The patch of red on the radar screen had settled squarely over Bedlam County. Jeff recalled enough from his days practicing tornado drills as a school boy that the warning sirens meant that a funnel cloud had been spotted. He nervously punched in Brady's digits, ready to warn his companions against the coming storm. The phone fell from his hand as the music of an unanswered ringback tone drained the color from his already pale and gaunt face.

> *When there's lightning - it only always brings me down*
> *Cause it's free and I see that it's me*
> *Who's lost and never found*
> *I cry for magic - I feel it dancing in the light*
> *But it was cold - I lost my hold*
> *To the shadows of the night*
> *There's no sign of the morning coming*
> *You've been left on your own*
> *Like a Rainbow in the Dark*

Between Frank and the good reverend, neither had much of an idea what they should be looking for. Even if trying however, Frank couldn't possibly overlook the sight before his tired eyes.

"Toto," he whispered breathlessly as he settled the unsteady beam from his flashlight onto the stone wall, "I don't think we're in Kansas anymore."

Beneath the varied layers of dust and cobwebs, scrawled onto the stone wall in what could only be blood, was a single word – REPENT.

"I think we've found something, reverend," Frank noted, leaning down for a closer look. He heard the sharp intake of breath from Collins as the man drew back in revulsion. "Yep, my thoughts exactly,"

The ring of Frank's cell phone shattered the silence, startling the two nervous explorers. Frank slid the phone from his pocket, flipping it open. "Yeah," he answered angrily, keeping his light trained on the wall.

"Twisters Frank, heading this way – you need to get your asses out of there."

Frank closed his eyes, concentrating on the muted sounds around him. From beyond the stone walls and over the thunderous storms raging outside, he could hear the wailing of emergency sirens.

"Shit – things were just starting to get interesting, too." Frank's knees popped as he stood. The first sign of age he had shown since the entire affair began. "I imagine you've talked with Brady and he's wrapping things up, too?"

Jeff's hesitation sounded warning bells in Frank's already troubled mind. "Brady's phone must be acting up...I couldn't get through."

Frank noted the clever way Jeff worded his statement and drew his own conclusions from the young man's worried tone.

"Son of a bitch!" he cursed, "Keep trying him. The reverend and I will circle back and see if we can find him."

Frank ended the call with Jeff, shaking his head in frustration. Turning to alert Collins to their change in plans, Frank found himself alone in the TREAT-MENT room.

"Perfect, just fucking perfect," he muttered, the pale beam from his flashlight passing over the darkened corners of the giant room. Odd contraptions of steel and wood littered the floor; each painfully mysterious in appearance and function. A fleeting flash of light from inside one of the *treatment devices* caught his eye. He approached slowly, his booted feet kicking a path through the rubble. It took a moment for his flashlight to pierce the shadows before him. As his weary eyes adjusted to the light, he recoiled, nearly tripping over the cluttered floor.

Rising before him, Frank gazed at a large wooden chair covered in dust. Suspended from atop the high back of the chair was a metal helmet of sorts; a simple ring of steel below what appeared to be a vice of some sort. It was the sight of what rested beneath the helmet that sickened Frank. Bound to the treatment chair by rusted manacles across both arms and legs; skeletal remains dressed in a ragged blue uniform which Frank quickly recognized.

The skull had been crushed down, collapsing into the jaw bone and leaving several vertebra dislodged from the spinal column. Frank scanned the light across the tangled mess of bone and cloth, letting it rest on the badge and name tag- LT. J. Bowling.

Frank reached forward, plucking the badge from the tattered remains of the Michigan State Police Trooper he had never thought of as a friend.

"You bastard – dying on me before I could shove that damn cigar down your throat."

Wiping his thumb across the dusty surface of the badge, Frank paused, "Rest easy, Jim - I'll be back," he whispered, tucking the golden shield into his pocket.

Frank Griggs departed the TREATMENT room, retreating along the cluttered corridor in search of Brady. Collins, for the moment, was merely an afterthought. Passing the decaying sign directing passersby to the Morgue, the retired sheriff's nervous stomach crept into his chest. *Nothing good ever happens in a morgue!*

Chapter 34

RAISING THE DEAD

Brady had always wanted an Ouija Board as a kid. Something about the thought of communicating with ghosts had always intrigued him. Maybe it was his obsession with reading Stephen King, from haunted cars and hotels to vampires, the dead seemed very much alive in the works of his favorite author.

Alone in the confines of the asylum's icy morgue, Brady clutched Ellis' bracelet, unsure of how one actually goes about summoning a spirit. *Hell, if a five-year-old can do it,* he mused – thinking of Abby – *then I sure as hell ought to be able to figure it out.*

He peered around the room, noting the bank of metal drawers on the far wall. Nine iron boxes, he cringed, imagining what they may still contain. *No way am I checking to see if they're empty!*

The light from Brady's flashlight danced around the shadow-filled room, reflecting off the oversized porcelain table dominating the center of the tiled floor. Rusted stains traced down the table's sides, spreading in jagged fingers across the cold floor. Brady was left to imagine what gruesome acts had been committed – flesh and bone memories leaving the stench of death to linger long afterward in the abandoned room.

While working at The Tribune, Brady had on occasion found himself lurking about the Cook County Morgue. Always nasty and full of god-awful smells, morgues were notorious for dark humor and loose lips. Here, however, in the crypt beneath the Lake View Asylum, secrets were plentiful and Brady was in no mood for laughter.

The room was much bigger than Brady had imagined even possible. Creeping forward into the darkness, he expected his light to eventually fall across a wall or doorway. Instead – the thin beam continued to slice deeper into the darkness. Finally, after what seemed like an eternity, the glow from Brady's flashlight revealed an end to the massive room.

Although still tiled in the same pale green color, the far wall was stained a deep rust color. Tracing his light along the length of wall, Brady was sickened by what it revealed. Anchored deep into the walls, heavy chains hung, ending in thick manacles.

Brady followed the trail of chains down the wall, his light dimming as it neared the corner. He crept forward, convinced that something waited in the shadows. His clumsy feet stumbled through debris. Redirecting the light to the floor before him, he found himself amidst a sea of skeletal remains.

"What the fuck?" he wondered, raising the light from the floor and back to the shadows ahead. Through the gloom, two red orbs blazed like beacons. With a final nervous step, the light from Brady's flashlight fell across the last set of chains. Clasped together by time in the rusted manacles, with rotted rags hanging from its shoulders hung the skeletal remains of what had assuredly been a most unfortunate soul. From within its empty eye sockets, a pulsing red light emanated. Brady heard the scraping of bones as the skull twisted – turning its attention upon him.

The bracelet in Brady's hand came to life, snaking its way tightly about his wrist, biting into the exposed flesh. Brady looked from the glowing eyes to his arm and back again a chilling voice tight with rage filling the room.

"I do believe you requested a dance."

Abby awoke from her nap screaming. Gruff immediately began to howl as April and Maddie came running in from the next room.

"Right here, baby – mommy's right here," April sat cautiously beside her troubled daughter, still weary from their last encounter. She took Gruff's lack of a growl as a permissive gesture on the part of her daughter's furry guardian and wrapped her arms soothingly around the child. Maddie hovered nearby hands clasped nervously over her face.

"It's okay, baby," April stroked Abby's blond hair, rocking her back and forth on the edge of the couch. "Mommy's right here. Nothing is going to hurt you."

Abby slowly caught her breath, wiping her tear-stained cheeks on her mother's shoulder. "It's not me, mommy,' she said between sobs, "it's Brady."

April looked nervously from her daughter to Maddie. The sheriff's wife shook her head slowly, not understanding the child's fears.

"What is it, Abby? Why are you afraid for Brady?"

The answer came with a crack of thunder overhead, accompanied by a bolt of lightning which instantly made the darkness beyond the windows light like fire. As the light exploded outside, inside the world went dark. All of the electrical appliances went dead as the power went out with a spinning finality that left behind nothing by a murky silence. April, Abby and Gruff all looked to Ms. Griggs as the sudden silence was pierced by the first shill sound of the warning sirens erupting through the storm. Maddie ushered her guests to the basement.

Brady was unsure which disturbed him more, the blood dripping to the tile floor from the constriction of the plastic bracelet about his wrist or the surreal conversation he was preparing to undertake with the mass of bones chained to the wall.

"Well," Brady glanced down at his bracelet biting into his wrist, "can I assume that this blood debt has been repaid?"

The voice in the room laughed.

"I seem to recall your grandfather being equally as humorous," the disembodied voice stated. "Of course, his laughter died with a single bullet. Pity, really. Much of this…nastiness could have been avoided if he had not taken the coward's way out."

Brady's years of verbal sparring with his father-in-law had proven very enlightening. He could now recognize and deflect goading attempts for confrontation. While the ghostly voice teased, Brady contemplated possible next moves. His reckless planning had only taken him so far – roughly here – and he quickly found his once-clear thoughts now overtaken by panic.

"That's one way to look at it, Ellis," Brady was slowly backing away from the skeletal form chained to the wall. "I can call you Ellis, right?"

The red orbs brightened as the skeleton's boney arms rose, snapping the chains free from the wall. With two staggering steps, the thing that was Ellis stood before Brady.

"Why yes," it hissed, "that would be just fine." It leaned closer, "I do believe you were about to make a point."

Brady paused, collecting his thoughts, before raising his eyes and setting his chin. "Cowardice is one way to look at his actions," Brady stated, shaking atop two very unsteady legs. "Although it seems to me that it took a fair amount of courage to pay your price. Blood for blood, right – that's the going rate for vengeance these days?"

Ellis' eyes burned with rage. "What do you know of vengeance – of the price one must pay to find it? Only a man who has lost everything looks to vengeance to fill that void." A boney hand shot forward, grasping Brady by the wrist. "The time has come, my clever young friend, for you to learn of loss."

Frank stumbled forward through the darkness – no sign of the good reverend. *Crazy old man is on his own*, Frank concluded, more than a little put off by the man's disappearance.

The .38 in former lawman's hand provided an illusory comfort; he knew that bullets would be of very little help given the current situation.

Frank's worried attempts to reach Brady by phone had proven fruitless – the savage storm outside was surely not helping the situation. Frank did his best not to worry about Jeff's chances of riding-out the brutal storm unscathed in his lightning-rod of a mobile tin can.

As he approached the hallway leading to the morgue, he finally heard voices, barely audible above the sound of the storm. Brady's usual confident tone was shaken, but still easily recognizable. The other voice, although having just the slightest hint of familiarity, remained a mystery. Frank halted, dousing his light, and waiting for his eyes to adjust to the darkness. A few moments later he crept forward, gripping his useless .38, and softly humming the theme from Ghostbusters.

Brady's world gave way to blackness as he drifted between consciousness and…something else. The closest his racing mind could come to quantify the experience was a frenzied sense of déjà vu; everything seemed foreign yet familiar at the same time.

My flashlight! Where's my fucking flashlight, he panicked, urging his eyes to more quickly adjust to the darkness. Ellis' chilling voice responded.

"No need for light, Tanner. It is through my eyes that we look -- and they are more than accustomed to the darkness."

Brady tried unsuccessfully to close his eyes against the disturbing vision that was slowly coming into focus before him. It took a moment for his racing mind to settle, but when it did he knew that what lay before him was no hallucination, but more remarkably, a memory.

Cradling the squirming bundle of rags against his chest, Ellis knelt in the back of the ambulance. Emily's cries for help, once intermingled so strangely with the raucous laughter of the men, had ceased. In its place an empty silence reigned.

The Packard roared to life, once again lurching toward what Ellis could only imagine was the asylum. The car's previous stop revealed little, although the sound of a seagull impressed upon Ellis a proximity to the lake. Beyond that clue, the whereabouts of his beloved remained a mystery.

Ellis' grip on reality was slipping; the events of the last several hours replaying on a continuous loop in his weary mind. His thoughts bounded from one memory to the next – Emily strapped to the table in the morgue, Clovis' bloodied hands between her outspread thighs, their escape through the trees beneath the burning sun, the demeaning encounter with local law enforcement, and the final separation in the back of the bloodstained ambulance. These brutal images, although shared with the love of his life, would forever be burned into his soul – a wound beyond healing.

Brady watched in horror, a voiceless scream searing his throat. He was both angered and sickened by the confused images. As witnessed through Ellis' memory, Brady felt an odd sympathy for the man he had singularly identified as a soulless, blood-thirsty monster.

"That, Tanner, is your first lesson on loss." Ellis' disembodied voice floated through the darkness. "Funny thing about loss," Ellis continued, "is that once you truly embrace it – there is nothing you cannot achieve." Brady's eyes, although wide-open, remained sightless, his body shuddering beneath the burden of Ellis' tragic memories. "Achieve? The shattered lives you've left in your unforgiving wake, the souls you've tormented – this is your grand achievement?"

Brady's question was answered in silence. The darkness closed around him, squeezing the breath from his chest. His sightless eyes rolled back white as Ellis pulled him once again into his dark recollections.

The Packard's thin tires came to a grinding halt, momentarily stirring Ellis from his sinister musings. The bundle of rags lay quietly in the corner. Always a man of thought over action, the timid boy who had grown into a taciturn man poised himself on the slick floor of the Packard and prepared for the doors to open.

His wait was brief. The doors swung outward on rusty hinges and Ellis leapt from the darkness into the sunshine beyond. Eyes closed to the painful rays of the sun, Ellis felt Bill's thick hands close over his shoulders, wrestling him into a headlock.

"Dammit, boy," Wyatt's nasally voice intruded through the struggle, "why make things more difficult than they need to be?"

Ellis opened his eyes, casting his hate-filled stare into the greasy man's face. Bill's beefy forearm was wedged beneath his chin, painfully squeezing the breath from his heaving chest. Ellis could feel the man's erection stiffen into the small of his back. He was confident Wyatt was sporting similar lumber.

"Doctor wants you – but I'm sure we have time for a bit of fun, first." Wyatt's tongue danced behind a disgusting smile.

Ellis' reaction was shocking in both its speed and brutality. The bulge in Wyatt's white pants collapsed beneath Ellis' perfectly placed kick, sending the small man to his knees with an agonized groan. With Bill's grip around his neck momentarily distracted, Ellis buried his teeth into the orderly's forearm, tearing free a mess of flesh.

Ellis ducked free from his captor, spinning the man to the ground. He glanced briefly at Wyatt, noting with satisfaction the man's agonsy before turning his attention once again to the larger of the two goons. The sorry man clutched his bleeding arm and whimpered at Ellis' approach.

"I never touched you," he cried, "never touched you – you fuck-ing freak!"

Ellis hesitated, Bill's blood running from the corners of his twisted smile. The switch flipped. The monster that everyone envisioned when first setting their sights on him had finally been unleashed. Spitting the flesh to the ground, Ellis savored the look of fear in the orderly's teary eyes.

"William, William, William," Ellis teased through bloodstained teeth.

"No worries – there's plenty of time for us to get acquainted."

Ellis pounced. Although outweighed by more than one-hundred pounds, Ellis' adrenaline-fueled attack overwhelmed the mountainous orderly. Blinded by fury, Ellis savagely pummeled the prone man – fists and fingers tearing into the man's soft flesh. Quickly, Ellis' arms were slick with fresh blood and his torn nails hung from tired fingers.

So caught was he in this frenzied state of cruelty that Ellis failed to notice the long shadow of Dr. Wesley Clovis fall across his shoulders. The last thing he heard before the shovel struck the back of his head was the whoosh of displaced air, and what he thought was the muffled cry of a baby.

The coppery taste of blood was heavy in Brady's mouth as the nightmarish images slowly faded from his mind, leaving him once again in the pitch black of nothingness. He rolled his tongue along his teeth, convinced he would find bits of flesh clinging to his incisors. He was never so gladdened by disappointment.

"It's an acquired taste," Ellis' ethereal voice taunted him through the darkness.

Brady's patience, like his sanity, was wearing dangerously thin. Ellis' loss, although brutal in its grizzly detail, was no less tragic than his own. Loss found its way into most people's lives.

Karen's untimely death with their unborn child, not to mention the passing of both parents, carved out deep chunks of the man, husband and father he had hoped to be – leaving a hollow void inside that nothing seemed able to fill.

Brady's rambling thoughts stopped dead on that thought – *father he had hoped to be*. Ellis' loss wasn't as deep as he believed.

"Your son, Ellis, the baby – he's alive!"

Instantly, Ellis' piercing red eyes flared to life in the darkness. Like a thunderclap Brady's mind exploded – a torturous ache worse than he ever imagined possible. Brady could feel the specter's boney fingers digging into his thoughts – searching for the truth within Brady's clouded memories.

This unearthly connection with Ellis' tormented soul provided Brady a window into the sinister depths of the monster's thoughts, feelings and tragic recollections. Brady felt like a tourist in his own mind, watching over a skeletal shoulder as Ellis' rotted fingers dug through Brady's memories like the pages of a dust-covered scrapbook – the photographs in no specific order.

His ethereal companion probed deeper into Brady's memory-banks, uncovering the jumbled emotions about his grandfather's suicide – a man he had never met yet seemingly shared so much with, the forgotten-grief of a stillborn baby sister he knew only as *Baby Kate*, and then jumping forward to the last confusing conversation with Collins about the baby...and Lionel. Deeper still, Ellis lingered at the murky image of Brady resting at the bottom of Asylum Lake, greeted by the ghostly specter of his lost love.

As the pain and shock ripped through Ellis and into Brady, the memory took a solid form, a sense of reality that Brady had for so long blocked from his fractured mind.

As the memories tumbled forth, Brady was crippled by Ellis' agonizing revelation of the horrible birthright he has passed on to his only son -- all in this twisted pursuit for vengeance. Brady could feel the searing rage within the tortured soul cool, icing over with horror at the wicked legacy he had left this world – the innocent lives he had stolen. It was the fate of his beloved Emily however, that finally extinguished the last spark of Ellis' merciless wrath.

"There can be no more blood. Forgive me."." Ellis' ghostly voice had softened in defeat. "Free her, Tanner, my beloved – and forgive..."

Brady's precarious bond with the dark spirit shattered beneath Ellis' final plea, shaking the morgue's tile floors and walls, releasing the shackled skeletal remains from their iron bonds.

Oh shit, Brady worried, raising his aching body from the dirty floor. *What have I done?* Groping through the darkness for his lost flashlight, Brady's eyes slowly adjusted to his grim surroundings. With a base-drum of thunder booming ominously overhead, the shaken reporter-turned-archaeologist-turned medium stumbled from the morgue, fleeing through the darkness in search of his friends.

Chapter 35

THE REUNION

It took ten days to restore power to the area - with crews from across the state working night and day to set things right. Although comparable to the legendary storm of 1958, most agreed that Bedlam had definitely been spared from the worst.

Brady spent those days surrounded by his rag-tag group of adventurous in the refuge of Frank's house licking his wounds—both of the physical and emotional variety. The Up North House had weathered the storm well, only suffering minor damage, but Brady was unenthusiastic about disturbing the scab that was just now forming over the secrets of his family. To dig through the yet undiscovered secrets of the home was a task waiting for him inside the log home.

The ladies, and Henry, had ridden out the storm quite nicely, tucked safely into the Griggs' fortified basement. Abby's emotional trauma, much like Brady's, was healing – with only an occasional nightmare as a reminder; her resiliency gave them all strength.

The good reverend had simply disappeared. Brady was unsure what to make of the old man's vanishing act, but instinctively knew that it somehow involved his continuing search for Lionel...and answers. He could not completely rule out one day crossing paths with Collins, but in no way was looking forward to the event.

Exactly two weeks from the night of their harried flight from the asylum, the Michigan Sate Police were dredging the bottom of Asylum Lake. Frank's initial attempts to plead his case for their involvement in his tale of the supernatural were met with polite declinations. His reverent presentation of Bowling's badge however, had changed their minds. Although many of the elder rank in file in Lansing remained convinced that Frank was just a dried-up old coot in search of attention, his service in locating a fallen brother earned him half a day of man power to put his delusional conspiracy theory to rest.

"Captain, we got something." The voice crackled from the walkie-talkie in the trooper's hand. Brady waited anxiously with Frank and April on the dock of the *Up North House*. Beside them stood Captain Graham Birdsong of the Michigan State Police – a serious-looking trooper leading the still unofficial investigation. The officer turned his attention from the dive team stationed in the lake to Frank. "Roger. What did you find?"

"Gallagher says it's a graveyard down there."

"A what?"

"A graveyard, sir. We've got at least twenty-five yards of scattered bones."

Birdsong stared silently from behind his mirrored sunglasses into the lake's glittering surface. After an eternity of silence, he again pushed the button on the walkie-talkie. "Affirmative." he responded, staring suspiciously down at Frank's grinning face, "Get Gallagher out of the water. I'll radio Lansing and request a full recovery team out here."

Brady retreated from the dock, holding April close as they made their way back to the strip of sand where Abby played. Gruff rested beside her, his paw encased in plaster. The dog's limb would heal, although a limp was almost guaranteed.

"Who's up for ice cream?" Brady asked through a partially-forced smile. Abby rose to her feet, brushing the sand from her shorts as she helped Gruff navigate the terrain.

"Me," she called, sliding her small hand into Brady's; delicate fingers brushing against the plastic bracelet that still clung to Brady's bruised wrist.

Gruff noted the bracelet, and with it the intermingled scent of his longtime companion, young new friend, and the underlying odor of death. Warily, he glanced from their intertwined hands to the activity at the center of the lake. The voices of the slowly surfacing dead whispered softly through the air. Ever vigilant, Gruff remained on guard against foes seen and unseen – living and dead.

Together they walked from the beach, past the dormant fire-pit along the worn path leading to the front of the Up North House. Jeff's RV was parked in the grass, providing the log home with a certain sense of hillbilly class it had been lacking. Brady smiled as they walked by the rusted Winnebago, wondering what internet conspiracies his friend was currently hatching. His smile, once forced, spread genuine across his exhausted face as Pearl Jam's Alive erupted from Jeff's sonically-charged speakers.

I'm still alive
Hey I, but, I'm still alive
Hey I, boy, I'm still alive
Hey I, I, I'm still alive, yeah
Ooh yeah, yeah, yeah, yeah, ooh

the storyteller

R.A. Evans is a husband and father of three small children. Between diaper changes, tea parties, and baseball games he finds time to catch his breath by golfing horribly, reliving his misspent youth playing video games, reading anything he can lay his hands on and, of course, writing. A graduate of Grand Valley State University, Evans started his career at a small town newspaper, and has spent the past fifteen years working in marketing/public relations. You can learn more about RA Evans at www.raevanswrites.com and contact him at raevans@asylumlake.com.